D0475374

CLOWN
IN A
CORNFIELD
2

FRENDO LIVES

ALSO BY
ADAM CESARE

Clown in a Cornfield

ADAM CESARE

CLOWN IN A CORNFIELD 2

HARPER TEEN

An Imprint of HarperCollinsPublishers

Library of Congress Cataloging-in-Publication Data
Names: Cesare, Adam, author.
Title: Frendo lives / by Adam Cesare.
Description: First edition. | New York, NY : HarperTeen, [2022] | Series:
   Clown in a cornfield ; 2 | Audience: Ages 14 up. | Audience: Grades
   10-12. | Summary: A year after the Kettle Springs massacre, Quinn and
   her friends Rust and Cole become the focus of online conspiracy theories
   that recast them as villains rather than victims.
Identifiers: LCCN 2022001875 | ISBN 978-0-06-309691-2 (hardcover)
Subjects: CYAC: Conspiracy theories—Fiction. | Murder—Fiction. |
   Survival—Fiction. | Clowns—Fiction. | Haunted houses
   (Amusements)—Fiction. | LCGFT: Novels. | Horror fiction.
Classification: LCC PZ7.1.C46498 Fr 2022 | DDC [Fic]—dc23
LC record available at https://lccn.loc.gov/2022001875

Typography Jenna Stempel-Lobell
22 23 24 25 26   PC/LSCH   10 9 8 7 6 5 4 3 2 1

First Edition

For Jen. Again.

ONE

David Rush was an Eagle Scout.

Was.

In addition to his scout training, he had secured an ROTC scholarship for his first two years at Missouri State and frequently spent weekends camping with his uncle, Lt. John Rush, a retired medical officer in the United States Marine Corps.

If there was anyone in Paul Tillerson's B-field that fateful night who possessed the know-how to survive the carnage—possibly even lead the other victims out of danger—it was David.

David Rush had the skills to survive.

And his attackers knew that.

Which is why he was one of the first targets of the ambush.

What follows in this documentary is not conjecture. These are facts, confirmed and verified by a panel of independent researchers and forensic specialists.

"Is this going to be gory? I can't deal with gore. Especially eye stuff. And finger—"

"Shhhh."

—first crossbow bolt to enter David Rush's body entered below his knee, severing tendons and chipping bone. The pain must have been excruciating.

"Ew."

"Shut up!"

—vestigators unanimously agree that the second bolt entered David's rib cage while he was lying on his stomach, already prone. Despite being fired at close range, this second shot missed all of David's vital organs. Which means that he would have been able to survive both of these injuries if he had received light triage and been taken to a hospital.

But there was no hospital. An hour after he had been shot, the injured David Rush was finished off by the

group's ringleader with a single, smooth cut across his jug-
ular vein.

"Where is this going?"

"No, I'm serious, be quiet. You got me to watch this thing.
Now let me watch it. She's my roommate and I want to—"

"Okay."

—as widely reported by the mainstream media, the
perpetrators of the Kettle Springs Massacre were each
dressed as Frendo the Clown, a character used to promote
Baypen corn syrup and the town's unofficial mascot.

But, as the next hour will show, this is one of the very
few accurate details circulated by the media in the days
and weeks after the crimes. What follows will—

"My bullshit sense is tingling. Where did you find this,
Pete?"

"My uncle."

"By any chance an uncle who thinks the president is a
lizard person?"

"I'm kicking you both out soon. I can't hear."

"Sorry."

—nica Queen. Matthew Trent. David Rush. It will
sound shocking. Maybe even offensive to some viewers,

but the truth is that there were only three teenage victims of the Kettle Springs Massacre. Not twenty-six as reported. And the killers were not Sheriff Dunne and the townsfolk. Nor was the mastermind Arthur Hill, the town's main jobs creator. No—the killers were the students of Kettle Springs themselves.

The police, the FBI, the media corporations that control our television and internet and want to keep us in a perpetual state of fear, all were complicit in this cover-up. All furthered the false narrative of twenty-six helpless school-age casualties. Why? Why would they undertake such an elaborate false flag operation? Why lie to the American people? And who were the real victims, lured to first the field and then the Baypen refinery that night?

"Okay. True. This does seem far-fetched, but hear it out."
"SHHHH!"

—to understand why, we have to take a closer look at the real sociopath at the heart of this story. The first person in Kettle Springs to don a Frendo the Clown mask in anger. The organizer of the entire plan. The girl who leveraged the pain of a divided small town, a divided nation, and has gone on to make that schism even worse.

The girl who dragged a hunting knife across David Rush's throat while he lay begging for help.

4

The girl who hatched the plan to kill and frame the town's authority figures.

A girl who, before the murders, if you were to believe everything you hear on the news, had been living in Missouri for less than a week at the time of the attack. None other than—

"Quinn Maybrook."

"See! Told you. She's been lying!"

"Oh please. That isn't real footage. I recognize the costume. It's from that Lifetime movie they made."

"Keep watching. It's not about the footage, which, yeah, is a little janky. They have facts. I was skeptical, too, at first, but—"

"Shh. Do you hear that?"

"Oh fuck, hide it, hide it."

Quinn Maybrook stood in the doorway and saw her face on the laptop screen before Mason could fumble the computer closed.

Then she shrugged.

It wasn't worth getting mad about anymore. She couldn't get away from this shit. No matter where she went. Not even after a long day of classes, not even in her own dorm room.

Figured.

She was familiar with the specific video they were

watching. It was the most popular one for some reason. The "documentary" was titled *The Baypen Hoax*, and even though Quinn, Cole, and Rust had successfully petitioned to have the original video removed from Facebook, the same "documentary" was re-uploaded to YouTube multiple times a day, the takedown notices unable to keep up. The facts in the video were all wrong, of course. And the conclusion that Quinn, Cole, and Rust had committed mass murder and then framed their victims—Sheriff Dunne, Arthur Hill, and the rest of the town's adults—was as laughable as it was convoluted. There were even sequences where Quinn's face had been deepfaked (poorly) onto the actress who played Ronnie Queen in one of the made-for-TV movies. Bad as the effect was, the image seemed to stick with an audience eager to see what Quinn would look like wearing a Frendo the Clown costume herself.

Never discount the gullibility of people on the internet, though. Janky production values and all, there were people who believed. Or at least *wanted* to believe, needed that outrage in their lives like a handrail.

Quinn had thought Dev was smarter than that.

"If you're going to watch conspiracy theory videos about me, there are better ones. More fun ones," Quinn said. She didn't know why she was engaging with this right now. "There's one where I'm secretly Cole's half sister and we framed Arthur Hill to split his fortune. That's a good one. And one where I was trained by the Zodiac Killer at a defunct summer camp in Virginia. Also good."

Sitting on the carpet, Dev swallowed a big gulp of air. Guilt stuck in her throat.

Quinn didn't wait to hear what excuse her roommate was going to stammer out. She hitched up her computer bag, leaned into the dorm room, and plucked the pillow off her bed.

"Oh, and FYI," she said, "David Rush wasn't even a real person. But Rust Vance really *is* an Eagle Scout, so that's probably where they got that tidbit from."

Dev started to get up from the floor, where Pete and Mason, two boys from down the hall, were sitting cross-legged and staring at the carpet.

Good. Let them squirm.

"Quinn—I'm sorry, we were just . . . ," Dev started.

"I guess I'll go sleep in the study lounge tonight," Quinn said, and slammed the door in Dev's face as she approached.

Quinn had only made it a couple of feet down the hall when she heard their door open again. She forced herself not to look back.

"I'm sorry!" Dev yelled. "I'm really sorry!" Her apology was loud enough that she must have embarrassed herself, because their door squeaked closed just as quickly as it was opened.

Quinn and Dev had only known each other for a few

weeks. They hadn't talked much in that time, despite sleeping in twin beds five feet apart, facing each other. Every night was like an awkward sleepover. Even so, most of their conversations had been Dev apologizing to Quinn. *Sorry, but I mixed up our shower caddies and used your shampoo. Sorry, but did you take Econ notes? Sorry if I'm loud on the phone, but it's still early where my parents are.*

And there were more apologies. Dev was sorry about the smell of her microwaved breakfast burritos. And also sorry that the RA had found the contraband microwave she kept in their shared closet.

Even with all these annoyances, Quinn didn't dislike the girl. She didn't think much about Dev at all, outside of pitying her for the hard time she seemed to be having adjusting to city life; the long hours she spent on the phone with her parents; and the trunk of arts and crafts materials, markers, and bracelet looms that she kept under her bed. But now the thought of Dev gossiping with those boys, speculating about Quinn's complicity in a mass murder . . .

Quinn was angry. So angry it'd be hard to sleep.

In the hallway, a few faces prairie-dogged out of their rooms to see what was up, who was doing all this yelling and stomping. It was a long walk. Quinn and Dev were the last door at the end of the hallway. The lookie-loos caught a glimpse of Quinn marching to the elevator before they each disappeared back inside.

Oh. Her. The Clown Girl. Figures.

It wasn't that everyone in the country believed the lunatic theories they saw online. No, those were fringe ideas with tiny fringe audiences. Most of America knew what really happened in Kettle Springs. Or knew a close-enough-to-the-ballpark version of the truth, which varied depending on the documentaries they'd seen, the podcasts they listened to, or which cable news station was on at their parents' house. But a few rejected that truth, thought Quinn was a criminal mastermind who'd roped two small-town gay lovers into a heavily armed assault against traditional American values.

It was only a few weeks after the attack that the conspiracy theories and abuse started. And as a result, Quinn had spent most of the last year with her social media deactivated to try to step away from the toxic stew of lies online and stem the constant—and sometimes quite detailed—death threats. She didn't have Instagram or TikTok on her phone, but still she never went anywhere without the device. It connected her to the people she loved. It could connect her to help.

Before leaving for college, she'd sat with her dad at the kitchen table and they'd performed timed drills to see how quickly she could set the phone to emergency mode. Then they'd tested which was faster, emergency mode or dialing 911 the traditional way. If she needed, Quinn could reach the Philly police without even looking down at her phone screen.

The dorm elevator smelled like chicken fingers, and Quinn could see why. Someone had let half a nugget slip from their late-night snack, probably while trying to hit a button for their floor, judging from the streaks of ketchup.

Quinn pressed *M* for Mezzanine. This building used to be a hotel, before the university bought it and converted it, quickly and cheaply, into freshman and sophomore suites. During that construction, they'd also portioned up the ballrooms of the second floor into residence life offices and study lounges.

The elevator car shuddered, and Quinn stared at the oily splotch of ketchup.

For the rest of the students in this building, college life was all fun and parties. With a little bit of learning thrown in. Maybe college wasn't the total freedom they'd imagined, but it was much more freedom than they'd ever had at home. Quinn's classmates had a bustling city at their front door. They knew about that one corner store that didn't card. There was a small dining hall in the building's basement that served fried food any time you were hungry, even at— Quinn checked her phone—nearly midnight.

Quinn wished she felt the same way. Was *able* to feel the same way.

She wanted to enjoy the curly fries. A little over a year ago, after pulling into Kettle Springs for the first time, coming back to Philly for school had been the plan. The dream.

This, being here, being back in the city she called home, was what she'd wanted. She'd wanted to be far from Missouri, live right on Broad Street, a few blocks' walk from City Hall and the heart of Philadelphia. But now that she'd seen death—now that she'd killed to survive—Quinn just couldn't get as excited about an eight a.m. Intro to Lit class, or how much detergent was enough in the dorm's strange washing machines, or complaining that her roommate was taking so long in the shower. The alienness of college, its freedoms, all seemed like inconveniences at best, dangers at worst.

DING!

The elevator doors opened onto darkness.

The building's second floor was often like this when Quinn came down late at night, looking for a little peace, but the darkness was still sometimes unnerving.

Quinn readjusted her pillow under one arm and waved a hand over her head.

There was a mechanical click somewhere, a circuit switched on, and cool bright fluorescent lights lit the hallway.

The lights were on a motion sensor. The darkness was good, actually, Quinn told herself. It meant she was alone down here.

Quinn walked forward into the hall, her phone buzzing with a text. She looked down.

Oh. Surprise, surprise. Dev was sorry.

Quinn opened Messages and silenced the conversation. She did *not* silence her phone. She never silenced her phone, even while she slept. There was always a chance that her dad or Cole or Rust could call with an emergency.

It was quiet down here, abandoned on this floor that the school hadn't bothered to remodel from when it was a hotel. Even with the sound-dampening qualities of the carpet and the popcorn ceilings that must've dated back to the '70s, Quinn's footsteps seemed to echo. The university offered cleaner, more modern places for students to study at night, but this one was closest, and a place where Quinn Maybrook could be alone. Maybe the only location on campus without classmates whispering into their hands, a barista asking her for her autograph on the back of a receipt, or a group in the dining hall trying to "accidentally" catch her in the background of a selfie.

At the end of this hall there was a large, open room with circular tables, booths, and a small kitchenette to make coffee or tea, but Quinn wasn't headed that way. Instead, she turned on her phone's flashlight and directed it into the slim, rectangular windows of the doors on either side of her.

These were private study rooms. They were empty now, but during midterms and finals were so in demand that they had to be reserved ahead of time.

She peered into a few windows before settling on a room

with three chairs and stepping inside.

"Shit."

A blanket.

She'd left her room in such a hurry, she hadn't grabbed a blanket. It was fine. At least she had her bag, which meant she had her laptop, her phone charger, and the small collapsible combat baton she kept for self-defense.

Quinn rarely arrived back at the dorm after dark, but on Thursdays it was unavoidable. Her only elective was a film class that consisted of an hour of lecture on Friday mornings and a two-hour screening block the night before. Tonight's film had been *Man of a Thousand Faces*. Rust would have liked it. It was an old black-and-white movie starring an old black-and-white movie star that was *about* an even older black-and-white movie star. She'd been enjoying it well enough until there was a scene where the actor was in clown makeup. Then she had a hard time focusing on anything but the faces in the screening room around her. How some of her classmates were watching for her reaction.

Quinn placed her laptop on the desk and opened it, not to use the computer but just to make it look plausible if anyone peeked in that she could be studying. She then pushed the three chairs together in a line to make a kind of bed.

She put her pillow against her back and stretched her feet out, trying to get cozy.

In the hallway, through the long rectangular window,

she watched as the overhead lights clicked off, one by one. She liked that. Liked that the timer attached to the motion sensor was pretty short. It let her know there was nobody else on this floor with her. This dorm, of all the housing on campus that allowed freshmen, was the only one with a single entrance. This entrance was guarded overnight, and every guest, even if they were students, had to sign in and leave their IDs kept in a flex-folder behind the desk for the length of their stay.

In the dark, feeling safe, Quinn scrolled her phone and hoped she'd soon get sleepy.

Apple News was all depressing stories. But at least she wasn't featured in any of them. Two months ago, there'd been an entire week where she hadn't shown up in any Google Alerts. Which was nice, but it was the calm before the storm. Two weeks and a few days ago had been the one-year anniversary of the Kettle Springs Massacre, and the retrospective think pieces had been out of hand. And the coverage was still ongoing.

She left the News app and went to Messages.

The top message, most recent, was Dev.

Quinn left the girl muted and unread.

Under Dev was her father, not in her phone as "Glenn Maybrook" but as "Dad." His last message—was it this morning or had he sent it before she went into the screening room for the movie?—was a simple *Love you.*

Under Glenn Maybrook was a group chat she'd labeled "The Boys."

That was Cole and Rust.

Then there was an automatic message from the last time she'd ordered takeout. And under that, inactive for days, was a three-person group text labeled "The Girls." Tessa and Jace. Were her best friends from high school still "The Girls" if she had only seen them once since moving back to Philly? Nothing had gone wrong, not outwardly at least, the last time they'd been together. Tessa was even living here, on campus, a five-minute walk from Quinn. But there was something about the way they both looked at her. Like they had questions they weren't sure they were allowed to ask. Like Quinn was someone famous that they used to know. Or maybe that was too self-serving. Maybe Tessa and Jace looked at Quinn like a curiosity. The damaged girl they used to know.

She didn't want to think about that right now, wonder if she still had two of her closest friends, so instead she opened up the text with the boys and tried to focus on something that made her happy. Something she'd been looking forward to.

Where are you now?

She waited a few seconds; then when neither of them replied, she buzzed their phones with an emoji. If they were trying to sleep? Then tough. She wanted to know how close they were.

CH: *Motel outside Pittsburgh.*

She smiled, then responded.

Motel? You're in my state! Can't you just drive it in shifts? You'd get here tonight.

CH: *It's a very long state. If you didn't know.*

Ha. I know. You two be safe in Pennsultucky. Try not to be an asshole.

RV: *What's that?*

Oh he can text.

RV: *I do if I'm not allowed to sleep.*

Quinn started to type them out an explanation of Pennsultucky, but halfway through looked up, the smile on her face wilting.

She'd been so absorbed in the conversation, so looking forward to her friends coming in for a visit tomorrow as part of their road-trip week away from Kettle Springs, that she hadn't even noticed that the hallway lights had switched back on.

There was somebody out there.

Was it Dev? Had she come down to apologize in person since her texts had gone unanswered?

Had Quinn been so wrapped up in texting Cole and Rust that she hadn't heard the elevator ding?

She didn't stand from her makeshift bed, but did stare at the skinny privacy window that faced into the hall.

There. Softened by the carpet, but still distinct, she could hear footsteps.

Footsteps and something else. Between the steps there was a kind of dragging sound. Something rubbing against the wall.

The sound came closer. And Quinn, her legs still propped up on the bed she'd made, moved her hands to her computer bag.

A shadow fell over the wall opposite the window; then whoever was casting the shadow stopped. They were *trying* not to be seen.

She unzipped the top compartment on her bag and reached inside.

The combat baton was not legal to own in Pennsylvania. Or most of the states that bordered PA. But for thirty dollars, shipping included, she'd had a couple of them delivered to her Missouri address no problem. Rust had suggested the baton. It was light, easy to carry . . . discreet enough for college.

Quinn gripped the handle of the baton, but didn't take it out of the bag. If she needed to take it out, she would also need an extra second to flick her wrist and extend the steel bar, tipped with a textured steel knob, to its full length.

"Dev?"

A face appeared in the window. It was certainly not Dev.

It wasn't a fellow student, either.

"Knock knock?" the man at the window said, and smiled.

As he stepped forward, filling the sliver of window, she could see he was wearing maroon coveralls.

Quinn's hand unclenched. Her heart rate slowed. Those coveralls meant he worked in the building. That he was one of the maintenance crew.

Quinn nodded and the man opened the door a crack, just wide enough for his face.

The man had a couple days' worth of salt-and-pepper scruff, a wrinkled neck, and a bad tooth that she could only see because he was smiling so wide.

"You aren't sleeping down here, are youse?"

Youse. She'd missed that.

"No. I'm studying."

Was there a rule against sleeping in one of these rooms? She didn't think so. She'd done it before. But she didn't feel like debating that fact if there was.

"Where's your books, then?"

Where's your cleaning supplies? And let me see what you're dragging behind you. But she didn't say that. Instead she said:

"Do you know how expensive course textbooks are?" She pointed to her laptop and added: "PDFs."

"Well, I'm going to be running my vacuum, so I'm sorry if it disturbs you."

She nodded. "No problem."

He started to let the door close.

A vacuum. He's a maintenance man with a South Philly accent who's wheeling a vacuum behind him. And you're ready to bash his head in with a two-pound steel baton. Dad's right— therapy should be more than once a week.

She felt silly. Then angry that she felt so silly.

As tired as she was—and she was tired all the time— anger was the one thing Quinn never seemed to run out of energy for.

"Hey," the maintenance man said, stopping the door before it could close. "You're her, aren't you?"

Quinn slowly put her hand back into her bag and wrapped her fingers around the baton.

"Yes. I'm her."

His expression changed. His mouth was a line. She could no longer see the bad tooth. What kind of videos would they find, in this guy's search history? Was he more of a *Baypen Hoax* or an *Antipatriot Agenda* kind of guy?

He seemed to carefully think about what he was about to say next, then started:

"I want you to know, I—"

DING!

He stopped what he was saying, snapped out of whatever starstruck or indignant path he was about to take their conversation down, and looked to his left to watch the stretch of hallway that led to the elevator.

Over the last year, Quinn had been part of so many interactions that started with "I want you to know . . ." Sometimes they ended with ". . . how sorry I am for all that happened to you."

And sometimes they didn't. Sometimes it was something cryptic like "I know what you did."

A few moments later, Dev was in the doorway, holding the blanket from Quinn's bed folded in front of her. Quinn told her she could come in, and the maintenance man left them without a word, just nodded to Quinn with sad eyes. Or were they angry eyes?

Quinn gave up one of her three chairs so Dev could sit down and they could talk through the girl's apology. Quinn figured now, while she had her roommate in an extra-apologetic position, that it was finally time to tell her how Cole and Rust would be visiting for the weekend.

In the hallway, the maintenance man began vacuuming, and Quinn realized she never did get to hear what he wanted to say.

TWO

The motel drapes were thin and did little to stop morning light from flooding the room.

The light put an amber tint over the walls . . . which made the grubby motel room look even worse.

Rust had been awake for hours, watching his surroundings change from the cool muted-television blue of night to this soiled hue of morning.

Lying next to Rust, with the top sheet pulled up over his face and twisted at the top like a cocoon, Cole snored.

It was not a soft, endearing movie-star snore.

No, Cole Hill's outsize TV-ready persona disintegrated when he let his guard down. It was rare that Cole let his control slip away, but it was unavoidable when he slept. In sleep, Rust's boyfriend honked and sputtered like any other mere mortal. Worse than most mere mortals, perhaps. *Maybe he should get checked for apnea*, Rust thought.

And of course, then there were the night terrors, though Rust knew Cole wasn't having one now.

But it wasn't Cole's snoring that kept Rust awake.

Ruston Vance didn't sleep much anymore. Sure, he could fall asleep no problem. Especially on the nights he stayed over with Cole, where the company meant things felt safer. It was *staying* asleep that was the issue.

Rust shifted in bed. At first to actually get more comfortable, and then again a few moments later because it felt like time to get back on the road.

"Come on. Stop," Cole said without removing the sheet from his face. "It's, like, dawn." Cole knew exactly what Rust was trying to do. And he was right.

"It's almost eight," Rust said. "We'll hit rush hour."

Cole pulled down the sheet, squinted at the light of the room.

"No, we won't. And don't act like hitting a little traffic *one time* in Indianapolis means you're an expert."

"If you want to respond to all her 'Where are you guys?' texts while I drive, then be my guest, sleep in."

"Fine."

"Fine."

Cole pulled the sheet up over his face like a sleep mask.

This was a bluff. Cole liked driving. Rust had only driven

a single shift in seven hundred miles.

Rust waited.

He looked at the small, stained bed around them, then tweezed a bit of fuzz off his elbow. His skin did that now with some fabrics. The sheen of his scar tissue was like a magnet for lint.

"Fine, fine . . . Let's go," Cole said. "The covers smell like bagged cabbage anyway."

Cole jumped up, started stepping into the jeans he'd crushed last night and left on the floor next to the bed. He stretched up before fishing his T-shirt from where it'd slipped behind the bedside table.

Cole looked good as he was petulantly getting dressed, but this wasn't how Rust treated his clothes. Certainly not in a room like *this*.

Last night Rust had folded his shirt and jeans and placed them on the highest surface he could find. Not that Rust could be accused of being a neat freak, or even germ-conscious. He'd field-dressed too many animals for that. He just didn't want mice or roaches—which this motel probably had plenty of—scurrying over and nesting in his flannels.

Cole didn't think about this kind of thing. Cole had grown up with a maid service that came in twice a week. In a big, clean house. A mansion, really. He didn't seem to realize that the rest of the world wasn't Hill Manor. There was also no way Rust would suggest Cole pick his clothes up off the floor. Any time he offered advice like that, it became a fight. Not that the fights were ever more than a few minutes, some heated words defused with a kiss. But Cole would get defensive if he thought Rust was judging him for growing up privileged.

Rust stood from the bed but didn't dress immediately. He couldn't. He went over to his duffel bag, removed the small, travel-sized tube there, and went into the bathroom.

Starting with a fingertip squeeze of lotion—nothing prescription or fancy, just the generic brand from the pharmacy—Rust began moisturizing the areas where he'd been burned last year.

His scars were the price he'd paid to survive. The cost of a resurrection. And they would grow scaly and chafe if he didn't take care of them. The fire messed up the pores and sweat glands when it damaged his skin.

Ear. Neck. Left arm, upper. Right arm, lower. Stomach. Lower back. A three- or four-inch rectangle below both knees.

The routine had become automatic, but it felt strange to be doing it here, in a roadside motel in Pennsylvania.

Last night, he'd woken up and in a rare moment of "Let me google that," Rust had done the math: this was over twice as far as he'd ever been from Kettle Springs.

And today they were going to go farther.

He couldn't help it. The idea made him nervous.

Being called "Redneck Rust" had never bothered him. There were worse nicknames. Plenty of them. Also, something about it rang true. Rust *did* enjoy things that were simple, old-fashioned, and he didn't view "growing up on a farm like your grandparents before you" like it was some kind of death sentence.

But something about a city . . .

Something about how in five hours—four and a half if they sped, which Cole would—they'd be in Philadelphia . . .

The thought put him in a Redneck Rust mindset, but in a bad way. He worried that once they were hanging out with Quinn's new friends, or her old friends from Philly, that he wouldn't be able to keep up. Cole would be fine. But Rust would get quiet, locked up in his own head and overwhelmed.

Or maybe that wasn't the reason he was uneasy.

There would be so many people.

Unlike Cole, since the massacre, Rust had stayed out of the spotlight the best he could—just a few interviews to make sure his story was told right. But to be in a city with that many strangers, some of them were bound to recognize him. Especially if he were standing next to Cole and Quinn. Add to that these crazy fuckers on the internet saying that they'd been aggressors, not survivors, and they—

There was a quick knock at the door.

Cole opened the bathroom door a crack to peek in, not

waiting for a response. There was a slight smile at one corner of his mouth.

"Hey Harvey, I gotta pee."

Harvey. Like Harvey Dent. Two-Face, the Batman villain.

This was not a pet name Cole used when anyone else could hear. It also wasn't as mean as it sounded. Rust was fine with it, really. It was a little gallows humor from Cole Hill, someone who'd been standing atop an *actual* gallows not that long ago. And had been put there, condemned to die, by his own father, Arthur Hill.

Rust had bad dreams and would never be able to forget the smell of his own cooked flesh, but there were days when he knew too well that for Cole Hill, things were worse.

Even if Cole was better at hiding it.

Great at hiding it, actually, an Olympic gold medalist in concealing his anxiety. And Cole's secret, how he was able to stay a few steps ahead of the darkness, was keeping busy.

Cole's magnetism, that star quality that had gotten him in this trouble in the first place, was also his saving grace. A winning smile and a quick wit saw him through TV interviews and talking-head spots, and were essential to his social media, where he engaged in what he called "celebrity advocacy."

And that was only a small portion of how Cole spent his time. As the executor of Arthur Hill's estate—at least all the funds that the government hadn't frozen as part of ongoing legal fallout—Cole had taken an active hand in rebuilding Kettle Springs. He'd invested in new businesses on Main Street. Not only that, but he'd vetted and handpicked new management for all the killer clown–owned businesses he'd taken controlling interest in. This after their former owners had gone to jail—or had been interred in the Kettle Springs cemetery.

Rust had been by Cole's side during it all. The management of all Cole's new assets was so demanding that both of them needed to take what Cole called a "leap year." And what Rust called "I don't think I was going to college anyway, but sure."

But make no mistake: Rust was proud of Cole. Intensely proud.

His boyfriend was doing immeasurable good for the town. For the country, really, by using his platform to speak out against violence and hate in all forms.

There were also days when Rust was concerned. Not only that Cole was working too hard, but that all of this was too public. Too heated. Cole was making himself a target.

A year ago they'd been shot, choked, stabbed, blown up . . .

No matter how vigilant Rust was in watching over Cole, if someone wanted to do his boyfriend harm, eventually they'd catch Rust sleeping. Cole was still pissing people off, which was his way, even if now he was no longer doing it through immature stunts and prank videos. One day, Rust feared those pissed-off people would strike back—and one day, they'd succeed.

"Ready?" Cole asked, his lips somehow a half inch from Rust's ear.

Rust nodded, fixing the second-to-top button on his flannel, the shirt tacky against his freshly lotioned skin.

They walked out into the October sun, the day bright but breeze-cooled, the blacktop of the motel parking lot smelling warm.

"Do we, like, need to check out? I paid in full last night."

Rust shrugged. Both of them were so confident at home, but that confidence went right out the window on the road. What did either of them know about motels? Kettle Springs had one, on the outskirts, but they'd never been.

"Let's give them their keys back at least."

So Cole headed over to the small office with the wire-mesh-encased front desk to take care of that while Rust tossed their bags into the trunk.

Tucking the bags away, Rust looked down.

Well. Cole wasn't spending *all* his money for the betterment of the town. He'd kept a little for himself to enjoy.

It was a ridiculous car for someone a few months out of high school. But then again: Cole sometimes reveled in being a bit ridiculous.

A 2021 Dodge Challenger SRT Hellcat. Black, like the 1974 Challenger that had been junked after parking it in Tillerson's B-field. It wasn't that Cole's old car couldn't have been salvaged. All it would have taken was new tires and a couple of parts special-ordered. But Cole didn't want the memories associated with it. The new Challenger was the same color and model, but there was fifty years of difference between the two vehicles. Even though they'd been sitting in the sleek car for days now, Rust still marveled at the Hellcat. It was like a spaceship. A spaceship with heated seats.

"Want to start us off?" Cole said, crossing the lot.

He underhand tossed the keys to Rust.

Rust *did* want to start them off. He liked driving. At least highway driving, when traffic was sparse. He hadn't liked when they'd passed through St. Louis or Indy, how close all the other cars seemed.

"Can you put in directions?" Rust asked, coming around to the driver's side.

Cole was already on his phone, no doubt deep into an email back to some lawyer or real estate agent.

"Huh?"

"I said—" Rust began, leaning his arm across the car roof, trying to get Cole to make eye contact.

Which was when Rust saw it, the second before Cole looked up. The little smile. Same he'd been wearing when he'd peeked in on Rust in the bathroom.

But now the smile was for someone else.

The smile was a reminder of the other thing that Ruston Vance was concerned about.

Rust opened the driver's side door, getting behind the wheel. Cole got in beside him.

"Is that Quinn?"

"Huh?" Cole asked again, this time his dreamy smile gone, making a show of readjusting and checking the rearview mirror. Guilty fidgeting.

"Did Quinn just text you?"

"No. It was just someone else."

"Who?" Rust asked, knowing.

"Come on. What is this? Am I under arrest or something? I'm not allowed to respond to a text?"

Well. That answered it.

Even if the trip meant Rust traveling out of his comfort zone. Ruston Vance was happy to be away from Kettle Springs.

This was a week when Cole wouldn't have a chance to see Hunter Duvall. And Cole wouldn't be smiling like that, in person, with another guy who he swore was just a friend.

THREE

Outside, a car drove by blasting music. The volume was too high, too loud, too booming.

And suddenly Jerri's mind was back in Tillerson's field: Her music was drowning out the screams of the dead and dying. Bodies collided on the dance floor. Elbows mashed faces. Sneakers crushed hands. Panic.

Jerri looked over from where she was huddled behind the walls of the DJ booth. She got down on her belly, arms outstretched. Reaching. Reaching, her shoulders aching.

If she could only pull the plug to shut the speakers off, then at least the upperclassmen at the party could hear where the shooting was coming from.

So they could try to run away.

"Get to the field! Quick!"

And then time skipped forward and she was in the field.

Jerri found Dorothy. Her sister. Her burnout, asshole sister who hadn't spoken to her in weeks before asking Jerri if she wanted to DJ this party. Partly to be nice, but mostly because Jerri was the only person in Kettle Springs with a deck and speakers.

God. Asshole or not, Jerri was so happy to see Dorothy. They joined hands and ran together, as fast as they could. Two sisters. Trying to escape, trying—

But the field was a trap.

Jerri Shaw heard the sound of a bowstring *thrum* and opened her eyes.

She looked at her fingernails for a few seconds, ragged and chewed, then up at the wall.

Hanging in Ms. Slade's office was a poster that said in rainbow letters: "You Matter."

Jerri wasn't in Tillerson's B-field.

No, it was a year later and she was in the cramped counselor's office of Kettle Springs High.

"What?" Jerri asked.

Jerri wasn't trying to be rude; she honestly didn't remember what Ms. Slade had asked. It wasn't like normal remembering when she got like this. It was like living. Jerri had been *in* the DJ booth. She felt it all again. Time wrapped back around. Only each time she was back in that night, the struggle to get the music turned off seemed longer, small details changing, like was she pulling the cord from a generator or just detaching copper speaker wire? Memory was funny that way, when it'd had enough time to get mixed up with nightmares and anxiety dreams.

She often wondered what else she was misremembering about that night, maybe even suppressing—

"I was saying that you aren't *required* to talk to me," Ms. Slade said. "But if you're going to keep coming to our sessions, you *do* need to keep your eyes open."

Jerri said she was sorry and rubbed her eyes to check for tears. Dry. That was good.

Ms. Slade sat straighter in her chair, moused her desktop screen to life.

Click. Click.

The light of the monitor reflected in Ms. Slade's glasses.

"A's and B's for the first quarter." She pitched her head down, looked over the top of her frames at Jerri. "But I suspect that some of those B's could be A's."

Ms. Slade did this, when Jerri didn't want to talk about her feelings—she started treating their time together like college counseling. "Yes, you're a freshman, but this is high school now. Grades are starting to matter. They . . ."

Ms. Slade kept talking, but Jerri found it hard to concentrate.

Jerri asked herself if these grief counseling sessions were better than attending second-period gym class.

She looked out the window and into the field behind the school. A sweaty Courtney Mazer took the knees out from under a sweaty Mia Novak, grass and dirt clods flying up. It was soccer today.

Yeah, better to be talking with Ms. Slade.

"I'll try harder," Jerri said. Was that the right answer? Were they still talking about her grades?

Ms. Slade kept talking, lecturing her about GPAs and extracurriculars.

Jerri kept watching the soccer match.

The team in the yellow pinnies was getting killed.

Someone grunted loudly and took a shot.

And like that, Jerri was back in it.

"He's back that way," Jerri whispered, feeling sweat cool on the peach fuzz of her upper lip. She pointed behind them. "I'm pretty sure."

"Then we go this way, bud," Dorothy said, a hand on Jerri's back, urging her sister forward.

Bud. That was what Dorothy used to call her when Jerri was little. The three-letter word was too commonplace to count as a *real* nickname, but Jerri found comfort in hearing it. It was better than the other things Dorothy had taken to calling her. Things she said within earshot of their mother, Mom not even getting angry, because maybe secretly she called Jerri those things, too.

Dorothy was crying, mascara so dark it looked like blood

in the moonlight. Jerri's own tears were just starting. But Jerri was crying with relief. Somehow she'd found her sister in all this chaos. She thought they were going to make it out of here alive.

"Come on, don't slow down," Dorothy said, squeezing Jerri's hand. "We can do this."

They made it three more steps before the arrow smacked Dorothy in the face.

The impact snapped Dorothy's head back so quickly that Jerri heard the vertebrae and ligaments in her sister's neck pop and grind, stretched to their limit.

Jerri screamed as something warm and wet splashed the side of her face, and she watched her sister's body crumple to the dirt.

A few seconds later, Frendo the Clown stepped into the row with Jerri. While the other killers Jerri had seen had been wielding crossbows, the Frendo that killed her sister was holding a compound bow.

The clown's head tilted quizzically to the side.

"And your doctor?" Frendo asked.

But he asked with Ms. Slade's voice.

"Huh?"

Jerri was back in the office. Coach Nielsen's whistle blowing outside the window. Time to hit the locker room. Second period almost over.

"Any more confusion?" Ms. Slade asked. "Any more"—she

searched for the right word, in the way only a well-meaning but underequipped school administrator turned "grief counselor" could—"questions about gender?"

"I, uh, have one?" Jerri said.

"Good," Ms. Slade said. "That's great." The woman looked back at her computer, like there'd be a missing homework assignment or an email that'd help her get off this subject.

And now that the memory was this far into being replayed, Jerri had to finish it.

"How old are you?" a female voice asked. The real voice behind the Frendo mask.

This Frendo was a girl, like Jerri.

No. Not a girl. Older. A full-grown woman.

Jerri could see that, in the shape of the costume. The hips under the jumpsuit.

"I-I-I'm . . ."

"How old!?" the woman demanded. As she did, the tip of the arrow was leveled at Jerri's heart. Bowstring still drawn. Ready to kill her like she'd killed Dorothy.

"Twelve," Jerri said; she'd raised her hands before turning and kept them that way. "I'm twelve!" Actually, she'd been thirteen for months. She wasn't consciously lying. At this moment she *felt* twelve. Felt younger, actually, smaller than her slight ninety pounds. Cry-for-her-mom-and-hide-under-the-kitchen-table years old.

"God. You're too young," the woman in the Frendo mask said, speaking to herself. The killer pointed her arrow down at the dirt. But Jerri didn't move.

This Frendo's shoulders were set, body language that meant some kind of decision had been reached. Still looking down, the woman in the clown mask said a single word: "Get." ·

Jerri didn't move. The woman behind the mask sighed, twice, so deep and quick it was close to hyperventilating.

The black holes of the plastic clown mask glanced up, fixing Jerri in Frendo's stare. "Did you hear me?" the woman said. "You need to run in the same direction you were headed for at least five more minutes. Then you stop and you stay put. Even if you're cold and scared, you stay at that spot in the field until morning. *Do not* go back to the barn. Don't run for the road. They'll find you if you try any of that. *We* will find you."

Jerri kept her hands raised. Her shoulders burned but she didn't move.

"Can you understand me?"

Jerri nodded, slow, her neck feeling rusty and pained. The blood on her face cold like her sweat.

"Then show me that you understand me: Run! Get!"

Jerri ran, half expecting this to be a trick. That an arrow would soon lodge in the back of her skull. An arrow to send her to see her sister.

But no arrow came. And Jerri listened to the woman's instructions, ran for what felt like five minutes and then crouched in Tillerson's B-field, listening to the screams and the occasional gunshot.

Jerri stayed in one place, past the chill of the morning dew, until the sun was slatting through the cornstalks.

Eventually a state police officer found her and tossed a blanket over her damp sweatshirt.

"You're all right," he'd said. "You're all right, kid. They didn't get you. What's your name?"

"Jerri."

Then. A moment later. The same word, annoyed.

"Jerri?"

"Oh, sorry. Yes?"

"I asked how are things with your peers?" Ms. Slade leaned forward, elbows on her desk. "Can't be easy being the only person in your grade who was there."

Would it really have made a difference? If she had friends who'd watched their older siblings die the way Jerri had watched Dorothy die?

"It's fine. I don't really talk about it."

"With your friends?"

What friends?

"With anyone," Jerri said, knowing that admitting she didn't have any friends would be a red flag, something else Ms. Slade would want to talk about.

Ms. Slade nodded. Looked at the clock. She must have been counting the minutes just like Jerri was.

"Although," Jerri said. Remembering something she'd read online. In the comments on a post that wasn't hers. It was actually one of the girls who'd just been playing soccer who'd said it. "Sometimes I get the feeling that . . ."

"Yes?"

"That the people who weren't there to see it for themselves . . ."

"Yes?"

"That no one believes me."

And like that, she was crying, and there was still so much of the day left to get through.

FOUR

Glenn Maybrook screamed.

But first he scowled. He wore this sad-sack expression for eight blocks, choosing to walk from his office in the Municipal Building to the edge of town where Main Street met with MO-135.

It would have been a quick drive, but Glenn hoped the walk would calm him, give him a chance to mentally prepare. It didn't. The walk just gave his stomach acid a few extra minutes to churn and bubble.

Reaching the base of the signpost, he took a few quick breaths before looking up. Then another moment to remove his glasses, clean them, and replace them on his face.

Even having some idea what he was about to see, he still screamed. Screamed in both shock and despair.

The image on the billboard was not Frendo the Clown. No, Duvall was too smart for that.

The billboard—which used to be an ad for Baypen, before Glenn's time, and up until yesterday had been a red-and-yellow "Your Business Here" sign—featured a *legally distinct* clown.

The clown lacked the porkpie hat, and there was a slightly different color scheme to his makeup. This not-Frendo on the billboard was using a chainsaw to carve into a jack-o'-lantern. The clown bore down with the weapon, and the pumpkin's features contorted in pain as seeds and pulp flew in either direction.

Beside this image, the advertisement read: "Revved Up Yet? You're Almost There. Stay Right."

Under that was the logo for Duvall Farms Haunted Hayride and Scream Park.

A motorist drove by, honking at Glenn. Or maybe they were honking at the sign, disgusted. Glenn didn't recognize the truck, but it had a sun-faded KHS memorial ribbon on the bumper. Which meant that the driver was local. Maybe even someone who'd lost a son or daughter.

Glenn waved and shouted, "I'll get it down!" even though the truck hadn't slowed, couldn't hear him. He was the mayor now. He had the power to get this problem sorted, one way or another.

With shaking hands, Glenn opened his phone and dialed

Eli Duvall's direct line. Oh how Glenn hated that there was a reason for him to know the number for Eli Duvall's direct line.

Duvall picked up on the second ring and wasted no time making Glenn even more upset.

"Heya, Glenn. What do we think?"

Glenn could hear the smile in the man's voice. He imagined that Eli Duvall had been sitting by the phone, cigar and a glass of cognac ready and waiting. But it was unlikely that Duvall thought that much about the hapless mayor of Kettle Springs.

"This sign is possibly the most offensive thing I've ever seen, and I believe I'm going to sue you back to Branson, Mr. Duvall."

"Oh, you are such a character, Glenn." Duvall laughed, then dropped his voice down lower. "It's not that bad. You've heard me say it before, but the town can't be so afraid of embracing its image and poking a little fun at itself. Turning a negative into a positive, if it'll attract a bit of business. Come on now, Glenn. You're a capitalist, aren't you?"

"People died. Kids died. It's not a joke. Not to me, and not to this town. And I'm not Glenn. Call me Mayor Maybrook. Please."

Either the connection stuttered or Eli Duvall *tsk*ed at being corrected. "Well, all right then." It came out *whey-ar-rightthane.*

42

It had taken Glenn a while, but he had gotten used to the way the people in Kettle Springs talked. It was a subtle accent. They spoke slow, their *F* and *W* sounds a bit muted, an offshoot of the St. Louis accent, he'd been told.

Glenn had spent the last year learning more than the regional dialect. Glenn had been getting a crash course in midwestern geography and culture. For example, he now knew that Branson, a city in southern Missouri along the Arkansas border, was where the Midwest stopped and the South began.

"Ya there, Glenn?"

That accent. It was cartoonish. It had to be a put-on. Or at least dialed up for folksy effect. But it wasn't Eli Duvall's southernness that upset Glenn. No, that would be prejudiced. Glenn was a midwesterner himself. Or at least he was now. He'd adopted this town as his home and his responsibility. He may not have talked like his neighbors, but he was one of them.

So it wasn't Eli Duvall's accent. It was every other aspect of the man that upset Glenn.

Duvall was a businessman who'd made his name in Branson, the city that served as the entertainment capital of the Ozarks. Branson was home to dozens of theaters that hosted jukebox musicals and celebrity impersonators, road-side attractions like laser tag and ATV tours, even a couple of theme parks. Glenn, born and raised in Philadelphia, had never been and had never even heard of the town before moving to Kettle Springs a year ago. All his knowledge about the area had been imparted to him by his executive assistant, Kendra, who vacationed in Branson with her family every summer.

"Let's start again. Since I've clearly upset you, Mr. Mayor." Not what Glenn had requested to be called, but they were getting there. "I had this billboard designed, printed, and hung at great expense. Personal expense. I did it as a favor to you and the town, and then I pick up the phone and the first thing I hear is a threat? Is that how they do things on the East Coast?"

"It's—"

"No, let me finish, Glenn. Because do you know what this sign gets me?"

"I—"

"Nothing. It gets me nothing. By the time they can see it, the guests are already in Kettle Springs. I as good as have their money in hand at that point. But I chose to undertake this act of . . ." He changed what he was going to say. "I chose to give you this *expensive* olive branch with one weekend left in my season."

"Now, don't think I don't appreciate the gesture, but—" Glenn started to say, and then stopped. Why should he give this guy even an inch? He'd never been good with people like Eli Duvall. Men who lived in their own reality. Men with disposable income and inflated senses of self-worth.

"Glenn," Duvall said, "this is exactly what you asked me for. To redirect the traffic that's been missing the turn. Keep 'em on the highway and from getting caught up on Main Street. And I moved heaven and earth to get it done for you before Halloween."

Tourists missing the turn was a problem, to be sure. And this would partially solve it. But Duvall knew full well that the real issue wasn't added traffic on the streets of Kettle Springs.

The problem was Duvall's clientele. No. That wasn't true. Mostly his clientele was every young person within a two-hour drive of Kettle Springs who had twenty bucks. Young people weren't the problem; they were just looking for something to do. More problematic was that fraction of Duvall's customers who weren't kids looking to have fun. The serial-killer groupies, the true-crime junkies, the people who'd been swayed by videos like *The Baypen Hoax* and wanted to get a glimpse of where the "alleged" events had happened. Duvall's business was inviting all these unbalanced murder tourists into town, so Duvall's business itself was the problem.

Thinking about it, Glenn felt his blood pressure spike. Duvall's ghoulish, tone-deaf business.

Glenn wasn't even against the idea of a haunted house. If it were done respectfully and was maybe a couple of towns over. Glenn—you wouldn't think it because he was neurotic and excitable even *before* he'd been kidnapped and forced to be a battlefield surgeon for killer clowns—actually *enjoyed* haunted houses.

Since Quinn was little, Glenn had been bringing her to Terror Behind the Walls, a haunted attraction at an old prison turned historic site in their former Philadelphia neighborhood. Every October before her death, Samantha Maybrook, Quinn's late mother and Glenn's late wife, would say she was too scared to go, that maybe she'd join them next year. But both Glenn and Quinn knew Sam wasn't really afraid; she just wanted it to be something special that father and daughter did together.

So a haunted attraction wasn't itself in bad taste. But having its advertising revolve around killer clowns chasing guests through cornfields? Pushing it. That wasn't even the worst part, though. The "farm" in "Duvall Farms Haunted Hayride and Scream Park" was actually Paul Tillerson's B-field. The *exact* site of the Kettle Springs Massacre. Duvall owned all of Tillerson's property now. The barns, the silos, and the primary and auxiliary fields.

Duvall even owned the farmhouse, though his family didn't live in it. Glenn's daughter had killed someone in self-defense in that house.

Eli Duvall had moved into town and set up a quick

seasonal attraction to profit off the death of the town's children. He was scum. He was—

"Glenn?"

Shit. He was still on the phone.

"Glenn. Are we good?" Eli Duvall said.

Glenn sighed, readjusted his phone against his face, the glass sweaty against his ear even though it was quite chilly out, and began:

"No. We aren't good, Eli. But at the moment I'm not quite sure what there is that I can do about it. Especially, like you said, since you've only got one weekend left in your season. I and many of my constituents have made it very clear that we do not want you here, profiting off our pain, making a mockery of the real-life tragedy that took place on that property. We did not make the licensing and zoning process easy for you, but somehow you persevered."

Duvall started to interject, but Glenn didn't let him. "But if I *do* think of something, some way to get your billboard ordered down or maybe even shutter your entire sleazy business in these next three days, you'll be the first to know. And if I *don't*: I hope you and your family have a happy Halloween and then take your blood money and get the hell out of my town."

Wow. Had Glenn really just said all of that? He was proud of himself.

"But my wife and my kid *like* it here, Glenn," was all Eli Duvall said in response.

Then the line went dead.

Glenn swallowed, playing the interaction back.

He glanced up at the not-Frendo, the clown digging a chainsaw around inside a pumpkin's brainpan.

Had Glenn Maybrook just made a very big mistake?

He wiped his streaky phone screen against his shirt and started walking back to his office, putting the sign to his back.

Not that he had anything to tell her, but he opened his messages and started drafting a text to Quinn. He kept most of the day-to-day operations of running the town from her—no need to worry her about his stress, especially since much of it had to do with moving Kettle Springs out of its past.

For example, earlier this month he'd successfully convinced the city council to replace Founder's Day with a generic Fall Festival. Same revenue for local businesses, 100 percent less connection to what instigated a mass murder.

Like everything about the one-year anniversary, it had gone surprisingly smoothly. Too smoothly, if he was being paranoid.

Hey. Good luck in—

It was Friday. What classes did she have on Fridays?

Bloop-boop!

The sound of the police cruiser scared him, made him

anxious, even in the daylight, even when he was on foot.

The car had crept up alongside Glenn without his noticing. Gravel crunched; a power window lowered.

"You look pale. Should I call the doctor?" Sheriff Lee asked. "Who is also you?"

She smiled even if it wasn't really true about Glenn being the town doc. At least not anymore. Kettle Springs now had two GPs and a podiatrist. Still no hospital or emergency medicine, though. That kind of care was an hour's drive.

Glenn put his phone away, smiled back. More than pale, he must have looked pretty pathetic, his shoes matte with dust, jacket crumpled, shirt collar spotted with sweat, standing and shivering on the outskirts of town in the fall sun.

Sheriff Marta Lee, in contrast, always looked put together. Her arm resting out the driver's side of her cruiser, nails painted, hair back, professional but still styled.

"Did you see the sign?" Glenn asked, crouching a bit to be eye to eye with her.

"Hard to miss."

"And?"

"And why do you think I'm headed back in? I'm going to find Duvall's BMW and cover the entire windshield in parking violations."

Glenn nodded, uneasy.

"That's a joke, Mayor Maybrook. Can I give you a ride into town?"

He got into the cruiser.

Kendra in the office may have helped him keep city council meeting procedures straight, and maintain budgetary deadlines, but Marta Lee was Glenn's real partner in running Kettle Springs.

There'd been a few other applicants for the job of sheriff, so unlike Glenn, she hadn't run unopposed, but she was the only person he'd wanted in the position and the only one he'd even considered endorsing.

Marta Lee was an outsider. Like Glenn. She'd been one of the police officers on loan from the St. Louis PD to help the feds deal with crime scene investigation, security, and risk mitigation. After the mess was cleaned up and the story told in the national media, she'd looked at the town's former sheriff—George Dunne, may he burn in hell—and the harm he'd caused. Marta Lee had wanted to show that not all law enforcement officers were like that. So she'd stayed.

And she *wasn't* like George Dunne. She was a force for good.

"Duvall will be out of here the second he thinks he can make a buck somewhere else—you know that, right?" Sheriff Lee said. "We can wait him out."

"He might not be. He says the event's temporary. Probably is. But have you seen the highway on Friday nights?" Glenn hooked a thumb out the window to indicate 135, which curved out of sight behind the homes and businesses of Kettle Springs. "There's traffic. Actual traffic. That land is making him money. And he owns it all. I wouldn't be surprised if he's already breaking ground to turn the Tillerson place into a roadside museum. Something permanent he can do year-round. 'Come tour the farmhouse of horrors!' or whatever."

"The Salem of the Midwest," Marta said, looking forward. Her shoulders drooped, letting her hands slide down to the bottom of the steering wheel.

"That's what he says, and there are plenty of local businesses that wouldn't mind that. Lots of voters, too."

"Not all of them."

"No. Not all. But I've been there once. Even in the off-season, you know what you see a lot of people dressed up as, while they're walking around Salem, Massachusetts? What the town's known for?"

"I've never been."

"You can guess."

Glenn stared out the window at his town. The life in it. A year ago, it looked nothing like this. It had been shuttered businesses and "Everything Must Go" signs. And in between those dead spots, there had loomed the painted face of a Depression-era clown.

Not only were the businesses back, but the clown was nowhere to be seen on Main Street. Wasn't that something to celebrate? So why did Glenn feel so uneasy? So exhausted with Eli Duvall and having to deal with the handful of knuckleheads who managed to find their way into town when they were headed to his attraction.

It was because even now, even after everything, you could still see the ghostly outline of Frendo's face peeking out the pharmacy window and in the chalk stain on the specials board at the Main Street Eatery. And that's all you saw when there was a news story or a documentary: they showed pictures of the town as it *was*, and the images lingered. The iconography persisted.

"Do you want me to drop you at the parking lot or in front of the—what's going on here?" Sheriff Lee's posture changed with her voice. She turned all-business, all-cop, in an instant.

"I don't know, it looks like—"

And before either of them got an answer, someone's face bounced against the hood of the police cruiser.

FIVE

It was Friday afternoon, school was out, and the world sizzled with possibilities.

Not for Jerri Shaw. All she had to look forward to was sweeping spilled popcorn. And maybe some more crying and another panic attack later, if things with her mom got bad.

But everyone *else* in Kettle Springs had possibilities.

Especially the upperclassmen, many of whom worked at Duvall Farms, but there would still be plenty of time for them to party when the haunt closed at midnight.

Jerri stood under the Eureka's marquee, watching a group of juniors. Not directly watching, like a stalker, but watching out of the corner of her eye. As cover, she smoothed the bubbles on a Halloween window cling, a vampire bat. Ms. Reyes had stuck the decoration to the outside of the ticket booth, where it had been picked at and peeled back by passersby.

Tyler Nguyen, Sandra Wright, and Vin . . . what was Vin's last name? It didn't matter.

The two boys flanked Sandra while she used a compact to check her lipstick. The boys not only had their backpacks, but each carried a duffel bag. Those extra bags must have contained their work clothes. Their *costumes*.

Not that Jerri kept a list, but of the trio, she thought only Sandra had been present at the Founder's Day Massacre. She was friends with Dorothy and had probably been extended an invitation. All three had been sophomores last year, which meant that Tyler and Vin had been JV squad, unlikely to be invited. Sandra had only a younger sibling, a brother in Jerri's grade, so she probably hadn't lost any family that night.

As they approached, Jerri could see that it wasn't just the lipstick, but Sandra was also wearing a dusting of white pancake makeup and had applied baby blue contouring at her cheeks.

Was the girl supposed to be a vampire? A zombie? Whatever role Sandra Wright played at Duvall Farms Haunted Hayride and Scream Park, it was something undead. Undead *and* hot, Jerri thought, turning back to what she was pretending to do before the other kids could catch her looking. Looking and blushing.

They were coming this way, were going to pass the

Eureka. Maybe they'd stop and check out the marquee, then read the posters. All-Night Spookarama. Well. A double feature, so not really *all*-night. Kettle Springs didn't have an official, legal curfew, but staying out past two a.m. simply wasn't done.

The event had been Ms. Reyes's idea. But Jerri had helped pick the movies. She stuck with ghosts and possessions. Nobody in town wanted to see a slasher playing anytime soon. If Tyler, Sandra, and Vin finished with work early enough, maybe they could even stop by after. At least in time for the second feature.

Jerri hadn't attended Duvall Farms Haunted Hayride and Scream Park and had no intention to. But she wasn't angry that the attraction existed, like so much of the town seemed to be, like her mother was. Just because Jerri couldn't fathom being back in that field where her sister died and she'd been shot at and stalked, where she'd caught pneumonia waiting to be rescued, didn't mean Jerri couldn't see the appeal. She'd seen videos of the attraction. Even watched a few live walk-throughs. Pumpkin-headed demons that lunged forward on hydraulic rigs. Possessed farmhands, their overalls stiff with stage blood. Surplus coffins and prosthetic teeth. It was all *pretend* horror. Safe horror. There was something to that. Therapeutic screams. Even the handful of killer clowns were different enough from the *real* Frendo to be harmless.

Maybe if the Duvalls were running the event again next

year, Jerri would apply for a job. She'd been working at the Eureka since the day she turned fourteen and had been off-the-books "volunteering" for a few months before that. Jerri liked work. She liked the sense of purpose. She liked Ms. Reyes. And, most of all, she liked being out of the house.

"Excuse me," someone said, coming down the sidewalk from the other direction. Whoever they were, they probably didn't mean Jerri. Jerri generally tried to stay invisible until a person forced her to acknowledge she wasn't.

"Excuse me, young man," they said again.

Oh. They *were* talking to Jerri. She fixed her expression into a flat smile, realizing that she was standing outside her place of work and this might be a customer service question.

"Oh. Excuse me. Ma'am."

Jerri didn't even have time to be ticked at the misgendering, because the guy standing in front of her was . . . a lot.

Just the sight of him shocked Jerri into silence, wilted her resolve.

Tall white socks peeking out the tops of black boots. Cargo shorts on a cloudy, fifty-degree day. On his belt were a number of small holsters and pouches; Jerri could see a Swiss Army knife, a flashlight, and a phone. He had his T-shirt tucked into his shorts, and over the shirt was a canvas vest with various pins, some with angular, esoteric symbols, but more with tiny writing and slogans.

The guy was in his thirties, maybe forties. It was hard to

tell. He had a receding hairline but not a single gray hair in his thick beard.

"Sorry, but the box office doesn't open until five," Jerri said.

She wanted this guy gone.

"That's okay. I'm not asking about a movie."

The words came out creepy, but to his credit, even he seemed to recognize that.

"What I mean is, some friends and I are in town as part of an investigation, and I"—as he spoke, he took a small device out of one of his many vest pockets—"was wondering if I could ask you a few questions? You live in town, right? You're a local?"

With his vest shifted, Jerri could better see his T-shirt. She couldn't read the whole thing, but had seen enough shirts *like* it to fill in the blanks. The shirt read: "Think for yourself. Search 'Baypen Conspiracy.'"

"That's okay. I'm supposed to be getting to work."

"It'll only take a second. Just a couple of questions."

"Sorry, but I'm really busy."

Trying not to make eye contact, Jerri slung her backpack off one shoulder and began to look for her keys. If she'd unlocked and propped open the doors of the Eureka, like she should have when arriving at work, she could have been inside right now, but there was no use wasting time on would've, could've. She riffled in the bag, feeling the keys jingle somewhere deep, but not able to reach them.

Her search seemed to make her new friend twitchy, so she stopped digging.

He ducked his head, trying to get her to look him in the face.

"I can see it in your eyes. You're young. But you were there, weren't you?" Any shred of good nature left Vest Guy's features, his beard going from a soft oval to a square as he set his jaw. He pressed a button on the handheld recorder, and a green LED began to flash. "Just a quick statement, for the record. Please. What did you see that night?"

For the record . . . This guy was talking like a cop, or like a reporter, but he was neither. She'd seen creeps like him, hanging around, harassing others. He was one of those—

"Is everything okay, Jerri?" Jerri glanced over. She'd forgotten why she'd been loitering outside the Eureka in the first place. She'd been watching Tyler, Sandra, and Vin.

Tyler knew her name! Which meant Sandra and Vin did now, too, if they hadn't already.

"We're fine here," the man in the vest said, holding up his hands, still defensive but already starting to show his belly in surrender. Now that he was outnumbered.

Coward, Jerri thought. It was something she'd thought before. On that night. When they'd killed her sister.

"Jerri," Sandra said. Now, close up, Jerri could see that Sandra was wearing eye contacts, novelty ones that blacked out all the color in her irises. It was hard for Jerri to even look at her, this corpse bride. Sandra had always been beautiful. Dark, clear skin and perfect hair, but the costume makeup elevated that beauty to the level of fantasy. "Is this guy bothering you?"

"Now look," the man-child in the vest said. "Nobody's bothering anybody. I was just asking questions. I like your makeup, hon. Happy Halloween."

"Halloween's not until tomorrow, sport," Tyler said.

"Er, Happy Halloween *weekend*, I guess." The man in the vest redirected his recorder to the juniors, trying to look professional, to regain the confidence he'd possessed when it had only been a single freshman girl he was cornering. "You're all older. Were you out in the field the night of the alleged attack?"

Sandra looked to Tyler and Vin. The boys seemed to come to an agreement. Jerri didn't know why, but it made her feel safe. Her heart was hammering but slowing down. This would turn out to be a fun anecdote she could tell Ms. Slade at their next session, about how her upperclassman *friends* scared off a weirdo.

"Do you know who Dorothy Shaw is?" Sandra asked the man. "Who she *was*?"

"Uh. What?"

Tyler and Vin took two big steps toward the guy in the vest. He matched them with a step back that left him balanced on the edge of the curb.

Jerri looked down at her feet and, in doing so, caught a glimpse of her own hands. The ones that were still never where she wanted them. They were trembling. Maybe she wasn't calming down. Maybe hearing people say Dorothy's name was making her—

Sandra didn't match step with the boys. Instead, she moved to Jerri's side and put an arm around her. Jerri's trembling stopped. Sandra smelled like matchstick smoke and mint gum.

"Dorothy was her sister, asshole," Vin said, dropping his voice to a whisper and indicating Jerri.

"No," Tyler said, jabbing a finger at the recorder. "You took it out. Don't put it away. Keep your interview going, big guy."

"Yeah. Everyone here is sick of this shit," Vin added.

"Sick of. Of . . . ," Vest Guy stammered, then found his courage. "Sick of lying? Sick of covering up? We have evidence! Measurements! Water samples! Ballistic trajectories! We know what this town is hiding!"

Farther down the block, a DoorDash driver was leaving the Eatery. He started to climb into his car, then stopped and joined the small crowd on the opposite side of the street, watching the commotion in front of the theater, all of the bystanders looking unsure what to do.

"I don't know what you kids think you're doing by trying

to intimidate me. I'm sure you think you're standing up for what's right or something. But you're going to end up on the wrong side of history."

Tyler and Vin traded a look, and then both took another step forward. The man with the vest and buttons was now standing in the gutter. It had rained yesterday and there were still puddles.

The man would be in the middle of Main Street if they kept pushing him.

"History? You're about to end up on the right side of your ass, shithead," Vin said.

"Nice," Tyler said under his breath.

"Thanks, man."

"Look out!" Sandra yelled, just as Jerri saw why:

There was a pouch on this weekend warrior's utility belt that none of them had seen.

Pepper spray.

Vin jumped back, retreating, and Tyler dove forward, ready to tackle the guy, but neither moved quickly enough.

The man in the vest flicked the plastic safety cap with his thumb and then depressed the spray nozzle.

Pfzzzzzzzzt!

The cloud was yellow. A dangerous, sickly yellow. Jerri didn't know why the color of the spray surprised her, but it did.

"Don't look!" Sandra's arm on Jerri's shoulder became a

hug, and then her other elbow wrapped around Jerri's head. Sandra's forearm squeezed Jerri's nose out of place, but covered her eyes by the time the mist wafted over to them.

Blindfolded by Sandra's grip, Jerri listened to the coughing and sputtering as it echoed, amplified by the neon and tin of the marquee. Then Jerri made the mistake of breathing in with her mouth.

The droplets of gas didn't taste like pepper, per se, but they were disgusting.

"I warned you!" the man screamed, pausing for a short cough of his own. "You were threatening me! There's witnesses."

"Fucker!" either Tyler or Vin yelled in response. Everyone's voices were pained and ragged, indistinguishable in the chaos.

Then, among all these sounds, putting an end to the swearing, gagging, and shuffle of feet, there was a wet slap, a screech of car tires, and finally a thud.

Sandra's arms loosened from around Jerri's head.

"I think it's"—she coughed—"okay now."

"Drop it! Put your hands flat on the ground," a familiar voice barked. Jerri looked up to see that a police cruiser had pulled in front of the theater, its left wheel bent against the curb.

Vest Guy was now on the ground and Sheriff Lee stood over him. Her hand resting on the butt of her gun, the weapon handy but not drawn.

Jerri had known Sheriff Lee since she was Officer Lee. Jerri liked the new sheriff. She'd been one of the most considerate voices in the days and weeks after what had happened in the cornfield. Jerri had been questioned quite a bit, trying to match her memory of events to which of the clowns could have killed Dorothy.

"I didn't do anything! They attacked me! Arrest them!" the man yelled—screeched, really—into the asphalt, hands at his side, still in the gutter, but now prone so that his cargo shorts were soaking in rainwater.

Mayor Maybrook was here, too. He stepped out of the police car, waving his arms in front of Tyler and Vin as the boys rubbed their eyes with the bottoms of their shirts.

"Stop. Stop touching. You rub and you make it worse. You're putting more in than you're getting out," the mayor said. "We have to flush your eyes. Come on. Follow me. Let's find you a sink."

Mayor Maybrook turned to Jerri and Sandra, pointing. It was clear he was in crisis mode. Glenn Maybrook was a high-strung man, normally, and now sweat popped on his face, fogging his glasses.

"Girls. Jerri. And . . . uh, friend." He didn't know Sandra's name. "Are you okay?"

Jerri gave him a thumbs-up, then looked over to Sandra. Jerri's savior must have gotten a partial blast. One side of her face was smudged and sweaty, the shoulder of her blouse white and blue from the makeup.

"I think so," Sandra said. "These dumb contacts saved me the worst of it, I think."

"Well, the haunt's finally good for something," Mayor Maybrook said in response, under his breath. Jerri was a fan of the mayor. He was like the town's nerdy dad. And he was dating Ms. Reyes, which meant he paid Jerri even more attention than he gave the rest of the survivors. The Massacre Kids.

There was the click of handcuffs, a sound Jerri wasn't sure she'd ever heard in real life but recognized from a thousand movies.

"What! Me? Why are you arresting *me*?"

"Assault of a minor. Minors plural, actually. As many counts as there are kids. You have the right to remain—"

"I'm being arrested for asking questions? It's my constitutional right! This is brutality."

"Only brutality's going to be if the dent your big head left in the hood of my car can't be pulled," Sheriff Lee said, readjusting on top of him. "The right to remain silent. You have the right to an attorney. If your broke internet friends can't Gofundme an attorney for you, one will be provided by the state."

"I don't know about you guys, but I can't hear a word the sheriff's saying," Mayor Maybrook said, loudly humming as he tried the heavy bronze doors of the Eureka and found them locked.

"Jerri, can you let us in? The men's room probably has the closest sinks."

"Yes. I see you. Move along!" Sheriff Lee yelled across the street to the crowd that had formed in front of the Eatery and migrated down the block to stand on the steps of the Municipal Building for a better view. Many of them were filming. A few of the faces weren't familiar to Jerri. Were they tourists? Maybe even the friends Vest Guy had alluded to? Sheriff Lee slammed the back door of her cruiser shut, Vest Guy inside, still yelling about the Constitution.

Sandra helped Jerri to her feet, and after a moment Jerri found the correct key and had the door unlocked.

Vin hissed, then coughed. He looked terrible. There was a thick string of mucus connecting his nose to his chin. "How long does this last, Mayor Maybrook? We've got a shift tonight."

Mayor Maybrook sighed. "I'm sure Duvall can spare you. And it's Doctor Maybrook—for the moment, I guess. Come on, guys. Let's wash."

Jerri pulled the door open for him, and they led the partially blind boys inside.

"Thanks, kid," Mayor Maybrook said. "Maybe stay out here. Sheriff Lee will probably want a statement. What a mess."

Glenn started to duck inside the darkened lobby, then seemed to think of something else and stopped.

"Eh, this, uh . . . Izzy will be okay I'm doing this, right? Using the sinks?"

Inside the lobby, the boys groaned in pain.

Jerri smiled. With all that had happened, Mayor Maybrook's awkwardness was still able to make her smile.

"Don't worry. Ms. Reyes will love it, actually. I'll put in the good word. Tell her what a man of action you were."

He flashed her a half smile, then let the door close behind him.

"Is the mayor like, your friend?" Sandra asked.

Jerri blushed. Not the way she'd thought she'd ever get to talk to Sandra Wright. But she'd take it.

SIX

Look at it.

A horror show.

A well-oiled terror machine.

Hunter Duvall shut the tractor's engine and, sitting up high, a few feet above the top of the cornstalks, he took a moment to appreciate his creation. He looked out across the field's acreage, the many structures and pathways of *his* haunt, and allowed himself to feel a deep, satisfying pride.

It was the best he'd felt about anything in his nineteen years, actually.

It was only a little after three p.m., the sun still high, hours before opening, but he could already hear tonight's screams.

And the sound got him excited.

Not a little excited. A lot excited. The act of frightening paying customers gave Hunter Duvall a near-sexual thrill.

Was that sick? Was it wrong?

Maybe. But he tried not to think about right and wrong.

Even with the fog machines switched off and the strobing effects of the haunt's colored lighting rigs obliterated by daylight, the attraction was still a thing of beauty.

They advertised the haunt as a hayride *and* "scream park," which implied a series of separate attractions. But that was a slight deception. There was only one attraction. One long experience spread across several stages meant to deliver a sustained, satisfying, and thematic haunted house experience.

The flow broke down like this: Guests arrived, parked, and were entertained by stilt walkers and scare actors as they queued to buy their tickets or to redeem the tickets they'd reserved online. Once they'd been given their wristbands, guests then entered a second queue to board the hayride. Each tractor could haul twenty-five to thirty guests, and the ride took roughly fifteen minutes, starting and stopping, ending a mile and a half from the ticket booth and offloading guests in the middle of the cornfield. Yes, this was the notorious Tillerson B-field. Once on foot, the guests waited one final time in a third line to enter the walk-through portion of the attraction—a winding, disorienting thirty- to forty-minute walk that would deposit them back at their vehicles. To prevent congestion and bottlenecking, the walk-through was segmented into four themed zones, each with its own entrance where groups of guests could be corralled by costumed staff and told to wait, if the zone ahead of them had begun to reach capacity.

It was Friday, Halloween weekend, and ticket presales were strong. Almost too strong. A lot of guests were looking forward to being terrified tonight. Hunter's segmented lay-out had worked so far, no major security or safety concerns, but with the sheer number of guests they were expecting, this final weekend would serve as a stress test. If Hunter's design passed that test, it would help him make the case that the haunt should return next year.

And Hunter wanted the haunt to return. He wanted it more than anything. Not only did he want the opportunity to expand and improve the attraction, but he enjoyed living in Kettle Springs. Even if Eli and Jane Duvall returned to Branson, he would probably stay behind. He liked the town and its people, one person in particular. He could see a future here.

But first he needed to do his afternoon maintenance and safety checks.

Hunter climbed down from the tractor, sure to stay mindful of the footholds. If he fell and injured himself out here, it'd be a long wait for help. The first of their employees, the scare actors and ticket takers, mostly high schoolers, wouldn't be arriving for another hour or two. With his feet on solid ground, he reached up and palmed the top of a skull that had been knocked askew, readjusting its eyeline so that it was watching the entrance to the thresher accident scene.

Running a haunted attraction wasn't a set-it-and-forget-it job. Hunter and the rest of the staff were constantly fighting against wear and tear. Guests got rowdy, touching props, sets, and performers when they shouldn't. When Hunter's dad had bought this land, there were only a handful of existing structures in the field, most of them unsafe to have guests walk near or under. The more famous landmarks of the field—the charred skeleton of the barn, the dynamited silo, etc.—had to be rebuilt and reinforced. But those didn't provide enough indoor space, so the Duvalls erected a handful of structures to protect Hunter's more elaborate sets and props from the elements. These temporary buildings were cobbled together quickly and cheaply with plywood, drywall, and even canvas tarps, and were constantly in need of repairs to keep them safe for guests.

Upkeep was a full-time job, but Hunter didn't mind. Every new problem was a learning experience, a chance to improve. An opportunity to build a better people-trap.

Because that's what a maze was, wasn't it? A people-trap. Even a maze that wasn't a maze, like the haunt, where guests couldn't get lost, no matter how much the pathway in front of them twisted and doubled back on itself. It might not have seemed it, but guests were never in danger, if they followed the house rules and kept their hands to themselves when an actor got in their face.

Years ago, in elementary school, Hunter had gotten into a fight with an older kid after the boy started trash-talking Hunter's dad. Looking back, it wasn't really the kid's fault. He was probably parroting something he'd heard his parents say. He'd called Eli Duvall a "slimeball" and a "fraud" and referred to the family attractions as "tourist traps."

At the time, Hunter had been upset, but now he understood that "tourist trap" wasn't really an insult. Trapping tourists *was* the family business. There was no shame in trapping tourists as long as, once trapped, they were entertained.

Laser tag, go-karts, escape rooms, and murder-mystery dinner theaters—Eli Duvall owned them all. He even held a controlling interest in the Ozark Howler, a mountain coaster and one of Branson's premiere ride attractions. Hunter's friends had parents who were bank tellers and landscapers, but Hunter had been born into the entertainment industry. And now, entering adulthood, he realized how lucky that made him.

Granted, Hunter *was* biased given all the work he'd put into the attraction, but he believed that Duvall Farms Haunted Hayride and Scream Park was the best thing his family had ever done. And though he'd only just graduated high school—and barely, at that—the haunt was Hunter's.

Yes, it had taken the whole family to make the dream a reality. His father put up the capital required to buy the land, for all the construction, and to prop up the payroll before the customers really started coming. His mother spent countless hours hunched at her computer with spreadsheets, tax forms, building codes, and licensing requirements. But it had been, to start, Hunter's dream.

For years he'd been begging his father to diversify into the haunted attraction industry and, when Hunter was old enough, to let him manage one. Real estate in Branson was at a premium, though, and Eli argued that a haunt required too much square footage. It had taken an event of *national* importance, and the promise of free *national* publicity, to get Eli Duvall, ever the huckster, even halfway interested.

Hunter put his hands together like he was about to pray, then parted the burlap curtain that portioned off the first indoor room of the haunt.

He stepped into the cool and dark, breathed in the stale fog juice for a second.

The room, a butcher's shop with fake human body parts hanging so that guests needed to bump past them to get through, smelled like dirt and sugary-sweet stage blood.

Of course, there was a cheaper way to build an attraction out here in the boonies. An easier way. The Duvalls could have planted and sculpted a simple corn maze, then hired a few actors to put on clown masks, pumped in some spooky music. But that would have made for a disappointing attraction. It would have been everything their critics claimed they were doing: a tasteless cash-in.

No, if the temporary move across the state and his father's investment were going to be worth it, Hunter believed that the haunt had to be good. Damn good. It needed to have scope and ambition, and last a satisfying span of time.

Even with the pinholes of light coming in through the abattoir's canvas roof, it was still too dark in here to see much. Hunter took a small headlamp from his pocket, pulled the elastic up over his hair, and clicked the light on.

Under the harsh white beam of the lamp, none of this gore was particularly scary or realistic. There were more expensive props up ahead, but it couldn't all be pro-level; some of this stuff was dollar-store Halloween decorations and Hefty bags. But if you added some red mood lighting? Had an actor, covered in clear plastic, posing as a dead body and then leaping out as a group passed? Gold.

Everything looked fine in the butcher shop, no upkeep needed. It had rained last night, but there were no puddles anyone could slip in, just the mildewy scent of dampness, and if anything, that moisture enhanced the experience. The condensation would make guests think that the blood splatter on the walls was fresh, that they were getting it on them.

Hunter exited into the sun, moving to an exterior set piece. The next scene had scarecrows scattered along the path. The prop scarecrows were rough, with wicker arms grasping wooden posts in a way that suggested a crucifixion. The scene was only mildly less sacrilegious than it sounded. One in every three posts was empty so that an actor, dressed as a scarecrow, could pretend to be trussed up, waiting for a victim so they could jump down to startle them.

Far from being a traditional corn maze, the haunt was much bigger than the cornfield itself. The cornfield was just the raw material to carve out for alleys and clearings. There were ropes of phosphorescent tape, cordoning off anywhere a guest might be tempted to head off the path. And as a result, needing to track down lost customers happened less often than Hunter initially feared it would.

Next, funneling guests into a single-file line, there was a vortex tunnel and beyond that—

Hunter's phone dinged with a special, custom chime. The rev of a chainsaw.

The sound didn't indicate a text, but instead a push notification. Cole Hill had posted something to IG.

Hunter looked down at his phone, but forgot he was still wearing the headlamp and got a blast of glare in his eyes. He switched off the light and slid open the notification.

He frowned.

This was not the Cole Hill content that Hunter Duvall wanted to see.

The story was a looping video of Cole's bare feet, propped up on the dash, the Philadelphia skyline out the windshield, and Ruston Vance driving.

Mother. Fucker.

Hunter wondered if he should just turn off notifications, if just the sight of Cole's boyfriend was going to upset him this much. It wasn't like he and Cole were together. They'd talked a few times. But Hunter was sure they *should* be together. They could be a Kettle Springs power couple. The boy millionaire and the teen entertainment mogul. If only Cole would see that—

Someone coughed.

Wait, what?

Nobody but Hunter should be out in the field this early in the afternoon.

Hunter looked up, cocked his head to listen. Nothing. Had he imagined the sound?

He stared into the dark circle of the vortex tunnel. The tunnel was an elevated platform with two sets of steel steps on either side. Guests entered, walking a narrow gangplank as a neon-streaked cylinder spun around them, mirrors on both ends making the tunnel appear longer than its twenty feet. Walking through the effect was disorienting and made you feel like you were entering a DayGlo nightmare world.

Hunter had placed the vortex here to act as a gateway to the haunt's next zone, a string of set pieces that involved killer clowns. With all the ingenuity and care he'd put into the rest of the park, Hunter still understood that killer clowns were what people were really paying to see. Even if the Duvalls never *directly* referenced the real-life horror of the Founder's Day Massacre, they did allow it to be their guiding inspiration.

The clowns of the Scream Park were actors dressed as black light–sensitive mutants with bulbous, distorted features. They wore demonic, pullover foam rubber masks. No porkpie hats. No pom-pom buttons. No 1930s clown makeup. No one was trying to be Frendo. It was one part good publicity, one part good business. Even without their clowns being *the* clown, it was more than enough to scare the shit out of most of their patrons.

That was why the placement of the vortex tunnel was so crucial. Guests heard circus music bleeding over from the scenes ahead of them. It built suspense. Antici—

The cough. Again. Louder now.

The sound ended with a wheezing through closed lips. Like someone was trying to muffle the cough, hide a sickness.

Hunter opened his mouth to ask if there was anyone there, but then thought better of it.

No. If there was a trespasser in the haunt—a trespasser in *his* haunt—then he didn't want to give them time to flee before he had a chance to see who it was.

Hunter stepped up into the tunnel, trying to be as quiet as possible despite being on metal stairs. With the cylinder around him motionless, not swirling like it would be tonight, he took baby steps, listening. Out in the clearing ahead of him, there were the sounds of movement. Then a tacky crackling that was not a cough. Hunter couldn't place the sound.

Who was here with him? High school kids? The haunt employed half the high school. He didn't think any of them were stupid enough to get fired before receiving their final week's pay.

Where was the trespasser? They sounded close to the mouth of the tunnel. Which meant they were likely standing in the shadow of the reconstructed barn.

The Duvalls' construction crew had been able to salvage some wood from the original structure where a lot of kids had died. It smelled like smoke and death. And Eli Duvall had insisted that the salvaged lumber be reused, reincorporated into this new barn. For history, he'd said, and to save on lumber costs. But Hunter knew it was more likely that Dad had done it to piss off the mayor.

Hunter reached the end of the tunnel, peeked his head out, and froze as he caught a glimpse of the intruder.

Their back was to him. Hunter couldn't see their face; all he could track was that they were wearing dark coveralls. It was hard to focus on many details beyond that. Because more interesting than the identity of the intruder or what they were wearing was what they were doing.

Hunter tilted his head up to take in the expanse of the barn. Ah, that was the crackling-dragging sound he couldn't place. The sound of a paint roller.

Big, each letter a few feet high, the trespasser had painted "FRENDO LIVES" on the side of the barn.

The graffiti seemed to glow in the late-afternoon light, the dark red paint almost 3D against the alternating fresh-plank, scorched-plank pattern of the rebuilt barn.

The man in the paint-streaked work outfit hadn't noticed Hunter approaching. He just kept working, using the long pole and roller to go back over the *E* in "LIVES."

This fucker was going to lose them business!

"Hey!" Hunter yelled.

The man, not overly tall, not overly gaunt, but some of both, didn't jump at hearing Hunter's voice. He was calm. Almost like he was expecting to be discovered.

"What the hell do you think you're doing?"

Hunter stepped down the stairs of the tunnel, down into the dirt of the clearing.

It was easy to forget, since Hunter walked this route

every day, multiple times a day, that something horrible had happened in this very spot. A group of teens, not much younger than he was now, had traveled to this clearing to have a party, and all they'd found was horror. Real horror, not the kind that Hunter had become an expert in.

The man who'd been painting the barn still hadn't turned, merely set the end of the roller down.

The roller displaced the paint in the tray with a slosh.

Black flies rose up from around the roller. . . .

They had been sitting on the edge of the tray. Bodies so swollen they flew in lazy slow circles.

The man finally turned to Hunter. He wiped his hands— no wait, gloves, he wiped his gloves—on his coveralls.

But his face wasn't a face at all.

The man was wearing a clown mask.

This mask didn't belong to the haunt, wasn't one of their designs. This mask wasn't latex pulled from a mold with a fine, movie-quality sculpt. It wasn't black light–reactive.

This mask was thin molded plastic affixed to the man's face with an elastic strap. *This* mask was so old, so well used, that there were cracks, chipped seams where the mask had been broken and glued together many times. Like it got a lot of wear.

This was a Frendo the Clown mask. And not a knockoff or a reproduction, but a genuine Frendo mask.

And the sight of it scared the hell out of Hunter Duvall.

"Hey. What the fuck? Private property. Get gone before I . . ."

Before he what? The clown kept staring forward.

The man in the Frendo mask didn't react. Just stood and breathed, chest and shoulders up and down. Intimidating in his near stillness. His dark coveralls were lumpy. Like he was wearing multiple layers of clothes.

The flies settled back onto the roller and tray. Hungry.

What type of paint drew flies?

Come on. Find your voice. This is your place. Your dream. And this fuck—

"Look. I know you're probably doing this as, like, a protest or something. But"—Hunter held up his phone—"I'm calling the cops right now and—and we, we press charges."

He moved his thumb over the phone to show he wasn't bluffing. He wasn't bluffing, right?

And then the guy in the Frendo mask did move. But not to run away.

He took two steps toward Hunter.

Every hair on Hunter's body turned into a needle.

This was fucked.

Hunter wanted to run, but he didn't. He held the fear in, felt it push out through his pores as cold sweat.

"Okay. I'm calling the cops."

Another step. The man was empty-handed; he carried

no weapon that Hunter could see.

But now, this close and with a slight change in the wind . . . Hunter could smell him.

The dark overalls hid the worst of the stains, but now that he was looking, Hunter could see the crusty runnels of caked filth, and smell the rot.

The scent knocked Hunter out of his stupor.

He dialed 911 and the operator picked up on the second ring.

"This is Hunter Duvall—" His voice caught, then cracked. He felt like a middle schooler. "Yes. I'm out at Duvall Farms, I have a trespasser here threatening me, and I'd like—"

But before Hunter could finish that request, the man in the Frendo mask turned, took five unhurried strides toward the end of the clearing, and disappeared into the corn.

"Hello? Mr. Duvall?" the operator asked in his ear.

Hunter sighed, watching the spot in the corn for signs of movement.

"Hello? Please stay on the line. I'm sending a car."

Fuck, Hunter thought. Then mouthed the word a few more times.

"Actually. You know what? I'm so sorry. False alarm. It was one of our employees."

"What? Sir, you can't—"

"No need to send anyone. Sorry about that," Hunter said,

then hung up with a quick and overeager: "Thanks!"

The last thing Hunter needed was the sheriff shutting him down tonight, the night before Halloween. And over what? Some internet lunatic wanting to tour the scene of the crime without paying the admission fee?

It took Hunter half an hour to find a hose long enough to wash the animal blood—he hoped it was animal blood—off the side of the barn.

By the time he was finished, the sky had darkened to dusk and the line outside Duvall Farms Haunted Hayride and Scream Park was two football fields in length.

The blood had been washed off, but the words were still there, faded. If you squinted, you could still see them:

FRENDO LIVES.

SEVEN

"Disgusting!"

"Truly horrific, right?"

"Yeah."

"So you like it?"

"I love it."

"Most people do," Quinn said.

She knew Cole would enjoy. But she was unsure what Rust would say. At the Eatery she'd seen him order dishes that were just as fatty, meaty, and cheesy as a Jim's steak. But there was a finickiness to Rust, an *If I didn't try it before I was ten, I don't like it* attitude that flared up at the weirdest times. It was the inverse of Cole's *I'll try anything once* adventurism.

Cole wiped his chin and passed the sandwich to Rust.

"Come on, don't make that face," Cole said. Whether it

was to switch up his style or because they'd been living out of suitcases—for the first time since Quinn had known him, Cole had stubble.

"I'm not making a face," Rust said, though he clearly was. Rust stared at the sandwich for a moment, then took a big bite of cheesesteak, looking like he was trying to spite Cole with his enthusiasm.

Quinn had ordered a single steak for the three of them to share. Whiz wit. Translated: chopped steak drowning in processed Cheez Whiz spread *with* grilled onions.

"Pretty good," Rust said from around his unswallowed mouthful. He didn't sound convincing.

"You're a goddamn spoilsport," Cole said. "Give me. I'll have your share. You don't deserve it."

Quinn laughed. It felt like, in the two months she'd been away, the couple had entered a new phase of their relationship. Sure, they'd just finished driving across the country together and had been with Quinn for less than two hours, but for every handhold or small show of intimacy that Cole and Rust shared, there was also some good-natured needling.

No less love, she thought—it was just being expressed differently.

"Before you fill up," Quinn said, "remember that this is just the first stop. We started here because everyone who comes to Philly wants a cheesesteak. But it's not our best local cuisine. It's not even our best sandwich."

As she spoke, she looked around them at the second-floor dining room of the restaurant. They'd gotten here between the lunch and dinner rushes and there hadn't been much of a line, but now the room was filling rapidly. There were at least two tables where patrons recognized them. As Quinn watched, cupped hands whispered and the news spread quickly.

She hadn't considered how visible the three of them would be together. She should have, but she hadn't. By herself and far enough from campus, Quinn could sometimes go whole days without being recognized. But Quinn Maybrook, Ruston Vance, and Cole Hill at the same cramped metal table at Jim's Steaks? There were people online who called them "the Three." And it wasn't just crime enthusiasts—most people who watched the news would be able to ID them.

Jim's had better steaks than Pat's or Geno's, which were the more touristy places slightly south of here, but Jim's still drew plenty of tourists. Whenever Quinn found herself accosted, it was usually out-of-towners who made the trouble. The folks who were in Philly to see the Liberty Bell, Constitution Hall, and to pose with Rocky were often also, it turned out, big fans of *The Baypen Hoax*.

"What's next on the tour?" Rust asked. He had his napkin balled in his hand. Had he spit out the big mouthful of steak? She hadn't seen him do it, but his mouth was empty now. Beside him, Cole was arranging the sandwich on the tray, letting the grease and cheese drip out, taking pictures of the whiz wit from multiple angles.

"We, um . . . ," Quinn said, losing her train of thought before looking up to Rust.

"Yeah, I know, I see them. Don't let it get to you," Rust said. There was tension in his voice. "But where to next?"

"Lorenzo and Sons."

"That's the big slice of pizza?"

"The biggest."

"And then?" Rust kept eye contact, trying to convince Quinn to focus on what was next just as much as he seemed to be trying to convince himself.

"Then a break from eating to walk the Magic Gardens, which he'll like because . . . ," Quinn said. "Hey." She tried to get Cole's attention without saying his name. He was still snapping pictures. "Hey," she repeated, leaning over the table to poke him. He looked up, blinked at her. "We're staying on South Street for a bit after this."

Cole wrinkled his brow. "Uhh . . . okay?"

"So we'll still be in the area. Maybe don't post those yet." She indicated his phone.

Then, finally, realization on his features.

"That"—Cole looked around them—"makes sense."

Quinn knew there'd been some travel over the last year

for Cole, but the bulk of that had been to St. Louis for the local network affiliates. In most cases the media had come to him via Zoom. Needing to move around a city while keeping a low profile weren't considerations he was used to taking.

Because if Cole posted a geotagged photo while in Kettle Springs? Like in the new Mexican restaurant on Main Street? Who cared? It wasn't the same as doing it in a city full of strangers.

"Don't worry. You can post them later," Quinn said. "And you'll have plenty more pictures after the Magic Gardens."

"Yeah," Cole said, "I can't wait. Pizza first, though. I'm still hungry."

So he *had* been listening.

Beside him, Rust stood too fast, his jaw set, metal chair skidding on tile. "Then are we done with this?" He pointed down at the mostly uneaten sandwich.

No, they weren't done, but Quinn heard the unease in his voice. Cole did, too.

"It's all right," Cole said to Rust. Then, louder, so the rest of the dining room could hear: "Guys, it's okay. Be cool. They're just curious."

The dining room was all small metal tables, some pushed together to accommodate families, with two walls of counter space so those in a hurry could stand and wolf down their cheesesteaks. Rust stood, tray in hand, ready to toss their lunch into the garbage, so that he was eye to eye with the diners at the counter space. He watched one group in particular. They were three men, all with buzz cuts. Either members of the military or—if Quinn and her friends were having bad luck today—civilians who liked to dress like they were in the military.

"It's okay, babe," Cole continued. Quinn wondered how often Cole needed to de-escalate situations like this. And how Rust felt about words like "babe." Maybe he didn't mind them when his anxiety overran his reason and started tipping into panic. "Again, be cool. Why don't you sit down and let's—"

"Excuse me," a voice came from over Cole's shoulder. The first person in the restaurant brave or oblivious enough to approach them was an older woman. She was wearing walking shoes, a baseball cap with a tail of mesh covering the back of her neck, and an American flag sweatshirt. In other words: a tourist.

"I know you're eating," the tourist woman started, "but I'd just like to say . . ." She was addressing Cole directly, not the three of them. It was possible, with his media visibility, she *only* recognized Cole.

". . . say that . . ." She seemed to be aware that the whole room was listening to her, slightly embarrassed.

Quinn tensed at what was coming next. Like the maintenance man last night, it was a crapshoot what any given person in the country thought about them and the role they played in the Kettle Springs Massacre. Or the Founder's Day Massacre. Or sometimes the Baypen Massacre. The name changed, depending on who was speaking it, but the massacre part . . . that always stayed.

Like with the maintenance man, Quinn thought about the combat baton tucked into her handbag.

"I don't mean to bother. I would just like to thank you, really. For all the work you do when you go on TV. It can't be easy to share that much of yourself. But you should know that it's appreciated. Our daughter is . . ." As the woman stumbled with her words, Quinn looked at the family behind her. There was an older man, her husband, presumably, a teen boy who was maybe in middle school, and a young woman in trendy athleisure wear, possibly a college student.

"My daughter is . . . queer?" the tourist woman said, testing the word out, trying to say it with the proper inflection. "Like you and your friend."

"Mom. Jesus. I'm twenty-six," the young woman, the queer daughter in question, said.

Cole smiled wide. "You're not bothering us. It's okay. Thank you, I appreciate that," he said to the tourist woman. Cole then leaned back in his chair and caught the daughter's eye. With a charming sort of sarcasm, he held up a fist in the air in a *Solidarity, sister* gesture.

The young woman smiled, but before anyone could say anything else, Rust cleared his throat.

89

The three men with the buzz cuts had pushed back off the counter and now surrounded their table in a rough semi-circle.

As harmless and endearing as she'd turned out to be, the tourist woman had opened the floodgates. She'd made it okay for the rest of the patrons to approach these three famous strangers.

One of the buzz cuts, his shoulders wider than his buddies, so their natural leader, spoke: "Is it true?"

Ah fuck. Here it goes.

Quinn could see Rust's neck flex, his scar tissue so tight it looked about ready to separate from the rest of him and make a run for the exit.

Quinn tensed as well.

But Cole remained Cole. Face blithely welcoming but a glint in his eye that said he might be bullshitting.

"Some's true and some's not, my man," Cole said. Being in the national spotlight hadn't *taught* him anything. Or hadn't taught him anything new; it merely honed his preexisting charisma and assholish charm.

"Depends on what you mean by true," Rust said. He shifted slightly, putting his body more directly between these three men and Cole. The change in body language was telling: if given the choice between protecting Cole or Quinn from danger, Rust would default to Cole every time.

That was fine. Quinn wasn't offended. Back in Kettle Springs, Rust and Quinn hadn't only been doing weapons training. They'd met three times a week in Rust's garage for strength and cardio drills. Quinn, who'd already been lithe and athletic before arriving at Kettle Springs, was now toned and muscular. And she'd continued that trajectory at school. The university had a clean, well-lit gym where she kept to her routine.

With both the gun range and the workouts, Cole had sat those sessions out. He preferred to fight with his mind.

"Did you really frag all those bastards?" the lead guy clarified.

"Yeah, did you waste an entire clown cult yourselves?" his smaller but more tattooed friend added, skeptical.

"Hell yeah we did," Cole said.

"So, uh," the lead buzz cut said, "can we get a selfie?"

Quinn felt her muscles relax, Rust let out the breath he'd been holding to puff himself up, and Cole laughed.

Cole stood, motioned for Quinn to get up, too.

"You sure can."

Cole put his arms around Rust and Quinn. Once squeezed together, Quinn had a better idea of Rust's discomfort. It seeped through his pores, wafting up through his jacket collar. This wasn't good. Quinn recognized it all instantly; she'd been there herself. The almost tactile smell of anxiety. Whether these guys they were currently posing with were "fans" or not: it didn't matter. Rust was about to snap.

"Three . . . two . . . one . . . ," Cole counted down, and led them all to repeat after him, "Screw you, Frendo!" as he depressed the shutter on one of the men's phones.

At that, most—but not all—of the people in the dining room laughed and applauded.

Rust began to pull away.

"Wait," Cole said, loving the attention, "one more for safety so that—"

"Boo!" someone said loudly. Not booing, but actually saying the word "boo." Quinn turned to see an old man in the corner, his family beginning to hush him, beg him not to make a scene. "Boo! Fake news!" He waved his hands across the dining room. "And you're all sheep. Don't you realize that they're murderers? You treat them like celebrities. Shame on you!"

The men with buzz cuts turned to the old man.

There was violence on their faces.

"Here, take your phone back," Cole said to the big guy, but he was too preoccupied, marching into the corner of the room. Cole set the phone down on the table, then, to Rust and Quinn, whispered: "Let's get the fuck out of here."

And they did, making their way to the exit before anyone else could stop them, before the shouting match between the old man and the three soldiers was anywhere close to being defused.

Out on South Street, with sun and fresh air that didn't smell as heavily of meat and cheese, some color returned to Rust's face.

"So where's the pizza place?" Cole asked, acting like nothing was wrong, trying to move on from the shitshow he'd just instigated.

"Right over there," Quinn said, pointing down the block. Rust leaned around the corner of Fourth and South to see.

"Can we skip it?" Rust asked. "It's too close. Someone could follow us."

"Fine with me," Quinn said. "We can walk to the Magic Gardens that way." She pointed to Bainbridge, the next block over. "There'll be less foot traffic."

"But isn't that too far too fast?" Cole asked. "Aren't your Philly friends meeting us soon?"

Quinn had forgotten about Tessa and Jace. And with good reason. A week ago, she'd told Cole and Rust that they'd be hanging out this weekend, but that turned out to be a lie. Quinn had never worked up the nerve to invite the girls. She was convinced they would have found a way to excuse themselves, so why should she open herself up to that?

"I meant to say earlier, but they aren't coming," she said. Then, not quite understanding why she'd lie, she offered:

"They have midterms or something."

"Whoa, really?" Cole said. "That sucks, I really wanted to—"

"Can we discuss this as we walk?" Rust asked. His eyes ping-ponged around them. The corner was practically empty. One or two pedestrians in either direction. Nobody had taken notice of them. Nobody was following them. They didn't need to be running away.

"Hey," Cole said. Then waved a hand over his own face. "Hey. Eye contact."

"Don't talk to me like that in front of her," Rust said. Growled it, really. He wasn't kidding with Cole; this wasn't like all the play fighting.

But Rust *did* make eye contact.

"Fair. That's fair. But remember, you're not sick," Cole said. "You're hurt, maybe. We all are hurt. But we're not the sick ones. They are." He pointed back up to the second floor of Jim's.

Quinn hadn't been part of whatever conversation Cole was rehashing, but she didn't need a recap.

She understood what he meant.

Trying to make sense of things, a year ago, in the days and weeks after, she'd had similar thoughts. How Arthur Hill's motive didn't make much sense. Or that it didn't make sense *unless* you considered the entire context, the steps it must have taken to get Dunne and the others on board.

Townwide, then nationwide context. Like Cole said, there was a sickness one needed to understand. And instead of shining a light on that sickness, spreading awareness, all the news coverage did was make things worse. Because first the opinion pieces reframed that coverage, then the comment sections under those opinions sparked and spun off into Reddit threads, and finally all that supposition and misinformation was collected up into internet documentaries.

Paranoiacs and conspiracists studying what had happened in Kettle Springs itself became a more powerful variant of that same sickness. The clearer that the motive was laid bare, the more that *actual* evidence was meticulously reported, the louder that nonbelievers shouted, "Parents don't kill their kids! They just don't! It's a hoax! It *has* to be a hoax!" And their germs of disbelief seeded doubt in others, a sickness bottled at Baypen and stamped with the too-wide grin of Frendo the Clown.

The thought reminded Quinn of something she wanted to ask Cole. So she interrupted the moment he and Rust were sharing: "What was that in there? Chumming it up with those hoorah guys? Are you an advocate for violence now, Mr. Hill?"

She was joking and she wasn't. All the #stopthehate work Cole did. The interaction back in the restaurant didn't seem to serve the brand.

"You'd prefer that I'd given the guy with the 'Don't Tread

on Me' bandanna tied around his arm an anti-violence lecture?"

"No. I guess not." She hadn't noticed the bandanna.

"It's not an act, you know. I want to do good in this world. But a big part of keeping us"—Cole indicated the three of them—"safe from guys like Radicalized Grampa in there is making sure we have support from a single slice of the public where we can get it." Rust tapped his foot. He'd heard this before.

It made sense. It was beyond "playing both sides" or "telling them what they want to hear." No matter how clueless Cole acted, even that was a technique he used to disarm potential enemies. Cole always knew what was going on in a given interaction and tailored his response to the specific person. He did the same thing in those TV interviews the tourist mom had enjoyed so much. On MSNBC it was more #stopthehate; for Fox News he leaned on the narrative that Quinn, Rust, and Cole were the ultimate Good Guys with Guns. It was Cole's high school experience, the cool guy who was comfortable with every clique, dialed up to one hundred, the stakes now life and death.

Still, Quinn couldn't be that way. Wasn't ready to even try. And she could see in Rust's expression that he wasn't, either.

"I'm with Rust, actually. Let's forget the pizza. We should get off the street," Quinn said. "Let's go back to the dorm. All the food on my tour is available for delivery. We can order in. Relax. The Magic Gardens will still be there if we want to try for it tomorrow. If not, it's just a bunch of broken glass and concrete."

Cole set his surprise into a slight grin. He wasn't used to losing. "Can we compromise? Get a few slices to go?"

And they did, calling a Lyft to take them back to campus once they each had a giant slice of pizza so big it necessitated two paper plates to hold.

In the Lyft, Cole and Rust sat in the back, Quinn in the front passenger's seat. Cole had parked his ridiculous car in an overnight garage near campus and didn't want to take it out. She didn't blame him.

Their driver didn't recognize them. Or maybe she did and was pretending not to. Either way she was cool, encouraging them to eat their pizza and asking at every light if they were okay with the temperature and radio.

Five stars. All the way.

By the time they arrived back at the dorm, all they had was a half piece of crust between them.

Rust and Cole filled out their visitor cards with the time and handed their IDs back to the man at the security desk. There were three or four guards who rotated working the desk, but this security guard, Joe, was Quinn's favorite. He was a retired alum who'd once told Quinn he'd taken this job for the free football and basketball tickets. That may have been part of it, but Quinn suspected that Joe genuinely liked watching over the kids. Making sure they stayed safe and had a good time at college.

"Be good, boys," Joe said, paper-clipping their IDs to their cards and placing each in the folder behind his desk.

"Always nothing but," Cole said, and Joe laughed like he understood the extent of the irony.

Quinn thanked Joe, then moved them through the first floor's common areas. These areas were weirdly empty for a Friday evening. There were usually a few groups milling, waiting for friends to get dressed and come downstairs so they could go out, and then a few more groups munching on French fries in their pajamas, just chilling.

They reached the elevators and before calling for one, Quinn warned them: "Just a heads-up, my roommate might still be in the room."

"She's allowed," Rust said. The pizza and quiet car ride had helped with his irritability, but he wasn't completely back to himself. Or maybe this was his baseline now. Maybe without Quinn a few houses down to exercise and shoot guns with, Rust had grown insular and sullen.

He was right, though. Dev *was* allowed to be in their room. It was somewhat unfair for Quinn to even ask her to stay away. But it was kind of Dev to offer to stay with the girls across the hall. And even kinder of them to be cool with it.

The elevator doors shut. And before they even started moving, Cole asked:

"Do you hear that?"

Quinn strained, listened.

"Yeah," Rust said. "What is it?"

It was an echoing susurrus, reverberating toward them down the elevator shaft.

It was an ominous sound. There was a fullness to it that triggered a cascade of pinpricks down the base of Quinn's neck.

The car rose and the fuzzy, amorphous sound resolved into a familiar bassline.

And then voices.

And then . . . wolves howling?

"That's *Thriller*," Quinn said.

The doors opened onto a party. Or the beginnings of a party. The early phases where everyone was still smiling and clear-eyed. No spilled drinks or hurt feelings yet.

And it was a costume party.

"Oh shit," a boy dressed as Captain Morgan said. It took a second for Quinn to recognize him as Mason, one of the boys who'd been in her room watching *The Baypen Hoax* last night. "They're here!" Captain Mason yelled down the hallway.

"We're here?" Rust asked.

Somehow, even seeing fake cobwebs pulled tight across

storefronts and freshly carved jack-o'-lanterns on apartment stoops, Quinn had forgotten that tonight, at midnight, it would be Halloween.

So much for the three of them spending a quiet night in her room.

EIGHT

"Don't cry. It's just movies."

"I'm not crying," Jerri said, but maybe that wasn't true.

Barely anybody had shown up.

Jerri didn't know why she was this upset. The Spoo-karama was Ms. Reyes's event. Jerri just worked here. But Ms. Reyes somehow inspired these kinds of feelings. To Jerri, she was more than a work mom and more like a mom mom. With dark hair kept in a permanently exasperated ponytail, she even looked like Jerri's mom.

Jerri didn't think tonight's show would sell out or anything. But she thought there'd be a better response to the double feature than this.

Seventeen tickets sold. And even fewer bodies in the auditorium. The turnout was enough to cover the rental and exhibitor fees for both films, but only when you added in popcorn sales.

Jerri cursed herself. She knew starting with *The Haunting* had been a mistake. Why hadn't she listened to her gut and tried to convince Ms. Reyes otherwise? They should have tried to lure in the young people of Kettle Springs, the small handful who were free tonight, with a newer movie. Then they could have sprung the classic on them as a second feature.

"Look. It's almost midnight," Ms. Reyes said. "We aren't selling any more tickets. I've got one more reel change, and then I'm swapping over to a DCP for the second movie. You go enjoy yourself. Watch the show. I'll man concessions."

Jerri nodded, like this was something she was interested in doing, when Ms. Reyes added: "You had a big day."

Which was true. She'd cried at school, in Ms. Slade's office, and it'd gotten crazier from there. She thought about the guy with the pepper spray; being held by Sandra Wright; and Mayor Maybrook flushing everyone's eyes with sink water. A rush of fatigue made her eyes tear up again.

"Good talk," Ms. Reyes said. Like a real mom, her patience was finite. She looked at her watch. "Speaking of last reel change. It's coming up. I gotta . . ."

And Isabelle Reyes walked away, unclicking the clasp on the rope that kept patrons from the stairs that led to the mezzanine. She bounded up the stairs two at a time, then disappeared toward the projection booth that only she was allowed inside.

Jerri didn't listen to her boss's suggestion to go take a seat in the auditorium. Instead, she stayed behind the counter and stirred the popcorn drawer because this was her job. She wasn't here to watch movies; she was here to sell Buncha Crunch to anyone who left to go to the bathroom between features.

The lobby of the Eureka had a three-story ceiling and a large antique chandelier that was as old as the building itself. The tip of the chandelier pointed down at the middle of the concession stand, and because of this, Jerri always stood to either side of the register.

And it wasn't idle paranoia that made her worry that one day the assemblage of metal and glass would fall and crush her. Cole Hill's initial investment in the Eureka had covered *most* of the theater's refurbishment. But the money wasn't limitless. Choices had to be made. Top of the list, and most costly, had been outfitting the projection booth with the digital system necessary to screen first-run movies. After that, Ms. Reyes had prioritized replacing the theater's HVAC. Then the marquee, a job where Ruston Vance helped research and organize the labor. Then new coats of paint, new rolls of carpet. Fixing the chandelier? No, they could only give it a good dusting and reinforce the chain. Complete rehab would have been too expensive. There wasn't even money to fix up the dry-rotted and rusted mezzanine to allow—

Tap tap tap.

Huh? Jerri looked up from where she'd been picking at her cuticles.

In the oversize lobby of the old movie house, the tapping pinged off lightboxed posters and the jewels of the chandelier. It took Jerri a moment to realize the sound was coming from *outside* the Eureka.

Someone was tapping at the box office window.

Eighteen tickets, Jerri thought, smiling. Maybe more, if it was a whole group of KHS students off the clock from working the haunt.

Jerri scurried out from around the concession stand and cracked open one of the front doors instead of searching her key loop to unlock the box office service door.

"Can I help you?" Jerri asked, sneaking up behind the customer. The guy turned, and she was immediately embarrassed to realize that she was talking to someone she recognized.

Hunter Duvall stopped knocking on the box office window and looked down at her.

There was a slight sheen of sweat on his forehead. He might have been out of breath, or drunk, but whatever was going on with him, he was trying to hide it. He swallowed hard before speaking.

"Hey," he said, then continued, fast and breathless, "Can I ask: When does tonight's show end?"

"It's um . . ." Jerri took a beat before answering, trying to remember not only tonight's schedule, but her own name and the English language.

If the upperclassmen of KHS were larger-than-life soap opera stars that Jerri liked to keep tabs on from afar, then Hunter Duvall, a year older and much rarer to spot around town, was even more intimidating.

Jerri found her voice in one of the only ways she knew how: talking movies.

"The program's not even half over. We started late. There was an issue with the trailer reel. Which is good news for you, because there's still a whole movie left. *The Conjuring.* The first one. The one with Annabelle in it."

"Okay." Hunter seemed to chew on this information. "Okay. Great."

"The box office is closed, but I can sell you a ticket inside, if you'll follow me."

"No. That's okay. I have to drive back to . . ." Then he changed his mind.

Whatever was going on with him, he was having trouble keeping eye contact with Jerri. She wished he'd look away long enough to give her a reason to look down at her hands. "Actually, would it be all right if I came in? Just for a second. I want to check if my friends . . . if my friends are in there. Whether they got here first."

Friends? Not that she was in a position to judge, but did Hunter Duvall have friends? Jerri could name most of the people in the auditorium right now, and she thought it was *highly* unlikely that any of them were Hunter's friends. The regulars at the Eureka tended to be older. The town cinephiles. One or two town drunks.

"Come on. It'll just be a minute. I'm not trying to sneak in for free. I promise. Please, Jerri."

"Jerri." Jerri said her own name. How did he—

"Your name tag."

She didn't know why, but that pissed her off. She'd gotten this way since Dorothy's death. Quicker to anger. Ms. Slade had given her a pamphlet about it, but the pamphlet hadn't helped.

Jerri thought about the seventeen tickets they'd sold tonight, of poor Ms. Reyes who cared so much about this town, and about how much money this guy and his family were siphoning away from the business. How the theater hadn't had a decent teen crowd since the haunt opened.

Bastard. She stood up straighter.

"A ticket's eleven fifty. And you have to buy a ticket; otherwise I can't let you in."

"Eleven dollars!"

"Eleven fifty. Special price for a double feature."

"That I missed half of!"

"So you're poking your head in to check for your friends or you're staying to watch the movie? I'm confused," Jerri said, a finger under her chin.

"I can't believe this," Hunter said, reaching behind his jacket. The movement alarmed her for a second, until she realized he was reaching for his wallet.

"Do you take credit cards?" he asked.

Jerri smiled and held the door wide open for him, ushering him toward the concession stand. "Everything but American Express."

Hunter stood impatiently while she looked through the register's ancient operating system for the "double" SKU. Then she took his card and, before swiping, asked: "Will that be all? M&M's or Sour Patch Kids? A Diet Coke, maybe?"

He stared forward. Eyes blank. Not amused.

She tore his receipt at one corner as his stub and handed back his card, and he continued into the auditorium without another word.

A minute later, the sweat on his brow more pronounced, breathing heavier, he left the theater and pushed out into the night.

Well. He really *had* been looking for his friends, she guessed. And hadn't found them.

With Hunter gone and no new customers coming anytime soon, Jerri stood by the far corner of the concession stand and peered through the auditorium door's tinted diamond window. Standing in that position, her back to the lobby, she watched the final reel of *The Haunting*.

She was proud of herself. She'd gotten an additional eleven fifty in the till, but it felt like more than that.

So even with muffled sound and an obstructed view, Jerri Shaw allowed herself to be absorbed by the movie.

She was so rapt, she never once turned to look at the lobby behind her.

Even as Frendo the Clown crossed through.

NINE

The room's door shook in its frame.

Little stood between them and the party that was currently raging.

According to Dev, this whole thing had started as a quiet pregame session in someone's room. But somehow, as people got into their costumes and group chats were consulted, it had become a case of *Why not just party here?* and the room party had grown to a floor party with everyone in the building invited, and soon seasonal novelty songs were being exchanged for some pounding Meek Mill.

Bags of Halloween candy bought and shoplifted from the CVS two blocks down Broad. Rooms cleaned out and the school-issue furniture pulled into the hall to give kids a place to sit. Some kind of *Be smart and keep it in your rooms* agreement had been reached with the RAs on duty, so drinking had to be done discreetly—"11B has Beam, 19A has lager"—shots were lined up in shower stalls, and bottles overflowed ice-filled sinks.

Even though Rust, Cole, and Quinn had arrived at an early stage of the party, they still had to push their way through a lot to reach Quinn's room at the end of the hallway.

A lot of hands for Cole to fist-bump and slaps on the back for Rust to flinch against.

A lot of "Hey, Clown Girl! What's up?" for Quinn to sneer at.

Quinn sat on the radiator, listening to the noise outside her room.

Cole and Rust sat on her bed. Both looking like they regretted every bit of driving out here to visit with her.

"When we first got here, that guy had said"—Rust looked over to Dev, who was sitting cross-legged on her own bed—"he said, 'They're here.' Are we some kind of guests of honor?"

"Yeah, I mean no no no, you're not. Sorry about that," Dev said. "We didn't even know if you'd be back in time. Quinn said she was taking you out to see the city. So we weren't expecting you. At all. Honest. But people know that Quinn lives here and—"

"And you *had* to let them know what I told you last night.

That my friends were coming into town for the weekend."

Dev frowned at Quinn, a sorry look about to become a cascade of verbal "sorry"s.

"No need to apologize," Quinn said, not wanting to hear it.

While the girls in the hallway had opted for sexy costumes, topical costumes, or a mix of both, Dev was wearing an off-the-rack honeybee costume that could have been for children. She wore the bulky fabric thorax over black leggings and a black turtleneck. Dev had accessorized the form-concealing yellow-and-black polyester with springy sparkled antennae and painted freckles of pollen across her cheeks.

It was a costume so lame it became endearing, and Quinn was finding it impossible to stay pissed at the girl. And she was *trying* to stay pissed. Even if the party had been spontaneous, Dev could have at least texted Quinn a warning to let her know what they were walking into.

They sat for a moment. Not in silence, because the music was too loud for silence, but at least without talking.

Cole looked at his phone. Rust closed his eyes and let his head rest against the wall, raising it after a second, probably because the vibration of the music was too strong, was rattling his skull.

Dev was twitching her lips and scrunching her eyebrows—her *I'm sorry* face.

Under Quinn, the radiator was beginning to warm. She

tried to focus on the heat and not Dev's stare.

"You *are* my guests, though," Quinn finally said. "So what do you want to do?"

"What are the choices?" Rust asked, keeping his eyes closed as he spoke. Implying that his choice was trying to sleep through this, shutting out the world.

Something slammed against the door. They all cringed at the sound. Except Cole, who was typing on his phone, unfazed.

Out in the hall, a burst of laughter, and someone else called someone a dick. Quinn couldn't know for sure, but she guessed a Nerf football or something similar had been whipped against the closed door. A mistake that wasn't a mistake, some mischievous drunk guy trying to get "Clown Girl" and her friends' attention. To get "the Three" to come out from where they were hiding and party with them.

"Choices are we stay in here," Quinn started, "or we try to leave."

"Leave to go where?" Rust asked.

"There are plenty of places, I guess. Maybe a restaurant? Get another Lyft and go bowling or something?"

"Yeah, I'd rather not," Rust said.

"There's also option three," Cole said, putting his phone back into his pocket.

"He speaks."

"Yeah, my sidepiece isn't texting back."

Rust opened his eyes at that, blinked.

Quinn was lost, because Cole's delivery barely sounded like a joke. *Did* he have a sidepiece?

"Sure, zing, good one. What's your option three?" Rust asked.

Cole spread his hands out like it was obvious. The reverb wasn't as bad now. The Meek song was over, and it was time for the playlist to switch to another holiday song. A bluegrass version of "Dragula" with a few boys on the floor singing along. Quinn wondered if this was a Spotify playlist or if some Halloween enthusiast out there was DJ-ing.

"We could go out there, have a drink, and loosen the fuck up," Cole said, a challenge in his voice.

"Are you serious?" Rust asked.

"He's serious," Quinn answered for Cole.

"It's a college party," Cole said, a pleading in his voice, looking around at all of them, even Dev, who wasn't involved in this decision-making process, as far as Quinn was concerned.

"Yeah, when you say it like that, I don't know what I have a problem with. When have we ever had a *bad time* at a party?" Rust's scars seemed extra prominent in the dorm room's lighting.

"Come on, don't be that way," Cole said.

Quinn could almost see Cole's reasoning. There weren't many safer places they could be. Downstairs, Joe, the security guard in his seventies, wasn't exactly intimidating, but he *was* a deterrent. Nobody was going to be walking into the dorm off the street. At least not easily. It was as safe a place as they were going to find.

"This seems like it's probably a private conversation," Dev said, inching her butt to the edge of her bed, her bee antennae bouncing as she uncrossed her legs. "So maybe I'll just go out there and—"

"Don't open that door," Quinn said. The radiator had reached full blast now. It was becoming uncomfortable to sit on.

Quinn stood up, which caused Dev to move back onto her bed, shrinking.

"It's a costume party," Rust said. "I *would* go. But I don't want to feel . . . out of place."

"Look. I get it." Cole clicked his tongue. "You two can live your lives like this if you want. But it's been a year. Over a year. If something was going to happen—say like if my dad was going to return and try to kill me again—don't you think he'd have done it already? Like on the one-year anniversary or whatever?"

Quinn didn't know how to react to his question. For all of Cole's joking and self-deprecation, they *never* talked about Arthur Hill. Or the fact that his body was never recovered and that the internet was chock-full of rumors he was still alive.

Also, they'd all three let the anniversary pass mostly without comment. They hadn't even *discussed* it. When nothing had happened, even though Quinn had been in Philly for the day itself, it had seemed disturbingly anticlimactic. Like they really were done. Like she'd memorized chokeholds and ammunition caliber charts for nothing.

Rust sat up, then laid a hand over Cole's shoulder. He was quickly shaken off.

"No. I mean . . ." Cole started again. "Yes. We're going to get looks. Yes, people are going to be weird. But my god, guys, I can't tell you how badly I want to have a beer somewhere other than sitting on my couch."

Cole reached for the doorknob.

"Or sitting on the toilet," Rust said. He was smiling now.

"Or while I'm crying in the shower," Cole added. Also smiling.

"Come on," Rust said. "You know if you go out there that I'm going with you."

"Yeah. Me and my shadow. But I just don't want to feel guilty about it."

"You don't have to."

"You'll tell me when you've had enough?"

Rust nodded.

"By using your words? Not just by being a quiet bitch?"

Rust nodded again, but looked pissed about it.

"Good."

They both looked back to Quinn.

Okay.

They were doing this.

They were going to a college party.

"Um," Dev said, her voice small. Rust and Cole turned to the girl, surprised. Quinn understood; half the time, she forgot Dev was there, too. "I know he was probably joking about the costumes thing, but I . . ."

Dev reached under her bed and pulled out a long plastic crate, a container that only fit because she'd put her bedposts on *two* sets of risers. Dev lifted the lid on the crate to show Rust and Cole all the construction paper, glitter, and markers she kept in her arts and crafts set.

"Ha. Now we're talking," Cole said.

"I chose a bee not just because I thought it'd be a *cute* animal costume, but because I really like bees. I think they're important and I respect them. They do a lot for the environment. If we didn't have bees, the planet would, like, completely fall apart," Dev said, handing out pairs of small child-safe scissors like a kindergarten teacher. "Now, before you start cutting, think: What kind of animal do you, more than *like*, which animal do you think is *important*?"

Cole used the scissors and gray construction paper to trim tufts of hair and two curved horns. A goat. *The* GOAT, he insisted.

Quinn, least enthusiastic among them, cut two triangles

for ears and glued on a black pom-pom for a nose. "I'm a fox," she said. And when Dev asked why she didn't use red paper or at least her orange markers, Quinn specified: "I'm an Arctic fox."

Rust used his green construction paper to shape a beak and poked two small nostril holes.

"A, uh, parrot?" Dev asked.

"A turtle."

"'Cause he's slow and wise," Cole explained, urging them to hurry up and staple on their elastic so he could get out the door and start his drinking.

"No," Rust corrected: "Because turtles are tougher than shit."

Ruston Vance had worried the mask would be claustrophobic.

He worried that he would get too hot in it, that the paper would soak up his sweat.

But now, after twenty minutes—or had it been more like an hour?—Rust was learning to love the mask.

Rust stood in the doorway to Quinn's dorm room, the empty suite at his back so he could retreat into its privacy, if he wanted to, and watched the party.

The masks were kind of stupid. Everyone in this hallway knew who was behind them. But there was something comforting in having a barrier, even a paper-thin barrier, between the commotion in the hallway and himself. Peering through his turtle eyeholes, Rust felt less like a participant, more like an observer.

People were being cool, leaving him alone, letting him just stand and take in the sights.

Rust watched as a vape was passed between girls discreetly, the gem on it glowing pot green instead of fire red. He watched as a couple exchanged phones, dialed in their numbers bashfully while stealing glances and giggling. He watched a guy stumble out into the hallway, then fall onto his friend and kiss a wet burp in his ear.

It was nice, watching all these things.

And then, when he was feeling about as comfortable as he'd felt all year, through his construction paper mask Ruston Vance could see down the hallway as the elevator doors slid open and Frendo the Clown stepped out into the hallway.

Quinn heard the gasps and the yells. But they didn't worry her. They sounded like any number of party yelps. She expected the noise would be followed by laughter, and somewhere a girl would be swatting playfully at someone's shoulder.

But when no laughter followed these sounds, Quinn felt her skin go cold underneath her paper mask.

She turned just in time to watch the elevator doors

close—a large man in a Frendo mask dressed in black tactical gear now in the hall with them.

"Bad taste, my guy!" someone yelled.

"Fuck off with that costume!" the girl next to Quinn shouted, then put her hands in the air and gave him an enthusiastic double thumbs-down.

The man was huge, a head taller than the nearest students that shifted uneasily out of his way. The Frendo mask scanned the party. He was looking for someone. This wasn't the Frendo that Quinn remembered from Tillerson's B-field. His black tactical fatigues had endless pockets and pouches, and the short-sleeved Under Armour top he wore under his vest and bandoliers revealed tanned, muscular arms and two sleeves of tattoos that stopped at his wrists.

"Hey!" Quinn could hear Rust yelling from behind her, not wanting to use her name. "Hey. Form up!"

They'd drilled for situations like this, using phrases like that. But, clearly, they hadn't anticipated this exact scenario. A long hallway with dozens of other bodies between her and Rust. It was not ideal.

Rust might have been being overly cautious, though. It was uncertain whether there was any real threat. The Frendo mask might have been someone's idea of a joke.

And the party seemed to be taking care of the situation itself.

Quinn readjusted her mask, peered into the room across

the hall, and squinted at the dimness. Cole was somewhere in there, drinking in the bathroom. Hopefully he'd hear the change in party sounds, get the hint that something more serious was going on, and come out.

Quinn looked back down the hallway, toward the elevators.

One, two, three, four. She counted doorways. She was in almost the exact center of the party, equidistant from the elevator and her room.

Someone dialed the music down so partygoers could better yell at the man in the mask. The *Ghostbusters* theme cut off exactly at the word "Who—"

The partygoers didn't all press flat against the walls, but a few of them did, and then a few of those inched toward the nearest open doors. A few stood their ground, either not yet noticing the Frendo or not caring, but enough of the partygoers were out of her line of sight so Quinn could watch what came next.

"Private party," Mason said. The boy who last night had been showing conspiracy videos to Dev took off his large red Captain Morgan hat, but kept on the fake beard.

Either drunk or brave, Mason walked up to the guy in the Frendo mask and pushed him, hard, in one shoulder. He motioned back to the elevator. "Get lost, Fren-Doe."

So quick that Quinn could barely register the movement, the man in the Frendo mask dipped his hand down to his thigh, drew a small handgun, a 9mm most likely, and shot Mason in the leg, dropping him immediately.

Fuck.

There was stillness in the hallway for a half moment, then chaos, bodies against bodies, arms clawing at walls and carpet, tripping over furniture to get away as Mason screamed and cried and held his leg.

Then, something that gave Quinn a small sliver of encouragement: instead of firing his weapon again, the man in the Frendo mask took his finger off the trigger and went back to scanning the crowd as he walked forward.

The man hadn't killed Mason.

That meant he wasn't *there* to kill Mason.

It was possible, but not likely, that he wasn't there to kill anyone.

The hulking man slow-walked down the hall, driving partygoers in front of him, gun at his side, rows of students breaking like waves.

Cole had appeared in the doorway across from Quinn, peering carefully around the corner.

"Oh shit. What do we do?" Cole asked.

He sounded drunk already. How long had he been in that bathroom?

Quinn reached into her bag and removed the baton.

"Get back to my room," she said to Cole. "Get to Rust."

Then a girl dressed as Elsa from *Frozen* bodychecked

Quinn, sending both off-balance as the girl scrambled for safety.

Doors began to be slammed shut, but too soon. Partygoers crowded outside those same shut doors, banging to be let in.

"But it's my room!" Pete cried, jiggling the door handle. He was dressed as some kind of superhero. An X-Man? Blue spandex sagged unflatteringly off him.

Quinn walked forward.

Not because she was brave, but because she wanted this to be over. Quinn was moving *toward* danger. She was swimming upstream, which was difficult at times, but most who saw her coming moved out of her way.

She'd been training all year for this.

She'd been—

The man in the Frendo mask passed in front of a closed door and whirled to his right just as the door was thrown open.

Two guys and a girl fell out into the hallway, rushing him.

"Get the gun!" one guy yelled.

"Go go go!" the girl said as she ducked low, going for the masked man's knees.

Not so stoic anymore, the man with the gun yelped as his arm was pressed up, straining in its socket, while a fourth partygoer, a tall and lanky guy dressed only in a

Speedo—Michael Phelps?—added himself to the pile.

The gun went off, but the bullet sailed harmlessly into the ceiling with a puff of plaster dust, and the students were undeterred.

The man in the Frendo mask screamed again. "Stop, stop!"

They didn't listen to him. They kept bending. They were going to tear the guy's arm off, dislocate his shoulder completely if they hadn't already.

Good.

Quinn was jogging now, the stragglers in front of her giving her wide enough berth so she could flick out her wrist, extending the tactical baton to its full length with a single smooth click.

Three more steps.

The guy was screaming in pain, had finally dropped the gun, and the boy in the Speedo was now kicking it down the hallway with his bare feet, toward the elevator. Not exactly great gun safety, but better than the attacker still having it.

Quinn reeled back and finally screamed to the dogpile: "Let him go!"

The guy covering the Frendo mask with his torso saw her coming and moved out of the way.

The textured tip of the baton cracked against the top of the man's skull, the rest of the pole flattening his ear with her follow-through.

All of them fell to the floor, the girl's hand crushed beneath the big tattooed man as he blinked out of consciousness and crumpled.

Quinn hit him two more times in the side of the head and was going for a third when someone grabbed her hand on the backswing.

"Stop it," Rust said. "He's down."

Rust who, in his other hand, had a small silver pistol trained on the man's neck.

It did make sense that Rust would have kept a gun in his overnight bag.

"Everyone okay?" Cole asked, and he was being serious, but it somehow read like a joke to Quinn.

Around them, people moaned. Mason was still screaming. Overlapping, panicked 911 calls were canceling each other out, nobody able to hear what they were saying or make any sense. Inside the rooms they'd just been drinking in, people were sobbing, calling their moms. Saying things like "It's okay"; "Everything's okay"; "I just want you to know that I love you."

Quinn hated this. All of it. Hated the world that would allow it to happen so often.

"Hey," Cole said, taking the baton from her, wincing at the blood and hair on the end of the nub. He was the only one of the three of them that still had his paper mask on. The GOAT.

Below her, the masked man's chest rose and fell slightly. She hadn't killed him.

Not yet, anyway.

That was probably for the best.

It would mean less time explaining herself to the police.

Quinn reached for the Frendo mask to peel it back. Something she'd done too many times in her life.

Sometimes déjà vu wasn't déjà vu. Sometimes it was just the same shit happening again and again until it drove you insane.

God almighty, Quinn was so tired of this shit.

But still, it had to be done. She had to see *who* it was behind the mask.

This time.

She hooked a finger into one eye hole and pulled . . .

"Who the fuck is that?" Cole asked.

She'd half been expecting the maintenance man from last night. But maybe that would have been too tidy. Would have wrapped things up too quickly.

The man had a cleft chin, was slightly bloated and bleeding out of one ear.

Like Cole, Quinn had no clue who the unconscious man in the Frendo mask was.

And she didn't have time to care.

Because in the last six minutes, Quinn had missed three calls from her dad.

And her phone was now ringing a fourth time.

"Hello?" Quinn said, answering.

"Oh god." It wasn't her father's voice on the other end of the line.

It was Dad's girlfriend, Izzy Reyes. Quinn was confused. How could Izzy have heard about what had happened so quickly?

But then she figured it out. Izzy was crying and frantic for a different reason.

"Oh god, honey. Oh Quinn. You need to get out here right away. You need to come home."

"What happened to my dad?" Quinn asked.

TEN

Glenn Maybrook was trying to be careful.

He didn't want to rush in.

And not only for Quinn's sake, but for his own mental health.

But today had been a lot. He'd already argued with Eli Duvall about the billboard, watched an out-of-towner tear-gas four minors, and spent three hours behind a two-way mirror, watching Marta Lee question the same Frendo "truther."

He deserved something good tonight.

He deserved to see Izzy.

The filament bulbs of the Eureka's marquee above his head hummed and seemed to radiate warmth. Seemed to, but there was still a chill in the evening air, so he pulled up his jacket collar to protect his neck. Glenn didn't do well in the cold. He barely made it through Philadelphia winters. Last winter in Kettle Springs, where the average temps dipped easily ten degrees lower than in Philly, had nearly made him rethink moving here all over again. Glenn wasn't looking forward to the winter, not at all, but still he'd be glad when Halloween, and its frustrations, was over.

Glenn looked down at his phone, peeling off his gloves and sliding them into his jacket pockets.

Five minutes ago, Izzy said there was five minutes left in the first movie. Glenn told himself to be patient and wait a few more minutes before texting again. She knew he was down here waiting. If he got too cold, he could step into the lobby. But honestly: he'd rather not chance seeing anyone else.

As mayor, Glenn had more than a few people he didn't want to run into. When he'd first taken the oath of office, one of Glenn's biggest worries was that he'd lose touch with his constituency.

He'd been so naive. The real problem was finding one moment to do his actual job when an "engaged constituent" wasn't barging into his office, ready to chew him out.

His phone buzzed.

Almost the credits. Switching over systems and will be right down.

Ah. So he hadn't been forgotten out here.

Glenn Maybrook smiled, even though the night was getting colder.

Frendo the Clown sat, watched the end of the movie, and tried not to move in their seat too much.

While there was a fresh-paint-and-new-carpet scent to the rest of the theater, the mezzanine was different. The floor was spongy with decay, and the seats made a terrible squeaking sound when you shifted. This row smelled like corrosion and motor oil. The front row, where Frendo decided it was too risky to sit, smelled a little better: like corrosion, motor oil, *and* Twizzlers.

On-screen, Eleanor, the film's haunted protagonist, was about to make a fateful decision.

In a few moments the credits would roll.

Now was the time to act.

This was the plan.

This was how the floodgates would open.

Frendo began to stand, but then fell back to the seat, rusted springs groaning.

They pinched the bridge of their nose. The pain behind their eyes intense. It was getting worse.

Worsening as Frendo thought, fixated on the question: *But how can I be in two places at the same time?*

In different time zones for that matter?

There was no time to contemplate this.

The movie was about to end.

Hurry. Any further delay and Frendo may still be able to complete their part in the plan, but there would be witnesses.

Frendo pushed through the pain, pulled themselves up, and rolled their mask down over their face.

It fit like a second skin.

Ah yes.

That felt better.

It'd been a whole year in Kettle Springs, and Glenn still wasn't used to the quiet.

Their Philly neighborhood had been relatively sleepy, but even there someone would have been on the street at this time of night.

Especially tonight. Because—what was it called? There was a name for the night before Halloween.

Oh yes: Mischief Night.

Not that Glenn wanted the teens of Kettle Springs soaping shop windows on Main Street, but it seemed *unnatural* that they wouldn't even try.

It was the repercussions of George Dunne and Arthur Hill's plot. The lingering fear, even though most of those involved were dead and buried, kept the kids of Kettle Springs on their best behavior.

It was so quiet that Glenn could hear the streetlight click over from red to green.

Here, in the stillness, waiting on Izzy—who he'd take home, her place or his, and make her spaghetti if she hadn't eaten, or warm some Chewy Chips Ahoy in the microwave if she had—Glenn was able to see Kettle Springs for what it really was. It was his home, and it was pretty great.

In that small moment, Glenn Maybrook felt absolute serenity.

Then he heard footsteps scuff the carpet behind the Eureka's double doors, textured antique bronze accents that gave the impression that a regal theatrical experience awaited within.

And then the door whispered open on its easy-close hinges, pushing toward him.

Glenn smiled, but it was a wasted expression, because the person exiting the lobby was *not* Izzy Reyes.

The first thought to break Glenn's serenity was:

No. Not you.

His second thought, fractions of a second after, was:

This can't be real.

Because not only was this not Izzy Reyes.

This was Frendo the Clown.

But this Frendo didn't *look* like Frendo the Clown. Not entirely. The features were all accounted for: red nose, wide smile, even Frendo's trademark porkpie hat. But these features had been rendered wrong. . . . This person was wearing a homemade mask. It was a mask assembled by someone who had a photo for reference, but no desire to opt for the accuracy of a similar molded plastic mask.

"What—" Glenn wasn't even sure what he was going to ask.

The fake Frendo was quick in closing the four feet between them.

Frendo slashed upward, hand becoming a line, their follow-through awkward, nearly spinning themselves around with the force of the swipe.

At first, Glenn was sure that Frendo had missed. Or that there was no weapon in Frendo's hand. Maybe this was some kind of prank. Mischief Night. The swing of the clown's hand had knocked Glenn's glasses off his face and sent them skidding into the gutter behind him.

But then, staring up into the lights of the marquee, he saw that some of the bulbs were crisscrossed with red. In the quiet of Main Street, Glenn could hear the sizzle of his own blood cooking against filament-heated glass.

Frendo had cut him, but with what and how bad?

Glenn started to raise a hand to his face to assess the damage. But his attacker was still coming.

"NO!" Glenn screamed, getting his arm up just in time to block another pass at his face. A jab this time instead of a swipe.

Something bit into the meat of his palm like a large insect. The angriest mosquito.

Clickclickclick.

There was blood streaming into Glenn's left eye now. Half-blind, he didn't *need* to see. Because he recognized that sound.

The person in the DIY Frendo costume was attacking him with a safety blade. The kind with razors you could reload, snapping off a length to replace a dull blade.

There was one more *click*.

The blade was poking through the back of his hand.

The details were bloody and hazy without his glasses, but he could see the glint of metal. The tip of the razor poked through the skin below the knuckles of his ring and middle fingers.

His attacker wiggled the handle of the safety knife and Glenn turned his arm, trying to make sure they didn't have the leverage to push and split his hand in half down to the wrist.

There was a metallic crunch between the bones of his hand. More than a sting or a bite this time, the pain was excruciating, so white-hot that he'd have sworn his hand was on fire.

His attacker pulled back the handle of the weapon, leaving a two- or three-inch segment of razor blade in Glenn's hand.

"Help!" Glenn screamed, hoping someone would hear. Where was Izzy? Where was anyone?

The attack felt like it had been forever, that his assailant was taking their time, but probably only twenty seconds had elapsed.

Clickclickclick.

Glenn winced against the sound of the razor blade extending. Frendo's weapon replenished after losing a few segments.

His hand ruined, the blood from his face now in his mouth, Glenn realized that nobody was coming to save him. He thought of Marta Lee. How, when she examined his body, she would consider everything that had happened to him up to this point as "defensive wounds."

This . . .

This was how Mayor Harlan Jaffers had died, too. He'd been one of the first to go the last time. He was *the* first, actually, if you didn't count Dr. Weller—killed about a week prior—as part of the same spree.

No, Glenn thought as he lashed out at Frendo. If he was going to die, he should at least go down fighting. It's what Quinn would want.

But by the time Glenn had thrown his first punch, Frendo wasn't where he'd aimed. Glenn squinted, his right eye beginning to cloud now, and swung again. The shape in front of him sidestepped again and closed the distance.

There was breath on the side of his face as Frendo began to run the safety knife across Glenn Maybrook's throat.

The knife caught the fabric and zipper of his jacket collar, giving Glenn a half second of hope that he might survive this, but then it found the thin flesh of his neck.

And began cutting.

"Hey!" a voice, shaky and young but still familiar, called out.

Glenn was so disoriented, he thought it might be Quinn's voice.

Then there were hurried footsteps.

Glenn could feel the grit of the sidewalk on the back of his hands, the first indication that he was now lying on his back.

The lights of the marquee blinked above him like a super-dense star-scape. A nebula.

"Mayor Maybrook!" Jerri Shaw screamed down at him. She was haloed by the lights like a teenager from another planet, a different plane of existence.

"Hold on!" she cried. "Ms. Reyes. Someone! Someone help. Ms. Reyes, please!"

Jerri pushed down on his neck, trying and failing to force the blood back into Glenn's body.

The last thing Glenn heard was Izzy's name and then . . . blackness.

ELEVEN

"Girl really rang your bell, didn't she, pal?"

The man handcuffed to the table rolled his neck. It was a tough-guy mannerism both detectives had seen a million times.

"I'm not your pal, pig."

It was the first thing he'd said all night.

"Oh, 'pig.' You hear that, Isaiah?"

"Anti-police hate speech. Next he'll be finger painting *ACAB* on the table in his own blood."

"I need a doctor."

"You already had one." He hadn't, but that was a little white lie. This wouldn't take long. "Remember? They said you're fine. Minor concussion." That had been from the paramedics who had bandaged the guy's head and shined a penlight in his eyes.

"Minor to moderate. Anyway, we're supposed to keep you awake. Keep you talking. So why don't you tell us a story, Bradly?"

The man flinched at being called by his name, then tried to hide his surprise.

"Oh, we know your name—Bradly Stoughton."

"See, I thought it was Stout-ton. That you leave the *gh* silent."

"That's how I said it, wasn't it?"

"You still put the huff sound in there," Zalinski said. Who were they supposed to be giving the business, Isaiah or the perp?

"Well, however you pronounce it, we already have your phone open, Brad. Really, a domestic terrorist that uses the facial recognition unlock function? Not bright. Real amateur-hour shit. It's only a matter of time before the Geek Squad finds a way to undelete all the messages you thought you scrubbed."

Bradly seemed to think about this; then his eyes unfocused and he slouched in his chair, the motion like a human record skip.

Zalinski snapped his fingers and Brad sat up straighter.

"Why don't you help us out and cooperate. What apps

and sites were you using to communicate? Closed groups? Any of the chans? Who were you talking with? Names help. Names or screen names. Each piece of info a suspect gives up now, in the immediate aftermath of an attack like this, helps take time off when it comes to sentencing. Usually."

"Usually," Isaiah repeated. This was good.

They had a good flow going. Good patter. They'd have this thing sewn up before anyone had to give a press conference for the morning news. A lone-wolf wacko who was now in custody; no casualties but a powerful reminder about campus safety and kids being aware of their surroundings.

At least, that was what they were hoping for.

"I want my lawyer."

"Do you *have* a lawyer, Brad? That sounds like premeditation."

"No. I mean, don't you have to, like, give me a lawyer?"

"See, earlier I implied you were not bright—that was premature. You're very bright, Brad. You've got us. We can have a public defender here for you once their offices open."

"But it's still way early."

"Very early. Still dark out. And that might take a while, so why don't you tell us why you shot that kid?"

Bradly Stoughton crossed his arms . . . or tried to—he didn't have enough leverage, the chain and eyebolt only about six or seven inches of give on either side. He then tried to fish something out of his pocket, but couldn't reach that, either.

"Or start by telling us how you got into the dorm in the first place."

"These are all questions we can answer without your help. We're already pulling surveillance footage. But like we said, cooperation makes you look good, Brad."

Brad figured out that by putting his right arm flush with the eyebolt, he gave himself enough slack to get the tips of his fingers to his left front pants pocket. Then, finding the pocket empty, he grimaced.

"Looking for your lock pick and file set? You really think we let people in custody keep whatever they brought in on their person?"

Isaiah had been joking about the "not bright" thing, but now he was beginning to wonder if Bradly Stoughton's massive head injury was making him sluggish and thick. Maybe they should have been getting him a real doctor. He had been unconscious at the scene. And bleeding. It was not exactly regulation to let something like that go untreated. But nothing about tonight was regulation.

"Pall Mall. Really? Wouldn't have guessed. The tattoos and the muscles. I thought you'd be a vaping kind of guy. Or at least smokes that read as more American."

"Marlboros, maybe," Isaiah said. "They've got the cowboy. You like cowboys, Brad?"

Isaiah didn't know they were going to the cigarettes this quickly. But Zalinski had the pack out of the evidence box and was holding it pinched between two fingers.

"Yeah. Bradly, if you were a cowboy, would you see yourself as more of a white hat or a black hat?"

Brad didn't look like he was hearing any of it. He watched the pack of cigarettes, his gaze fixed on the smokes.

"Uh-oh. I think we have an addict on our hands."

"Then let's start small. This is a no-smoking room, but I think we can say *one* smoke for Brad. One smoke if he answers one question. Fair?"

"Sure. Can even be an easy one. To get the ball rolling."

Zalinski slid the pack of cigarettes over the steel table.

Isaiah turned and dug around in the box for their next prop.

"Where'd you get the mask?"

Isaiah held up the clown mask as a visual aid. The plastic felt thin under his fingers. Old, like he could crumple the whole thing to nothing but the elastic strap if he pressed just a little.

It was an original. That was for sure.

Brad had the pack of Pall Malls open, his lighter out of the plastic, then narrowed his eyes, hands shaking, the chain between them tinkling against the tabletop as he tweezed a cigarette out.

"Brad? Earth to Brad?"

"Where'd you get this?" Isaiah raised the mask to his face, but didn't let the plastic touch his skin. The mask smelled like sweat and was stained with nicotine around the mouth. Brad had worn it a lot, not just tonight. Did he do the whole *Taxi Driver* bit, wear the mask and talk to himself in the mirror, shirt off, guns drawn? Frendo amping himself up for a rampage?

"I got it on eBay," Brad said.

"Oh, word?" Zalinski said. "How much?"

Bradly Stoughton had the cigarette to his lips, then looked up like what he was about to say was going to be very witty.

"More than you could afford, pig," and then, quickly, not singing it at all: "Just a drop of Baypen makes everything better."

Bradly used the back of his hand to flip the cigarette into his mouth, filter and all, and then began to chew.

Isaiah and Zalinski shared a look, only Zalinski giving voice to what they were both thinking: "What the fuck?"

It was Isaiah who realized what—as his partner said— was the fuck.

Isaiah dove across the table, getting an arm around Bradly Stoughton's head and pushing two fingers into his mouth. At first he tried going in through the front, but Brad bit down hard to block him, catching the tips of Isaiah's fingers. With Isaiah squeezing against his jaws, Brad's teeth didn't have enough leverage to break the skin, but Isaiah changed tack, sent his thumb and forefinger around the side of Brad's mouth, wedging open Brad's molars, fingernails in the space where the man's wisdom teeth were coming in.

The soft tissue of the guy's mouth was slimy, but Isaiah had to keep his hand in there—he couldn't let this guy swallow.

"Spit it out!" Isaiah heard himself yell. It was the way you'd get the family dog to let go of something that'd make them sick. Maybe even kill them.

Under him, Brad coughed and wet brown clods of tobacco hit the metal table.

Zalinski had a pen out, began combing through the material with the tip. That was fine—let Isaiah be the only one getting his hands dirty.

"I think that's all of it? I don't see anything in here."

"You crazy bastard," Isaiah said, looking down at his shirt. One of only three nice work shirts ruined. Blotches of blood from Brad's head wound across the chest and strings of brown spit on the sleeves. "No more cigarettes for you."

Isaiah and Zalinski looked at each other, both panting from the excitement, smiling like they'd just dodged a major bullet.

Zalinski skewered the pen tip into the cigarette's filter and raised it up so Isaiah could see what he was seeing: it'd been hollowed out.

And a small dusting of powder was leaking from one end of the filter.

Beside them, Bradly Stoughton started to twitch and seize, hands pulling wide against his restraints and foam overflowing at the corners of his mouth.

In less than a minute he was dead.

"Shit," Zalinski said.

"Shit," Isaiah agreed.

They were going to be in so much trouble.

TWELVE

Quinn was numb.

No, that wasn't accurate. Numb was a few hours ago. Now the sensation was like every inch of her body was recovering from an intense dentist visit. Novocaine wearing off, pinpricks and tingling, wounds beginning to pucker.

The three of them were quiet in the back of the squad car, arms interlaced, Cole and Rust dozing on either side with Quinn in the middle.

The boys had been in and out of consciousness on the plane. She hadn't heard them discuss it, but they knew she wouldn't sleep and it seemed like they were nodding off in shifts in order to sit vigil with her.

A vigil because the flight was three hours without cell service. Quinn found it impossible to silence the voice whispering that her dad was dead, that he'd died as soon as they'd gone wheels up and was now cold in his hospital bed or on an operating table or chilling in a morgue. Or dead on a helicopter, if the medical team had tried to airlift him from the small hospital in Hermann to one of the bigger emergency units in the city.

Sheriff Lee had met them at the airport, flashers on so nobody questioned her stopping in the "No Stopping" zone. She hadn't said much beyond the essentials: Quinn's father was still alive and out of surgery.

Sheriff Lee hadn't editorialized. Hadn't offered Quinn a few sweet and pat *Things will be okay* lies. And Quinn respected that. Quinn didn't know every detail of how her dad had been doing as mayor of Kettle Springs, but she knew enough to know that Sheriff Lee was his best and most competent partner.

The sheriff hadn't tried to hug Quinn. Which Quinn appreciated.

Quinn didn't want a hug. She wanted to see her dad.

"I can't believe I did that," Cole said. His words broke the silence in the back of the car, rousing Rust and Quinn.

They were still miles from the hospital. The sun only now burning off the dew on the fields and suburban lawns they drove past. It had been a little after four a.m. when they'd boarded the plane, one of only three direct flights a day between Philly and St. Louis. At least they hadn't had to wait around in the terminal for long; in fact, they'd almost missed their flight while being questioned by the police.

It was a gift that they'd been allowed to leave the Commonwealth of Pennsylvania at all. It couldn't have been standard police procedure, but maybe this was one of the perks of celebrity. If Philadelphia inspectors needed Quinn Maybrook, Ruston Vance, and Cole Hill: they'd know where to find them.

"What can't you believe—that you drank that much Jägermeister in a complete stranger's bathroom?" Rust asked, his voice sleepy but still laced with annoyance. To Cole's credit, after the party ended in gunfire, he'd sobered up quickly, but in the immediate aftermath of the shooting, he could barely hold his head up against the spins.

"No. Drinking gross shit with strangers is very *me* behavior. What I can't believe is that I gave my car to . . . what's her name?"

"Dev," Quinn said. She'd been quiet for so long that the sound of her own voice surprised her.

Cole hadn't *given* Dev his car. Just the keys and boozy directions where to find where he'd parked it. Then he'd Venmo'd her a thousand dollars to drive it back to Kettle Springs for him.

"Yes. There was probably a better way to handle that," Rust said. "A hauler service or cargo train or something instead of the girl dressed like a bumblebee."

"Oh, I'm sorry, John Hick. At that point weren't we just in a gun battle? Pardon me if I wasn't thinking straight."

It felt to Quinn like Cole had been sitting on "John Hick" for a little while.

"The rarest thing from him: an apology," Rust muttered. "And not really a 'gun battle.' I never fired a shot. . . ."

Cole groaned, but before he could get himself into more trouble with his boyfriend, Sheriff Lee interrupted the two of them:

"The doctors aren't going to let the boys in. It'll be family only. Do you need me to drive you back to town or is there someone who can pick you up?"

Cole and Rust looked at each other, Cole stretching high in his seat to see over Quinn's head.

"What? My father works Saturdays, and you know Sybil doesn't like to drive," Rust said.

"Oh, well then I'll see if *my dad* can swing by," Cole answered.

Cole was being a brat. Nobody wanted this right now, him invoking Arthur Hill for snarky deflection.

"Fine," Rust said. "I'll call and see if I can get a hold of him."

Rust talked about his parents so little, Quinn often forgot that he *had* parents. She'd met them a handful of times, and they seemed nice enough. But Rust never encouraged interaction, and those meetings had mostly been accidents, his dad getting home from work early and catching Quinn reracking weights in the garage. Rust's mom, Sybil, was a small woman who did bookkeeping and tax prep for local businesses, and his dad did something . . . agricultural? It was hard to tell— Jim Vance was so stoic he made Rust seem chatty.

"If not, I can drive you back later. Might be a while, though. I sent some materials to the crime lab in the city."

Materials. What could that have been? Did they have the weapon?

"And every deputy back home is on the streets, running down leads. So here in the middle is where I'll need to work, off my phone and laptop, until Quinn's dad wakes up," Sheriff Lee said, eyes on the road, blinker on, prepared for an exit. They must be getting close.

Rust turned to Quinn. "Even if it means staying in the waiting room, we really can stay. Just to be there for you."

"Yeah," Cole added. "For as long as you need."

When Quinn hadn't cried at any point during the night, even as Izzy Reyes had described over the phone how her dad had been attacked, how much blood he'd lost, she thought that her crying days might be over for good. Maybe over the last year her eyes had dried forever.

But now the tears came, with these two friends offering to wait for her.

"No. You should both go home. Sleep in your own beds. I'll call you later."

They sat for a moment, the sheriff's car turning into an industrial park, low office buildings beginning to surround them.

"Okay, but we might just wait for you anyway. I don't like being told what to do," Cole said, his voice soft, as he stroked the back of her hand.

Quinn hadn't realized they'd arrived until she read the words "Medical Center" out the window.

The hospital was smaller than she'd imagined. Its squat building blended in with the rest of the industrial park. A single-floor structure on a slight hill, awning-covered ramps for loading and unloading patients, and a bay at one side with an ambulance parked at the door.

Sheriff Lee turned behind her and caught Rust's eye: "Bring her to the front desk. I'll be in once I park."

Marta Lee could have more easily turned her head in the other direction and related her instructions to Cole, but she chose not to.

Even adults who barely knew the two boys knew which one they'd prefer to deal with.

The medical center *looked* different from the glass and concrete towers of CHOP, Jefferson, or Penn—hospitals Quinn had been to either for pediatric visits, because of her dad's job, or because her mom had overdosed again—but the small building *smelled* exactly like them:

Chemicals, wet paint, and dead gift-shop flowers.

They approached the front desk, Rust walking too close to Quinn. Either he was taking Sheriff Lee's instructions too seriously or he expected her to faint and wanted to be there to catch her.

Cole, for contrast maybe, walked a good distance behind them with his eyes down on his phone.

The reception or nurses' desk—whatever you'd call it in a place this small—was abandoned.

The whole atrium was abandoned, and she saw no activity down either of the hallways.

Instantly, Quinn hated it here. She looked behind the desk at the dusty phone systems blinking with messages, the decades-out-of-date computer monitors with their desktop icons burned in, and immediately thought her dad was dead. That no place this backward and shabby could save him.

"Um, Quinn?" It wasn't a doctor or nurse that came to meet them, but a young . . . girl? Yes, a girl. She looked vaguely familiar and fully disheveled. Her hair, the style either a pixie cut or a layered bob, was messy and unwashed, oil so thick it worked like product to hold tufts at weird angles. Her hands were out in front of her, fingers twisted into knots by anxiety. Her freckled skin was pale, mostly all over, but then there were spots where it was stained a dark pink. The girl trembled like a chihuahua, even though she was wearing a large oversize down jacket. It was a winter jacket, not the fall coats and long sleeves that Quinn, Cole,

and Rust wore, and from the size of it, it belonged to someone else. An adult much larger than the girl.

"Jerri. What are you doing here?" Rust said the girl's
name, and Quinn was able to place her.

She worked at the Eureka.

"I'm the one who found Mayor Maybrook." Jerri turned
to Quinn. "I mean. I found your dad. I did my best. I—I
stayed with him until help . . ."

God. The pink stains on Jerri's skin. The dark spots
Quinn could now see on the clothes under her oversize
jacket.

Blood.

Jerri's cuticles and the webbing between her fingers: her
hands were scarlet with blood, rinsed but not washed away.

"They're down here," Jerri said, then added: "He's sleeping."

Izzy Reyes must have heard them coming down the hall,
because she intercepted Quinn in the doorway, pushing her
back and out while wrapping her up in an awkward hug.

"Oh god, it's okay," Izzy cooed in Quinn's ear, keeping
a pressure on her hug and stepping back two more steps as
she squeezed, nudging Quinn farther away from the hospital room.

Was Izzy trying to keep Quinn from seeing her dad?

What did he look like? Had his condition suddenly wors-
ened since their last phone call?

Or was a hug simply a hug?

Quinn was rigid at first, then softened in Izzy's arms, her limp body propped up by the hug. She would accept the embrace, but couldn't bring herself to return it.

Glenn Maybrook had been dating Izzy Reyes since the summer, so it was likely that Quinn had hugged Izzy before. But those had been quick *Nice to see you* bend-at-the-waist affairs. The two of them had never been this close for this long, not ever. And it wasn't because Quinn disliked Izzy, or harbored any sort of conscious *You're not my mom* animosity. No, Quinn was mature about these things. It was that there'd never been a *reason* for the two of them to embrace like this.

After a moment Quinn decided that even if Izzy needed the contact, needed the comfort, that Quinn needed something more:

"Please let me . . ."—*let me go*—"let me see him."

"Of course," Izzy said, arms unlocking from around Quinn.

Izzy stepped back. She was taller than Samantha Maybrook and they didn't look much alike in the face, but now that Izzy's hair was out of her usual ponytail, Quinn could see that it curled almost exactly like her mom's had.

Her dad had a type.

Izzy took Quinn by the hand and led her into her father's hospital room.

She closed the door behind them, locking Cole and Rust on the other side. Quinn almost wanted to protest that, but didn't.

Quinn had come a long way in the last twelve hours, and she was close now. So close she could almost see him.

If she raised her hand and lifted the curtain partition, she would be with her dad.

But first she took stock of his room.

There was an empty bed in the corner, linens tucked in and folded. It was possible that, if demand called for it in this seemingly deserted hospital, her dad would have a roommate.

She listened to the noises of the room. Behind the thin curtain there were beeps and clicks. A heart monitor and other machines she couldn't place.

"Guess who's here," Izzy said to Glenn, her voice hushed and shaky. But it was the same way you'd talk to a baby or a cat. Rhetorical, knowing they couldn't respond.

Quinn finally looked toward her dad's bed as Izzy drew back the curtain. Even though the image of her dad wasn't as bad as what Quinn had been dreading and imagining, she still cried out at the sight of him.

"It's okay. It's going to be okay," Izzy whispered to her. Quinn understood where Izzy's optimism was coming from. People said these kinds of things in times of crisis, repeated these sorts of words, but Izzy hadn't been with them in

Tillerson's B-field or on Baypen's factory floor. She might have been some nice company for Quinn's dad. A distraction. A warm spot in a bed. But Izzy hadn't lived with this shit for the last year. Not like Quinn and her dad had.

From everything her dad had said, Izzy was cool, wanted to help the town heal by volunteering, hiring survivors at the Eureka, hosting community movie nights. But she hadn't spent a year dealing with death threats that ranged from possibly credible to internet shitposts while waiting for the FBI to investigate them.

Now someone had really done it. They'd tried to kill the town's East Coast libtard mayor.

And they tried to kill me at the same time, Quinn thought, trying to do the math and calculate the timing of when everything had happened. Within the same hour of each other.

There was a roadmap of wires and diodes affixed to Glenn Maybrook's arms, neck, and chest. But no intubation and no respirator.

That was good, right?

"He's breathing on his own now, has been since getting out of surgery," Izzy said, reading Quinn's mind. "He's got a long road ahead, a lot of PT for his hand and probably another few surgeries, but he *will* recover."

Where was his doctor? Why was Quinn getting all this info from Izzy? In fact, Izzy and Jerri were so far the *only* people Quinn had seen in the entire building.

What kind of fucking place was this?

She needed to talk to a professional.

Quinn's eyes focused on her dad's injured hand, mounds of gauze and medical tape holding his split digits together.

Materials, Quinn thought, remembering what Sheriff Lee had said in the car and piecing it together with something Izzy had said on the phone. They had part of the weapon because it had broken off inside her dad's hand.

After five minutes of Quinn squeezing Glenn Maybrook's good hand, watching his eyes move in a dream under his bruised lids, the doctor would eventually arrive and put Quinn at ease enough that she could collapse into the seat beside her dad's bed and fall asleep.

But before that could happen, Izzy stepped out and Quinn fixated on her dad's hand, his defensive injuries, then clenched her own hands into fists and asked the otherwise empty room:

"Why would someone do this?"

THIRTEEN

Rust watched down the hospital's tiled hallway as Sheriff Lee talked with the doctor.

"I found us a ride," Cole said. "So that we don't have to bother the sheriff or her deputies." He paused, then added: "Or Jim and Sybil."

Cole always called Rust's parents by their first names. It was disrespectful, but what, was *now* the time to ask Cole to be polite? Even so, Jim and Sybil Vance had gotten better with Cole, and he with them. Rust was encouraged that all three of them were at least trying. The Vances were still a long way from flying the pride flag on their front lawn, but things were going well enough that Jim spoke at the dinner table sometimes.

"That's good," Rust said.

Rust couldn't talk about this now; he was straining to hear what was being said down the hall.

Sheriff Lee crossed her arms, and Rust was able to get the gist of what she was saying to the doctor:

"Where have you been?"

"—we're short-staffed on weeken—"

"Where is the security guard I posted outside the room?"

"—there was a call over—"

"It doesn't matter. The mayor's daughter is here now, and I swear to god if he dies at this point, I'll disassemble this building brick by brick."

Sheriff Lee was taller than the woman in the white coat, seeming to grow even taller as they spoke. The doctor shrank back, curled into a question mark by the force of the sheriff's body language.

When Sheriff Lee's cop rage had subsided, the doctor nodded and nodded, mouthing apologies.

"Don't you want to know who it is?" Cole asked.

"Who what is?"

Rust wasn't feeling up to playing twenty questions. They'd been in such a rush that he hadn't moisturized today. He could feel his scars starting to flake. Rust's skin was one irritant that wasn't Cole's fault. But it added to the annoyances that were . . .

"I mean: Don't you want to know who's on the way to give us a ride back to town?"

"Who?"

"You're not going to like it. Probably. Now that I think about it, you might *dislike* it so much that you'll want to make other arrangements."

Rust sighed, scratched at his chin, nails riding the scar-tissue bumps where his facial hair wouldn't grow in.

Why was Cole doing this—why here and now? Had Cole spent so long away from the chaos of prank videos and flipping off authority figures that he was now finding new games to play, with Rust in his crosshairs?

Worse, was this what growing too familiar with each other looked like?

Or, worst of all the scenarios Rust feared, was this how Cole was pushing Rust away? Was Cole trying to give himself a reason to run?

The pieces fell together in Rust's sleep-deprived brain with a click so tactile he swore he could hear it in his inner ear.

"You've got to be kidding me."

Cole had asked Hunter Duvall for a ride home.

"He's the only person who doesn't work for me who texts me back!" Cole said. "And that includes *you*."

This again. Rust had a phone, but he hated it. Always was "accidentally" leaving it in his glove box, or on Cole's nightstand, or just turning it off and slipping it into his shirt pocket. He knew he should stay more connected—Quinn never went anywhere without hers—but not being available all the time was one small way that Rust tried not to let the fear rule his life. Prepare for anything, but don't wait for the call.

"When does he arrive?" Rust wasn't going to argue about his texting back, not again, not here.

Cole tipped his phone screen so Rust could see a map with a moving blue dot.

"Eighteen minutes," Cole said. He had a guilty smirk, even though Rust was growing convinced that Cole Hill was incapable of feeling guilt.

Eighteen minutes away. Even in Cole's new car, the hospital was over an hour away from Kettle Springs.

"So when did you call him to come get us?"

"He saw what had happened on the news and offered."

"The news?" Rust raised an eyebrow.

"Well, on Twitter."

The eyebrow stayed raised.

"Fine, I texted him when we were at the police station in Philly."

Rust nodded, let his eyebrow drop. The prosecution rests.

"He texted me, actually. Something about a fight with his parents or something, being up all night. It was a *lot* of texts, he seemed in a bad place. To get him to stop, I had to tell him what was going on with us. I'm sure it's all over the real news by now anyway."

Something about that last part halted the rising tide of anger and jealousy that was bubbling up along with Rust's stomach acid.

"The news," Rust said, not to Cole and not really to himself, either.

"What?" Cole asked, sounding genuinely confused.

Rust turned, looked both ways down the hallway.

Sheriff Lee and the doctor had finished their argument, and both were coming their way. Down the other end of the hallway, a tired-looking nurse exited a patient's room, checked her phone, and then dropped the device back into her colorful patterned scrub top. Across from them, sitting on the floor like this hallway was the waiting room, Jerri stared into the middle distance between her hands.

It was the biggest crowd the hospital had seen since they'd gotten there.

Pushing Cole aside, Rust tried to make eye contact with Sheriff Lee, then put his hand out to signal her.

"Sheriff. Are there going to be reporters here soon? The news must be breaking. . . . If they're going to be here with cameras, should we . . ." He jogged to her, caught her before she could enter Glenn Maybrook's hospital room.

Sheriff Lee looked up at him and stopped. Down the hall, the doctor looked awkward, unsure where she should be going, whether to follow the woman who'd just yelled at her.

"Rust. You don't need to worry about any of that. This

location is strictly need-to-know, and I've got Mayor May-brook's office waiting as long as possible before they issue a statement about the attack."

"But. Whoever did this, they could try—"

"Ruston." She removed her hand from the door, placed it on his shoulder. "This is not your job. Your job is taking care of Quinn right now. Making sure your friends feel safe and loved. I *have* deputies—a few deputies, at least—and I still have friends in St. Louis. I've been working at this for hours. Put a little faith in me, please." She flicked her eyes to Cole. "Go home. Take a shower. Get some rest. And"—she indicated Jerri—"bring that one with you. Nobody can reach her mom."

Sheriff Marta Lee pushed open the door to the room, ushered the doctor inside, and then closed it on them again.

Rust felt . . . *embarrassed* wasn't the right word. Not totally. But he did feel helpless.

He didn't like it.

Cole cleared his throat. "Look, I'm going to go wait out-side for him. Are you coming or not?"

"I don't think it's a good idea."

"Does that mean you're staying? For Quinn or just because you don't like Hunter?"

"No, I don't just mean me. I don't think it's a good idea to be taking a ride from Hunter Duvall. Either of us." He remembered Jerri. "Any of us."

Cole crossed his arms, newly intrigued. "Why?"

"We . . ." Rust tried to articulate something that was somewhere between a hunch and jealous disdain. "We don't know him."

"No, *you* don't know him. He's my friend."

"Well, your *friend*." Rust hated the emphasis he placed on the word. He could hear himself now, but couldn't do much to stop the words. The lapbar had lowered and locked on this carnival ride: no getting off until the spinning stopped. "He and his family are out in that field every night pissing on your dead friends."

"Oh, don't act like that's the problem! You sound like the Chamber of Commerce. It's a fucking haunted house. Don't use Janet and the rest of them that way. Like their memory's a tool to get what you want."

Cole snuck Janet Murray's name into the conversation like a sucker punch. When Cole talked about Janet, it was clear that there'd always been a kind of love there. That, of all of them, she was the one that had stayed in Cole's mind, the grief just under the skin like a splinter.

And invoking Janet's name should have caused Rust to stop. Or at least reconsider what he was doing. But it didn't.

"Look. He's new. His family is *literally* invested in keeping our town fucked up."

"What are you even saying?"

"I'm saying Quinn's dad was just attacked. We were just

attacked. At the same time. Down to the minute. This is not just some lunatic. This is coordinated. It's happening again. And I don't want you getting a ride from . . ."

"Who? Frendo Jr.? Are you even listening to yourself? This isn't a game of Clue. There's not a handful of suspects on a whiteboard. There are hundreds, thousands, of fucked-up people out there. And all those people sit in their threads and message boards and they hate us. All day every day. If you think the new kid in town and his family are behind this, then you are just as deluded as the conspiracy nuts. There's no way it's as simple as that. Chaos isn't simple."

Rust breathed, swallowed, felt his skin flake.

"All I'm saying is just think for a second. Why is he so interested in you? Why does he even want to be your friend so bad?"

"Because I'm good-looking, Rust," Cole said. Yelled, really. "Because I'm famous! Because I have money! And I don't give a fuck because I need a friend. I'm not going to cheat on you, the thought had never ever once occurred to me, but when you act like this . . ."

"When I act like this what? Say it."

Cole was crying now. Maybe Rust was, too. He didn't know.

"Stop," Cole said, low. Then, straightening up: "Just stop."

"I'm . . . I'm sorry." And Rust was. He'd never regretted

anything quite like he regretted how this argument had turned out.

"Are you my boyfriend or my bodyguard?" Cole asked the question.

"What?" Rust asked, even though he heard him. Understood him.

"You're so worried about keeping me safe that you're doing nothing for here." Cole pointed at his own head with two fingers. "Or here." With the same two fingers he poked Rust in the chest, hard. The fingers an arrowhead over Rust's heart.

Cole looked over to Jerri, who was now staring even harder at her hands, had clearly been listening to their argument.

Then Cole looked down at his phone, now buzzing.

"Come on, kid. Ride's here," Cole said to the girl.

Jerri kept her eyes down, but stood, began walking toward the exit.

Cole looked up to Rust, tears streaking his cheeks but not yet drying. "It's not too late for you to catch your breath and think about this. You could take the ride with us and come back home."

Rust rubbed one bootheel against the pattern in the tile, traced the space between lines.

He didn't look up.

"No. It's fine. I'll call Jim. Or get an Uber."

Cole sighed, then left Rust standing there, alone.

After a few minutes of trying to listen to the muffled voices inside the mayor's hospital room and not understanding a word, Rust took his phone out of his shirt pocket.

He held the button on the side to turn it on.

He blinked.

Goddamn it.

He blinked again, dislodging a fat tear that fell onto the screen.

He didn't want his dad to see him like this.

And how did he even use Uber?

FOURTEEN

This situation was awkward.

So awkward, weirdly, that it was helping. The tension between Cole and Hunter allowed Jerri Shaw—parts of her neck and chest still tacky with the mayor's blood—to focus on someone else's problems for a moment.

Had Cole and Rust just broken up? And with her in the middle? Literally the middle, because Jerri had to ride up front, sandwiched between Cole and Hunter Duvall. Hunter used his pickup truck for work and had stacks of foam board and plastic skeletons piled in the back seat, more in the truck bed.

The truck was like the one Rust Vance drove around town, but—despite the haunted house clutter—it was a lot newer than Rust's truck.

"That sounds . . . ," Hunter said, then tossed his eyes back to the road. They were far enough from the hospital and surrounding area that the landscape had begun to feel more familiar. Jerri was comforted as the space between buildings widened, filled with sky and fields and farms. The corn out the windows was earmarked to be used for grain, so the harvesters had not yet rolled the plants down. It was late enough in the season that nothing was green, everything faded and dried to golden amber.

"All of that sounds bad," Hunter resumed after a pause. "And not just the really bad stuff. I'm sorry if the fight with Rust was my fault. I certainly didn't mean it to be."

Hunter sounded sincere. But this was a different Hunter than the one Jerri had been talking with last night. Had it really only been last night? The Hunter in the driver's seat wasn't the one who'd been sweating, befuddled by an usher who'd decided to stand her ground and not let him into the theater without a ticket.

This Hunter was cool, effortless, like he had a plan.

"It's not your fault," Cole said.

"I mean, it *can* be if Rust wants it to be, if it keeps him from getting mad at you." Hunter looked back over to Cole.

Instead of turning her head to watch them, Jerri only moved her eyes, able to see their faces using the truck's rear and side mirrors.

Hunter was smiling now. And maybe he wasn't so

different from when she'd seen him last night. Maybe he was worse. Because there was a fatigue in his eyes that he was trying to hide with makeup. She had to think, since he'd left only minutes before Mayor Maybrook was attacked: Had he seen something last night? After searching for his friends and not finding them at the Eureka, had Hunter driven his truck around town looking for them late into the night? While he was crawling down the alleys and side streets of Kettle Springs, had he caught a glimpse of Mayor Maybrook's attacker? Could Hunter know who was responsible? Was he *himself* responsible?

The last twelve hours felt like a nightmare. No, more specific than that. She was living every story with a *Be careful what you wish for* moral to it. Where the main character desires something and they get a twisted, ironic version of that thing. She'd wanted to be part of their world, their drama, and like it or not, she'd gotten that wish.

All the months Jerri spent watching the older kids of Kettle Springs, the famous and the not-famous ones, tracking but never impacting the soap opera lives they lived. And when she didn't have enough information about their *real* dramas? She filled in the blanks with fantasy.

She imagined that Cole and Rust were going to get married next year. And that Cole's dad was still alive and going to get arrested trying to sneak back into the country to attend the wedding. That Tyler Nguyen was secretly a great singer who'd been training to surprise the school at the Christmas Talent Show. That Sandra Wright might date a freshman. Which wasn't so much a fully fleshed-out storyline as it was a series of daydream vignettes.

But now Jerri Shaw was being force-fed all the drama she could stand. More than she could stand, since the sinister dramas of Kettle Springs seemed to involve multiple fatalities.

Like a slow-motion version of the night Dorothy died, chaos and violence had begun swirling around Jerri again, and she was terrified of what came next.

First her sister, dead before her body hit the dirt, and now the mayor in critical condition . . . and what did both acts of violence have in common? Besides Jerri being there to witness? The identities of the attackers were a mystery. It had been less than a day, but would they ever figure out who'd attacked Glenn Maybrook? It had been over a year, and Jerri and her mom still didn't have a definitive answer as to who had killed Dorothy. The closest the FBI had come to catching Dorothy Shaw's murderer was assuming it'd been Gertrude Blevins. They had Jerri's description of the killer's voice, and Trudy had been the only female clown confirmed to be in the field that night. But it hadn't been Trudy's voice, had it? When the clown had shown a glimpse of mercy and told Jerri where to hide? And with Trudy's thin build, would she have had the strength to draw a compound bow? It just didn't . . .

"This might be too personal a question," Hunter said, readjusting his hands on the wheel. "So don't feel like you have to answer. I know we don't know each other super well."

"Nah, don't say that," Cole said. "We know each other plenty. Even if we don't hang out. Heck, I know what your bedroom looks like . . . from the internet."

Was this . . . flirting? Jerri had begun to fixate on questions of murder and death, and the boys in the truck's cab with her were *flirting*?

Hunter was blushing, the color coming up from around his makeup, the glow stopping under his eyes. But he shook the expression away: "It's not that kind of question. I'm trying to be serious here. Did you ever . . ."

He trailed off again, losing his courage. Hunter didn't sound like he was trying to flirt. Cole didn't seem to be picking up on that, but how could he? Cole lacked context, didn't know that Hunter had been frantic last night, sweating and searching.

"Ha." Cole elbowed Jerri, acknowledging her presence for the first time in miles. "He's shy, can you believe it? Don't worry, whatever you're going to ask me, Jerri can keep a secret, I bet." Cole was back to himself. Or at least back to the version that Jerri had seen on TV and the internet. Looser, more buoyant than he'd been in the hospital, where he'd first been solemn in front of Quinn and then frustrated as he'd started arguing with Rust.

And then, put at ease, Hunter asked his question:

"Did you ever get the feeling that your dad was planning something? I mean, before what happened with Founder's Day and the party and all that? Did you ever look at him, or talk with him, and think that he was getting ready to do something?"

Cole crossed his arms and didn't respond.

It was like a balloon had been popped in the truck cab.

Jerri looked at her hands. Even with flecks of Mayor Maybrook's dried blood still under the nails, staring at her hands was better than acknowledging Hunter's question.

"That came out so wrong," Hunter said.

Cole still didn't respond.

"I'm sorry. I way overstepped. I'm just tired and thinking about something—"

"Look, it's fine. It's fine. You came all the way out here to pick us up. I don't want to be rude," Cole said. The truck slowed as Hunter turned to look Cole in the eyes. Jerri looked straight ahead, like it was now her job to watch the road. "But that's the kind of thing I get asked by reporters. Or by randos online who like all my posts and want to pretend I'm their friend. You and me . . ." Cole paused for emphasis. "We're not that. So I'm just going to forget that you asked your question."

"Seems fair," Hunter said. "I appreciate it."

"Know that it's the only do-over you're getting," Cole

said. Jerri couldn't see his face to tell if he was kidding or not, but he didn't sound like it.

Hunter looked back to the road, and Jerri felt a little calmer. But only a little.

They drove for a few more minutes in silence.

"Hey look, it's you." Cole broke the quiet and pointed out his window.

They were approaching a billboard. A split billboard, one side featuring the Geico gecko and the other a creepy scarecrow wearing a clown nose and holding a rusty sickle.

Under the scarecrow were the words: *30 Miles to the Fright of Your Life.*

"That's not me."

"No, I know you're not, like, the person dressed as a scarecrow."

"Not what I mean. It's not *my* haunt, it's my family's," Hunter said.

"That gecko is fucked," Cole said, looking back at the sign.

"Yeah, it's cheaper when you pay for half a billboard. And that's not stock photography," Hunter said.

"What?" Jerri asked.

Both Cole and Hunter looked at her, then to each other, as if to say, *I didn't know she could talk.*

Jerri was just as surprised. It wasn't like her to speak up.

"A lot of haunted attractions," Hunter explained, "they'll

go online and get stock photos to use in their advertising. It always bugged me. All of our press, our print and digital ads, we either commissioned original art or we had professional photos taken of our actors."

"Very nice," Cole said.

Hunter slowed so they could get one last look at the scarecrow. "I bet you know them, the actor in the picture."

"'Actor'?" Cole asked. "I thought your staff was mostly high schoolers."

"They are. But we call them scare actors. That's the *industry* term."

"Oh, the 'industry term,' is it?" Cole rubbed his chin. "I graduated. So, can't say I'd know the kids who work for you."

"But she does," Hunter said, and tapped Jerri on the shoulder. "Come on, Jerri. Free admission passes if you can guess who it is in three tries."

Hunter smiled at Cole; the two of them seemed happy to try to get Jerri out of her shell.

But she liked her shell. Her shell was safe.

"That's okay," Jerri said.

"You saw the sign," Hunter said. "We still have thirty miles. Humor us."

Jerri thought for a moment. She laid out the junior and senior classes in her mind, tried to picture the faces she knew from afar like a yearbook. There were some older sophomores that also worked for the Duvalls, but not nearly as many, so she wouldn't worry about them.

"Look at that concentration," Cole said. "She's going to get it."

"How about . . . ," Jerri started.

"Wait," Cole said, putting his hand down like a seat belt. Then to Hunter: "What if she doesn't want to use the tickets?"

She didn't, but she wasn't going to say that.

"Can she return the passes for their cash value?"

"I mean, I'm offended, but sure," Hunter agreed.

This was nice. Having a game to play was nice.

So in that spirit, Jerri started to guess.

"Uh . . . so is the scarecrow . . ." She paused. Both to think and to keep the game going a little longer. "Is it Aaron Lacey?"

"Wow," Hunter said, making her think she got it in one, before taking his hand off the wheel and giving her a thumbs-down. "You really think Lacey is the right size? I have him tucked in the smallest hiding spot in the haunt—he's the only person who can fit without crouching."

Aaron Lacey *was* short.

Okay. Maybe that was a hint.

Jerri thought tall.

"Is it Vin . . ." Ugh, what was Vin's last name? "Vin . . ."

"Vin Cortez?"

"Yeah. Him."

"Errrrtttt!" Hunter made a very annoying buzzer sound with his mouth.

"Is that a good buzzer or a bad buzzer?" Cole asked.

"Bad buzzer. She's wrong," Hunter said, then to Jerri: "Why do you keep picking guys? Girls can't be homicidal scarecrows? That's sexist."

Another hint.

Then, without even thinking about it:

"Sandra Wright!"

Hunter blinked. "Yeah, wow. How'd you get that?"

Jerri shrugged. It was Jerri's turn to blush.

"Fucking nice. Never mind the hows, what does a ticket cost? My client would like—" Cole turned to Jerri. "Cash or Venmo?"

"It's okay." She giggled, actually giggled. "I'll take the ticket. It's Halloween and the past is the past and I want to do something . . ."

But before she could even finish saying the words that she didn't believe, she was thinking about being back in that field again. And then it was only a few seconds before she was crying and trembling, reliving it, her hands trying to hold in her tears and sobs and failing.

"Fuck," Cole whispered, then put a hand on her back. She flinched at first, but then allowed it.

Cole rubbed small circles on Jerri's back for ten minutes or so, until she stopped crying, and they sat the remainder of the twenty-eight-mile drive in silence, no more small talk or games of roadside "I Spy."

It was only once they'd passed the Kettle Springs county line, approaching the turnoff for Cole's house, that anyone spoke again.

"Don't turn," Cole said.

Hunter looked at him, a question on his face.

"Maybe drop Jerri off first. She's probably got people waiting for her. I have time to kill."

Maybe Jerri's mother was waiting for her. But maybe not.

They all looked down the private road toward Cole's large house. Hill Manor was the town's most visually distinct landmark . . . now that the skeleton of the Baypen factory had been bulldozed down, its basement filled in with dirt.

"Okay, I can do that," Hunter said, aiming the truck back toward town, turning onto Jerri's street before the homes and businesses were in sight.

"And maybe you want to come over for a beer?" Cole asked, like Jerri wasn't there.

Hunter looked at the clock on the dash.

It was 11:25 a.m.

"A little early, no?"

"A soda pop, then," Cole said, rolling his eyes.

"Yeah, that'd be nice. I could use the caffeine."

They brought Jerri home.

And instead of being worried about what her mother was

going to say, or whether she wanted to confront her about not picking up the phone for the police, Jerri found herself more worried for Cole and Rust. For their relationship. For what it was that Hunter had in mind for when he got into that big house. She wished there was some way to warn Cole about that other Hunter, the one she'd met last night with the frantic eyes. But there wasn't a way.

Jerri Shaw had a very bad feeling about what was going to happen next.

FIFTEEN

Eli Duvall watched the blinking light on the single-serve coffee maker and let his anger burn.

In his younger years he'd attended many seminars, many conventions, listened to so many goddamn books on tape. All because he'd wanted to learn everything he could about business. Young Eli had taken endless notes: tips about the art of negotiation, securing a supply chain, or cultivating an effective managerial climate. But not one "expert" had ever shared with him the truest, most helpful piece of business advice:

Anger was good.

Nobody successful wanted to admit that they owed their success, in whole or in part, to anger. But Eli, in over three and a half decades of entrepreneurship, had met plenty of businessmen like himself. Some didn't drink alcohol. Some didn't even drink coffee. But *all* of them indulged in a cup of anger, every once in a while.

Or, he should clarify: the *right kind* of anger was good.

Spite, for example, was a helpful variety of anger.

Say you own a car lot and you don't like the guy next door? Let that spite fuel you so you can work harder and afford to buy out your neighbor's lease and expand your own business.

Rage and resentment were also good. You just had to know where to direct them. Resentment was particularly great in a negotiation, if you knew when to show it, when to hide it. How to harness that anger.

And harnessing his anger was how Eli Duvall had dealt with Glenn Maybrook for the last two months. Eli felt his rage glow any time he had to talk to that twerp of a mayor on the phone, and it was even worse when he had to deal with the pencil-neck prick in person. But mayors, even pissant ones, weren't the kind of people you could blow up at. So Eli had to channel his rage, build dams and tributaries inside himself so that Glenn only received tiny blasts of perfectly directed hate.

And that strategy had worked, hadn't it? It was Halloween morning, wasn't it? The Duvalls had made it to the end of their inaugural season.

Mission accomplished.

And cashboxes full to bursting.

Cashboxes that Eli could go count, empty, and transfer into the safe if he could just get some fucking coffee first.

Here was another teachable moment: blind anger.

Blind anger was just wasted energy.

The light on the coffee maker blinked. Taunting him.

For maybe the tenth time, he lifted the handle to check that there was a pod in the tray.

There was.

Eli bit his cheek.

If he allowed himself to indulge this blind anger, he'd bash the machine to pieces. He even knew *how* he'd do it. This wasn't home, just a rental house he'd gotten cheap a few weeks before they'd extended the offer for the Tillerson land, but he still knew where in the kitchen the meat tenderizer was kept.

"Fucking thing sucks," Eli whispered.

He was angry.

But not so angry he was going to raise his voice and wake Jane.

Jane . . .

This thing with Jane hadn't been a problem he'd anticipated.

Moving to Kettle Springs for three months? Letting his lamebrain managers back home run every operation he had going in Branson? An enormous financial gamble to indulge the boy's long-held fantasy of opening a haunted attraction?

He'd anticipated plenty of problems.

But Jane Duvall starting to sleep on the couch wasn't one of them.

As angry as Eli Duvall let himself get, for business purposes, he'd thought he'd done a pretty good job of keeping any of that anger away from his wife and kid.

Not that he and Jane had the kind of marriage that won awards, if awards were given for such things, but he thought they were solid enough. He still loved her, all these years later.

But about a week into living in the Kettle Springs rental house, Jane spent her first night on the couch.

The habit had started innocently enough. Jane asleep in her clothes, printed spreadsheets, her laptop, and two iPads arrayed on the coffee table in front of her. She'd wanted the haunt to succeed just as badly as Hunter, maybe even more, since she doted on the boy. And, that first week, she'd run herself ragged helping with both the financial and logistic sides.

But after a few nights of that, of not having the "energy" to go upstairs to their bed, Jane had eventually stopped showering in the mornings. She'd swapped her rotation of casual work-from-home attire for a single housecoat. Then she'd started sneaking pillows from off their bed and leaving them downstairs on the couch. Even still, that wasn't the worst of it. Because at least then Eli saw her occasionally.

A few weeks later, with the haunt built, staffed, and operating smoothly, when there were no more logistics to worry about and the only financial work left would come in February or March for tax time, Jane had tacked up the bedsheets. She hung one sheet to partition the living room from the front hallway and another between the living room and the kitchen.

The living room was now "Jane's room."

Sometimes late at night, coming downstairs for a snack or a drink of water, Eli could hear her in there. The only sounds were the occasional keystroke on her laptop, an indistinct chatter of music and voices from her earbuds.

In the kitchen now, Eli opened the cabinet beside his head and returned his mug. There would be no coffee this morning, not here.

Then he approached the sheet that Jane had used to block off the kitchen.

These weren't even their bedsheets. They didn't own anything with this floral pattern. She'd either ordered them online or they'd been in a linen closet he hadn't even known the furnished rental house had.

He stood there for a moment, listening to the sounds of the living room . . . Jane's room, a label Jane herself had never said aloud, but the name Eli had mentally assigned to it.

He listened.

Sometimes she'd be awake late into the night and into the next day.

But there were no computer sounds now.

No shuffling of paper. No electric buzz of daytime TV on mute.

When they returned to Branson in a day or two, Eli hoped that things would go back to normal. He'd never confronted her about sleeping on the couch, hadn't really had the chance to discuss Jane's room at all, since things had been so busy. But maybe that was good. If they never talked about it, if he never asked her what exactly she was doing in there, then in a few months maybe this all would be a distant memory. Something they could forget.

There. There was sound.

He heard Jane sigh. It'd been weeks since they'd shared a bed, but he knew enough to recognize that it wasn't an awake sound.

Jane was breathing heavily in her sleep.

Eli raised his hand, suddenly wanting to see her, to watch his wife doze on the shallow couch.

But, no. He pulled his hand back. Best not to look.

He'd been yelled at before for peeking in on her. No need to risk it again.

When they were young, Jane used to talk in her sleep. It was something they'd joke about, even. Then, sometime after she'd given birth to Hunter, she developed a less funny quirk: Jane had started to scream in her sleep. Not big horror-movie screams where someone wakes themselves up, sweating. No, the screams were somehow worse than that. Jane screamed with her mouth *closed*, her unconscious mind trying to work the sound out through clenched teeth. The screams were usually loud enough to wake Eli, but not Jane, who would finish with a series of muffled yelps, then turn onto her side and continue sleeping. She never remembered the incidents the next morning.

Here in Kettle Springs, either exhausted or content to be on the couch and away from Eli, Jane no longer screamed. Not that he heard.

"I'm going to work, honey," Eli said, not expecting a response.

Then he stepped back from the bedsheet, took an apple from the crisper, put it into the front pouch on his laptop bag, left the kitchen, and headed for the front door.

If he didn't get some coffee, he'd have a headache within the hour.

It was a little out of the way, but he would stop in town, grab a to-go coffee from the Eatery, then continue to the haunt to count last night's take.

He walked out onto the porch and looked at the sky.

No clouds, just gray. The way October skies could sometimes be.

It was noon, maybe a little after. And it was Halloween, he reminded himself, as he crossed the small, dead lawn of their rental house to the BMW.

The kid still wasn't back with the truck. Not that Eli drove it. But playing chauffeur on an important day for the haunt . . . wasn't like Hunter.

Eli lowered himself down into the driver's seat and told himself to let the boy be. Let him live his life, let him make the wrong friends and make his own mistakes.

He'd earned it.

Hunter was a good boy, better than Eli had been at his age. Different from Eli. Very different, that was for certain. And with peculiar interests. But if those interests kept filling the cashboxes, depleting the haunt's onsite ATMs twice a weekend . . . good on the boy.

Eli pressed the keyless ignition, the car's engine nearly silent.

Ick. It smelled in here. Like an animal had crawled up under the hood for warmth and had died there.

Maybe as he drove down Main Street—windows cracked— he'd see some of the town's elementary school kids in their Halloween costumes. In Branson, trick or treating seemed to be sliding earlier and earlier in the day, with the younger kids done before the sun was close to setting.

It hadn't been like that when Eli was growing up, but the world was growing stranger and stranger and—

A shadow rose up in the back seat.

That there should be a shadow behind him, in the daylight, in his own car, was such an alien idea, Eli didn't even have time to register fear . . . or anger at the intrusion.

He didn't have time for anything as the metallic glint fell over his eyes and settled around his neck.

By the time he'd recognized that glint—it was dull and shiny at the same time. Galvanized steel, the kind used in . . . razor wire!—it was too late.

Almost too late.

He was able to get four fingers of his left hand up in front of his neck before the shadow behind him pulled the wire tight.

"What are you—" His own knuckles were shoved against his throat, pain in his hand and windpipe.

This was no joke. No kid taking props from the haunt to try to scare his boss. The wire wasn't foam rubber. It was real. It was really cutting into his hand.

There . . . there had to be a way out of this.

Yes, there was.

Get angry.

Eli Duvall looked up into the rearview mirror and raged at the clown in the back seat.

Cursed its stupid mask. Its dumb fucking red nose.

He felt spittle dribble down his chin.

This may have not been the approach to take.

Maybe he should have been begging.

The wire pulled tighter. Eli could see that the clown, Frendo, wasn't wearing traditional white clown gloves but instead reinforced work gloves.

Eli's hand was wet, blood running in thick lanes down his wrist, onto his lap.

That smell. How had he thought it was a dead animal? It was worse than that. Body odor and manure.

And the clown's mask. It was chipped and broken, with pieces of it fallen away, giving Frendo a weird double-mouth, a gap in his painted plastic smile revealing yellowed teeth and gray, grease-stained stubble.

Those broken teeth revealed more of themselves as the clown bore down. Eli heard the metal of the wire crunch as Frendo tightened his grip with his heavy gloves.

Here goes, Eli thought.

No anger in him anymore. All of it leaving his body as the adrenaline numb dissipated and the pain started flooding in.

Frendo began to saw, and Eli screamed as his fingers separated from his left hand.

Skin and bone barrier gone, there was nothing to stop the wire from cutting into his neck.

Frendo didn't accelerate his motions. The clown kept sawing in an even, unhurried rhythm. Back and forth, back and forth.

Eli's vision dimmed as a vein or artery was severed. Blood played against the windshield of the BMW like a rain shower inside the car.

In seconds the splatter became so thick that it eclipsed his view of the driveway entirely.

Frendo took a break to readjust his grip.

Weak from blood loss, before the wire worked all the way through his vocal cords, Eli was able to call out one short word:

"Jane!"

He yelled for his wife.

But even if she'd been able to hear him from inside the house, Jane was probably still asleep.

Jane Duvall was in Jane's room.

And Eli Duvall was dead.

And Frendo the Clown, himself full of anger, kept working the loop of razor wire side to side, just to make sure.

Because this was *his* town.

SIXTEEN

Most people went to the movies to escape.

Jerri Shaw was no different.

But most people didn't have the keys to the theater so they could make popcorn and lock themselves inside the building all afternoon.

Not that Jerri was going up to the projection booth to run a film. The film projector with its canisters, magnetic tracks, bulbs, cotton gloves, and reel changes . . . That intimidating process could stay a mystery, as far as Jerri was concerned. However, she did understand how to use the digital projector. Ms. Reyes had shown her in case of emergencies. In case Ms. Reyes wasn't around but the show needed to go on.

Ms. Reyes wasn't around, but the movie house should stay silent, out of respect.

Without a movie, Jerri sat in the large, empty auditorium and tried to take comfort in her surroundings. She was in her preferred seat, center of the fourth row, with the house lights dimmed to 25 percent, and had a bucket of fresh popcorn between her feet.

She had her phone in her hand, but didn't look down at it.

Not yet.

Instead, she stared up at the blank movie screen. Tried to let the smell and texture of the place calm her.

Jerri was supposed to be in her bedroom right now.

Earlier, when Hunter Duvall had dropped her off at home, Jerri had waited a few moments on the sidewalk before going inside, taking deep breaths to prepare to talk with her mom. She was sure she was about to be screamed at for worrying her mother. For making Joanne Shaw think she'd lost another kid. Not her favorite kid, but the only one she had left.

But when Jerri opened the front door, her mother didn't even look over from her perch on the couch. Jerri's mom was watching CNN, the landline phone's wireless handset on the cushion next to her.

To get her attention, Jerri let the door close a little harder than she normally would.

"What are you doing?" Joanne Shaw said, turning to the noise. "Don't you see what's happening?" She motioned to the TV, which switched away from a shot of the newsroom to a commercial for dryer sheets. "You can't go out right now. Get away from that door. Go to your room."

It took Jerri a confused moment to figure out what was happening. She noticed the slow red blink on the phone. That was why nobody could get through. The busy signal was not because Jerri's mother was frantically calling friends and acquaintances, searching for her daughter, but because she'd left the phone off the hook.

Joanne Shaw must have gone to bed early, before Jerri would have been home from working the late-night show, and woken up, switched on the TV, and let the news out of Philadelphia freeze her in place.

Joanne Shaw not only hadn't been looking for her daughter, but she hadn't known Jerri was missing at all.

Her mom had become like this after losing Dorothy. Over the past few months, things had gotten slightly better at home as the country racked up new tragedies to fixate on and the Kettle Springs Massacre became less of a nightly story. But if a before-a-commercial-break teaser on Fox promised new information about the whereabouts of Arthur Hill? If MSNBC was holding a town hall with a panel of experts and survivors? Joanne would clear her entire day to watch.

"Don't look at me like that."

Jerri blinked. Her mother blinked, too, top lip trembling.

"Don't look at me like I'm crazy," her mom said. "Something's happening. There's going to be a press conference soon. Go to your room."

Jerri didn't argue with her. She went straight to her room, only coming out to go across the hall for a shower to get the blood off her.

She should have been tired, but after lying in bed for an hour, watching the ceiling, unable to sleep, she decided to leave. She put on a fresh set of clothes, then slipped on the coat she'd borrowed from the sheriff. The coat was too hot for fall, its pleats stuffed with heavy down meant for subzero temperatures, but the sleeves and torso were large enough that, wearing it, Jerri felt like she was invisible enough.

She listened at her bedroom door, the non-regional cadence of a female news anchor echoing in from the living room, then lifted her bedroom window and headed to the Eureka.

In her palm, her phone buzzed. . . .

She looked down, startled and a little hopeful. Would it be Cole, checking in on her? Maybe Quinn Maybrook herself, thanking Jerri for watching her dad?

No.

Neither of those people had her number. She didn't have anyone who'd text her.

The buzz was a push notification that Jerri's screen time was down 7 percent this week.

The silver lining to mortal terror was slightly less time wasted on her phone.

While she had the phone open, she thumbed over to Instagram.

Along the top of the screen . . . fresh stories.

Dozens of them.

Dozens of pink-and-orange circles, beckoning.

Jerri followed most of her classmates. And most of the classes ahead of her. Everyone, actually, every single student at KSH that had a public account. Not that any of them knew it. Jerri followed everyone through a private account with less than five followers, an @ that wasn't her name, and an avatar that was a picture of a dandelion sprouting from a crack in a sidewalk.

There was a "real" Jerri Shaw on IG, too, but she rarely logged into that account. It existed solely as a lurker smokescreen, so that when kids around town wondered, *Who's this dandelion watching all my stories?* the answer wouldn't be that weird girl from Algebra I.

With the safety of anonymity, Jerri selected the leftmost story and let it play in the empty theater, her phone's sound on.

It took a moment to see it, but the flow of seemingly unrelated five-to-fifteen-second clips posted by different accounts at different times told a larger story about the last twenty-four hours in Kettle Springs.

Prayer hand emojis and animated stickers of flickering candles were superimposed over Mayor Maybrook's assistant, Kendra Stoppard, tearful, standing behind a podium. The watermarks in the corner of the photographed TV screens and laptop monitors changed from KMOV to KDSK. This must have been the press conference Jerri's mother had been so eager to watch. Jerri watched Kendra make the public announcement that, last night, Glenn Maybrook had been attacked.

The posts from six to ten hours earlier had meltdown face emojis and text that ranged from "smdh" to "Thank God Nobody Was Killed" to "Fuck Philly! Fuck the Clowns!" to a mug shot of Bradly Stoughton with his eyes x'd out. Jerri had read about that earlier, that the guy who'd attacked Quinn, Cole, and Rust in Philly had died in police custody.

Interspersed with these updates were posts from classmates.

The wordiest story was posted by Tyler Nguyen this morning, a screen cap from the Duvall Farms Facebook page:

"While our thoughts go out to all victims of violence, after consulting with local law enforcement, Duvall Farms Haunted Hayride and Scream Park *will* be *open* tonite."

Tyler offered no editorialization other than a flexing muscle sticker and a "Kettle Springs Strong" blue-and-gold ribbon.

Jerri let the progress bar on the top of Tyler's post elapse and was treated to a video clip that was . . . different than the rest.

Scarier.

"They were in my backyard," the caption at the top of the video read. Then, spaced to the bottom of the screen: "Who are they?"

Between those words, there was video footage from inside a house.

The camera moved from window to window, following two figures as they walked from the backyard out onto the street.

The video ended with the person in the house opening the door and yelling "Hey!" as the two shapes climbed into a car with a third figure behind the wheel and drove away.

A chill went up Jerri's spine. She needed to see that again.

This was posted twenty-nine minutes ago by Parker Robbins, a sophomore Jerri barely knew. Barely knew because Parker rarely posted. Something about that made the video feel realer, more unsettling.

Jerri held her finger down, pausing, trying to catch a clear look as the second figure passed by the window. The blinds obscured her view enough that Jerri couldn't make out anything about the figure's face. She tapped back, rewinding again, and let the video play. This third time she was able to see that the figure was wearing dark coveralls, adorned with patches and buttons.

Just yesterday Jerri'd been accosted by a man wearing similar patches on his vest. *Some friends and I are in town as part of an investigation*, Jerri remembered the guy in front of the theater saying, before the upperclassmen had shown up.

How many "friends" did that guy, Vest Guy, have? Jerri wondered.

But she didn't have long to consider the answer.

Because somewhere behind her, the theater still and empty, no sound from her phone because she still had her thumb on the screen . . . there was the unmistakable *creak* of one of the auditorium doors swinging inward.

Someone was in the theater with her.

Jerri ducked low, letting her new jacket envelop her like a turtle shell, making sure the back of her head couldn't be seen over the seat back.

She put her hand down over the screen, blocking the glare, then toggled to silent mode before locking the device.

Footsteps started down the aisle to her left, the carpet of the old movie house wafer-thin, the concrete underneath amplifying the sound of heavy shoes.

Last night the doors to the Eureka had been left unlocked, since both Jerri and Ms. Reyes had ridden in the ambulance with Mayor Maybrook.

Jerri thought she'd be doing Ms. Reyes a favor, coming in and locking up.

But had somebody come in earlier today? Had Jerri locked someone in here with her?

Jerri scooched her butt off the theater seat, easing her knees down to the floor. While doing this, she kept one hand on the cushion.

This was her favorite place to sit, not only because of its placement in the auditorium, for sound and picture, but because it was located in one of the rows that had been reupholstered during the Eureka's renovations. The cushion was foam, not springs like some of the older seats in the wings.

The footsteps were getting closer.

She needed to move.

She began to take her hand off the cushion, letting the seat fold back up.

It shouldn't creak.

It was a new seat.

She held her breath.

With oiled hinges.

Please. Don't. Creak.

Above her, there was a light. Whoever was walking down the aisles was using a flashlight to check between the rows.

She let her hand fully off the seat.

And the hinges let out a tiny squeak.

"Hello?" a male voice asked.

Jerri felt her heart slamming against her ribs. Imagined that while she'd been watching her Instagram stories, there hadn't been *one* person sneaking around the theater, but a whole team of them.

She imagined the last row of the auditorium, every seat filled, every spectator wearing a Frendo mask. All watching the back of her head and tapping razor blades against their knees, waiting for her to turn around and notice them.

"Who's in here?" the voice asked again.

Jerri didn't recognize the voice, but they didn't sound happy.

And they were almost to her row. There wasn't enough clearance to crawl under the seats toward the fire exit.

Her hands and knees were tacky with the sweetness of dried Diet Coke and melted Good & Plentys.

She began to crawl, hoping beyond hope she'd reach the end of the row before she was spotted.

The footfalls echoing through the empty auditorium turned into a light jog. Whoever was in here, they'd begun zigzagging between the rows, the flashlight's motions growing more frantic until . . .

Click.

The flashlight was extinguished.

He was toying with her. Must have been.

He knew she was here and . . .

"Don't take one more . . . er. Don't crawl one more inch," the voice said.

There was another click, and Jerri looked up from the

floor of the theater to see . . . nothing.

The flashlight blinded her to all but the one shadow poking through the glare: the outline of an arm gripping a handgun.

"What I mean is don't fucking move at all."

Jerri didn't.

SEVENTEEN

Rust Vance lifted the yellow "Do Not Cross" tape, ducked his head low, and crossed the uncrossable police line.

He was not in the mood to be told what to do.

And, if anyone asked, he'd been given permission to be here by the sheriff herself.

Not strictly true. But the sheriff had been in the room when Ms. Reyes asked if he could make sure the doors to the Eureka were locked.

"It's Halloween. I don't need my candy counter ransacked and my lightboxes filled with shaving cream. You know," Ms. Reyes said, indicating the hospital around them, "on top of everything else."

Looking down Main Street, Rust didn't think Izzy Reyes had much to worry about.

Even though it was Halloween—and a late Saturday afternoon—there were no kids on Main Street.

Their parents were keeping them home.

The way those same kids wouldn't be allowed out if there was a storm warning.

Rust cared about the businesses of Main Street. Maybe not as much as Cole cared, sure, but Rust cared. So it made him sad to remember that, a few years ago, Main Street was the place the children of Kettle Springs would start their night of trick or treating. They'd go door-to-door to their neighbors afterward, but before the close of business the store owners on Main would hand out full-size candy bars.

But that was before Victoria Hill, before the close of Baypen, before . . . the rest of it.

With all the economic regrowth, all the leases Cole had countersigned through his lawyers, the storefronts Rust had helped repaint, and the awnings he'd helped recanvas . . . this could have been the year Halloween in Kettle Springs started getting back to normal.

Could have, but . . .

Rust looked down at his boots. For a moment he'd forgotten where he was standing.

Next to his big toe there was a curved piece of yellow plastic with the number two printed on its side. The placard must have been left over from when the cops'd taken crime scene photos.

Rust wiped at his eyes, crust and sleep rolling free. He'd slept on the ride to town. It had started as pretending to sleep, when the Uber driver's small talk had turned into discussion of *The Baypen Hoax*—had he seen it? But Rust playing possum soon turned into real, deep sleep. That hadn't been smart. He was lucky nothing bad had happened. He'd used a fake name when registering for the app, and it didn't *seem* like the driver had recognized him, but . . .

Rust worked his way to the Eureka's front doors, careful not to step on any of the darker splotches of sidewalk.

He tried one of the large double doors.

Locked.

Then he tried the next.

Also locked.

Hmmm. He'd have to go into the alley and check the side door. Ms. Reyes, scattered as she was with everything going on, must have locked the doors before leaving.

That was . . . weird, but plausible, he guessed.

Rust pulled on the same door handle again, then *pushed*, just to make sure he wasn't making the kind of mistake you made when you were burnt out and half-asleep.

No. The doors *were* locked.

Rust shrugged and navigated back under the police tape the way he'd come, then headed around the corner to check on the side door.

"No, really," a voice said.

"Sure. I believe you. Sure. But this whole building's a crime scene."

Rust heard the struggle before he saw it.

"I can walk. Let go of—"

Rust nearly collided with Jerri Shaw.

Not only Jerri, but the sheriff's deputy who was holding her by the back of the neck. No, not by her neck, but holding onto her oversize jacket, the way a puppy or kitten could be picked up by their scruff.

Any time Rust saw an animal hold its young like that, it always looked like it hurt.

"Hey!" Rust said to the officer. "It's okay, she works here!"

"Sir, move along please, I . . . ," the officer started, then looked up from the girl he was carrying.

The man's demeanor changed as he recognized Rust.

"Vance," the deputy said.

The deputy holding on to Jerri Shaw's jacket was clean-shaven with bland features and broad build.

The man knew Rust, but Rust couldn't say he knew him.

The deputy was maybe a few years older than Rust. It was possible they'd even overlapped in high school. But the most Rust could say was that *maybe* he recognized the cop from around town. The town's police force had been massively scaled back. Marta Lee had fired every officer who'd served under Sheriff Dunne, then tried rebuilding her staff with officers without a single connection, family, business, or otherwise, to Dunne, Arthur Hill, or any of the other clowns. Which, in a small town, hadn't been easy.

The deputy loosened his grip, and Jerri shuffled forward a step before being yanked back. He still had her jacket balled in his fist.

"Whoa. Hold on there."

With Jerri more to one side, Rust could read the officer's nametag:

Miller.

A generic name for a generic man.

Cole—god, why did Rust keep thinking about Cole?—would have known this guy's first name and his whole family history, but Rust wasn't interested.

"So, this little dude works here? Even though I found him creeping around on his hands and knees?" Officer Miller knew full well it was a girl he was holding. "And *you,* Vance, just happen to be walking through the alley at the same time? Why don't you explain that to me? Because from where I stand, it's suspicious."

Officer Miller put his hand on his hip.

Close to his gun. Rust noticed that the holster was already unbuttoned. Had this dope pulled a gun on Jerri?

Rust stopped himself from mimicking the motion and getting himself into real trouble. Or dead. Not that he had a gun anymore. The one he'd traveled with was in a Philly evidence locker right now, and he hadn't thought to stop home to rearm himself.

When you're tired, you make mistakes, Rust reminded himself.

He breathed deep.

"Officer. *Her* boss asked me to come by to lock up," Rust said. Then he raised the three keys he was still holding and jingled them.

"Everyone's got the same story around here," Miller said. "Because that's what this one was doing, too."

Rust was getting frustrated. Over the last year Rust had been part of enough interviews, cross-examinations, and downright interrogations with state and federal cops that he never again wanted to hear the phrase *Let's go over it one last time*.

Which wasn't something that Officer Miller had said; it was more in his tone of voice.

"Officer Miller. Please," Rust said. "You're going to tell me you don't recognize Jerri? I think she's one of the Eureka's two employees."

Miller looked at Jerri, scrutinizing her face, and then back to Rust.

"I don't go to the theater. I got a Fire Stick for movies."

But something about having Rust as a witness must've made Officer Miller decide that whatever he'd been in the process of doing—detaining or simply harassing Jerri Shaw—wasn't worth it.

Miller let go of the girl and she tripped forward. Rust caught her. She felt like nothing at all under the down of her large jacket.

"Why don't you escort they/them here home and then get off the streets."

Rust hated Miller for a moment, and that hate jogged a shard of memory loose. Maybe Rust had known Officer Miller. Maybe he'd seen him bully a kid back in school. Or seen him fight someone smaller than him to impress a girl.

"And then get back to"—Miller paused, making a show of choosing his words—"your partner's mansion or wherever—"

Miller's radio chirped.

"All officers return to station for debrief. Lee's on her way back. Repeat, all officers 10-19," said the tinny voice on the radio clipped into Miller's belt.

"Out of the way," Miller said, pushing past them and disappearing around the corner toward the Municipal Building.

They stood for a moment. Jerri coughed.

"I went home, but . . . ," Jerri started, her voice low. Rust looked off down the alley so that she could speak without being stared at. The dumpster hadn't been emptied in a while, and there were clear plastic garbage bags of stale popcorn propping up the lid. "My mom told me to go to my room. She's been so freaked out, between what happened to Mayor Maybrook and what happened in Philadelphia. . . ."

Rust looked at the girl, then back out onto the street. A cop car passed, lights flashing but no siren. There was no traffic to usher out of the way.

He thought about Cole. How Jerri might be able to tell him something about their ride home with Hunter. But it wasn't fair of him to ask.

Rust had his phone on. If Cole texted, he'd answer. If he called, he'd pick up. But elsewise, there'd never been anything Rust Vance could make Cole Hill do. If Cole wanted to sit alone in his big house and brood, well, it was probably the safest place he could be. The only way Cole would be safer was if Rust were there to protect him.

Are you my boyfriend or my bodyguard?

Rust rubbed his chin.

He looked over at Jerri, sizing her up before he spoke. He could remember being that young, that awkward.

"I'm hungry."

"Huh?" Jerri asked, like he'd said it in French.

"I'm hungry. Let's get tacos."

And so they did, walking four doors down to Mesa Sabrosa.

They ordered at the counter, and Rust took a seat facing

the window so he could watch what was happening in his town.

If Cole needed time, Rust would give him time, he decided.

That time was from now until Rust and Jerri finished with this meal.

EIGHTEEN

Quinn was dreaming about something terrible happening in a hospital room. She dreamt she could hear her father screaming.

Then Marta Lee gently shook her awake.

"Someone wants to talk to you," the sheriff said.

They were in a hospital room.

Quinn blinked, taking a second. They were *still* in a hospital room.

"Our family has to stop meeting like this," Glenn Maybrook said.

His motorized bed was raised to a sitting position and his injured hand lay across his stomach, the fingers curled into a thumbs-up. Izzy Reyes stood beside him.

"I threw a few punches, but . . . ," her dad said. Quinn

wasn't used to seeing him without glasses. "I don't think you'll laugh if I say 'You should see the other guy.'" His voice was a pained rasp.

"I'll laugh at anything if it gets you to be quiet and rest," Quinn said.

She pushed up from her chair, and a hospital blanket dropped to the floor. Quinn hadn't put the blanket on herself. Izzy Reyes or Sheriff Lee—which of the two women had more *lay a blanket on you while you slept* energy?

Quinn approached his bedside.

How long had she been asleep? The hospital room didn't have a window. Had the sun begun to set?

She wanted to hug her father, but couldn't see a place to put her hands that wouldn't risk causing him pain.

"You look worse than I do. Go home," her dad said. "Go sleep in your own bed. I'm going to be fine. They say I just need a day or two."

"Try a week or two," Marta Lee said, jokingly disguising the statement as a cough.

As Quinn had slept, the bandages around her dad's neck had shifted, brownish-red raspberry spots of blood dotting the gauze.

"Did you tell him what happened?" Quinn looked to Izzy, then Marta Lee, who stood at the foot of the bed, her laptop in one hand, balanced on the railing. The sheriff really had been trying to do her job remotely.

"Yes. I heard about Philly," her dad said. "I'm glad you're okay, but I'm so sorry you had to go through something like that again, kiddo."

"I'm fine. Everyone's still alive." She wanted to say something else. Be more encouraging. Quip. But she didn't have the energy. She looked over to Sheriff Lee, then to Izzy. "Should we get the doctor?"

"She was just here," her dad said. "You slept through the whole thing. Even missed all the stuff about my catheter."

"Great."

He smiled weakly at that.

"But listen to me," her dad said, turning serious. "I love you. I'm so happy to see you, but you've been through something as well. You should be resting, too."

He looked to the sheriff. His seriousness grew even more pronounced. That scared Quinn more than anything else. Seeing her dad without glasses, not being a goofball: "Marta. Can you drive her home? Make sure she's safe?"

Quinn reached out and touched his knee. And he winced. Even his knee. Every part of him hurt.

"Yes. I can drive you," Marta Lee said to Quinn. "There's only so much police work I can do from . . ." She held up the laptop.

Quinn leaned over to her dad. "You'll go back to sleep? Rest? You promise?"

"Yes, but first going to see if the TV works so I can watch

my . . ." Glenn Maybrook was trying to switch back to dad-joke mode. Quinn knew his shtick well enough to guess he was going to say "my shows" or "my stories," imitating a grandmother she didn't have, but instead he started coughing.

It was a thick, wet sound, the blood spots on his neck seeming to flash redder with each convulsion. After a moment it quieted down.

"Sore throat," he explained.

Izzy helped him readjust his pillows so he could lie flatter, then handed him the remote to lower the bed.

"I'll stay with him," Izzy Reyes said. "If that's all right?"

She wasn't asking her dad. She was asking Quinn.

"Don't ask me," Quinn said, a little more edge in her voice than there should have been. "Ask him."

But Glenn Maybrook was already back to sleep, his head slumped to one side, chest rising and falling, bandaged hand still with its thumb sticking up.

Yes. Quinn *wanted* to leave. She especially wanted to leave if the sheriff was driving her. Because the sheriff knew things Quinn needed to know. Because Quinn was headed back to Kettle Springs for one reason and one reason only: to find the bastard who'd done this.

"I think he'd want you to stay, Izzy," Quinn said, then added, unsure how subtle she was being: "Thank you. For everything."

Izzy didn't respond with words, just let tears well in her

eyes and looked down at Quinn's father. Was it love? It was for Izzy; Quinn was becoming more convinced of that by the second.

Quinn stretched, lifting one leg, then the other, knees feeling tight. There were pins and needles up and down her legs and sides, a physical exhaustion that reminded her of volleyball practices.

And there were miles to go before she could get a good sleep.

Quinn leaned forward, careful not to wake him. She pushed her hair away from her face and kissed the air next to her dad's head, where his glasses would normally rest. Then, quietly, she said that she loved him.

"I'm ready when you are," Quinn said, rising. The sheriff nodded, folded her laptop under her arm, and walked out the door.

Quinn started to follow her, then lingered for a minute, now alone in the room with her dad and his girlfriend.

"Izzy," Quinn said, whispering, pulling open the school bag that'd traveled with her from Philly.

Izzy looked up, her expression confused, a little guilty, like she was preparing for Quinn to say something cruel. This woman didn't know Quinn at all. When things calmed down, Quinn would need to do a better job of having her get to know her, if Izzy Reyes was going to stay in their lives. And even if she wasn't, it was still the right thing to do.

"I know the sheriff said this is a safe place," Quinn started. "But there is no safe place. Take this."

Quinn pushed the grip of her tactical baton into Izzy's hands.

Izzy hesitated a moment before taking the weapon. There was an even longer moment of confusion before she seemed to understand what it was.

It'd never been logged into evidence in Philadelphia because, according to the taller of the two detectives: "An illegal weapon like this? Too much paperwork." And airport security hadn't inspected her carry-on close enough to catch it.

Izzy looked ready to push it back to her, but then seemed to realize that the two pounds of alloy steel was an olive branch.

It was fine for Izzy to take it. Quinn had more batons back home. And blades. And Rust's gun safe.

"I won't let anything happen to him," Izzy said. Like she was making both Quinn and herself a promise.

"Good. Don't."

And Quinn left the room.

"The front seat feels weird," Quinn said. They'd driven a few miles in silence, and it felt like, before her questions, she should start with an icebreaker.

"What's that?" Sheriff Lee asked.

"After being in the back this morning. And in Philly before that. Passenger's seat in a cop car feels weird, is what I'm saying."

Marta Lee grunted. Or laughed. It was hard to tell over the sound of the engine.

There was a shotgun between them, held by a heavy machined-metal locking mechanism that covered the trigger guard and stock.

Quinn hated that she noticed things like that now, that she could name all the different components of the gun.

Rust had taught her to respect weapons. How to shoot. But all the familiarity in the world would never get Quinn to *like* guns.

"So . . ." Quinn was about to be blunt, but she was too tired to think of any other way to ask the questions she needed answers to. "Are there any suspects yet?"

Marta Lee took her eyes off the road, met Quinn's gaze. Was that a smile, at the corner of her lips? Or did the woman's neutral face just look like that and Quinn had never noticed?

"Quinn. I know you've been through a lot, but are you law enforcement now?"

Quinn smiled, shrugged, tried to summon a good humor that she didn't feel. "More a concerned citizen."

Sheriff Lee sighed.

"Look. It's going to sound stupid, and I'm sure he doesn't

215

consider me his, especially because he has you, but . . . your dad's my best friend."

Quinn started to say something, but the sheriff kept going: "I'm not exaggerating. Maybe not my oldest friend. But right now, my best. I don't know how much he's shared with you, about the last couple months, but he's been working really hard for this town. And I've been there with him. Every day."

"I get it," Quinn said. "He talks about you a lot. Even if we don't get into specifics of what's going on with his job, I know that you work closely together."

"That's good. But what I'm pretty sure he hasn't told you is that he's got . . ." The sheriff readjusted her hands on the steering wheel.

"Enemies?" Quinn asked.

Sheriff Lee's eyes were back on the road, and crinkled a bit at the edges, hearing that word.

"I was going to say opposition. Heavy opposition. And that opposition makes a list. And I promise you, the first thing we do when we get back, after I talk with my office and get in the lab work, is I'm going door-to-door to talk with every person on that list. I'm going to—"

"Rattle some cages," Quinn cut in.

"That actually *was* what I was going to say."

They both smiled now.

"You know? I think I like you better than the last sheriff," Quinn said.

"Gee. Thanks."

They drove for a while then, Quinn allowing Sheriff Lee's words, her determination, to let some of the pressure off. It was clear that Marta Lee would never phrase it the same way, but the sheriff and Quinn were partners now.

"What did you mean by lab work?" Quinn asked, thinking back over their conversation.

"Huh?"

"You said lab work. Blood, fingerprints?"

Marta Lee sucked air in, looked away from Quinn, out the window. Corn now. Surrounding them. Reminding Quinn that she wasn't in Philly anymore, that the life she had there that had only just started to feel real was gone again. At least for the time being.

"Both. We have both."

"That's good, right? Having both?"

"We have more than both. We have the weapon, too. Or part of it. A few inches of snap-off blade from a utility knife."

Quinn thought for a moment. Then felt a surge of pain in her own palm, like the attack had happened to her.

"From his hand? You have fingerprints from the blade in his hand? How is that even possible?"

"It's not much of a print, that's how. And blood from the sidewalk. But . . ."

"Then what did the lab say?"

"Nothing that helps us yet. Look, it's not like I have to tell you this, but it's not like on TV."

"Then why even say that? If you know I understand?"

"Don't get smart," Sheriff Lee said, and the corner of her mouth did twinge up in a slight smile. The kind that showed teeth. "I'm just saying you don't feed DNA into a computer and it prints you out a picture of the suspect."

"But it gives you something to compare to."

"Yes. But don't get your hopes up there. Whoever attacked your dad, as best we can tell, they're not in the system. But they *were* stupid enough to leave us materials to check against, clues to who they are, and now the old-fashioned police work can begin—taking statements, finding inconsistencies in those statements, and following up."

"You sound excited about old-fashioned police work."

"I'm excited about seeing this shithead in handcuffs."

Quinn smiled. "Sure." *I'd rather see him dead*, she thought. But that was wrong. It showed how the last year had changed her, that she could so easily wish death on someone.

Quinn let herself lie back. Leather squeaked; the smell and feel of the seat enveloped her.

Sleep was coming again.

Her mind and vision were going fuzzy from exhaustion.

And while she was in that half state, they could have traveled one hundred feet or ten miles.

"Oh, what now?" Marta Lee said under her breath, but

loud enough to pull Quinn's consciousness forward.

There were two men by the side of the road. Barely in the shoulder, they stood on either side of an open hood, their car's hazard lights blinking between them. The car was a junker, so red with rust and paint so sun-cracked and faded it was hard to even tell a make and model.

The men looked like they were arguing with each other, and as Marta Lee slowed the cruiser, heading toward the opposite side of the two-lane highway, one noticed that a cop had arrived and began waving his arms.

Sheriff Lee cracked her window.

"Push it farther off the road!" she yelled to them. "You're going to get side-swiped." Then she added, lower, "Dumb bastards."

Both men were dressed in black. And Quinn could . . . see their skeletons?

Quinn blinked, tired enough that this detail felt like a dream at first, but then she remembered: it was Halloween.

Matching costumes. They were two men in their late twenties or early thirties dressed as skeletons, faces covered in amateurish skull makeup.

The man who'd been waving his arms looked both ways down the corn-lined stretch of highway and then jogged over to the cruiser.

"Officer! Thank god you're here."

It was twilight, but with his white-and-black face paint

highlighting his features, Quinn could see the man's worried, slightly stupid expression in the dark. The skull design had smudged and was melting off as the man sweat.

Quinn craned her neck between the seats to see that his friend had stayed with the car. He kicked at the gravel in frustration, and when that wasn't enough, he kicked one of the car's tires.

"We broke down and . . ." The man at the window was angling his head to speak into the two-inch crack Sheriff Lee had opened for him.

"Sir, I can hear you," Marta Lee said. "Can you please step back from my vehicle?"

"Oh," he said, and took a small step back, looking both ways again to make sure he wasn't stepping into the nonexistent traffic. "Sorry."

"Don't have time for this shit," Marta Lee muttered. She picked up the radio. "Motorists at mile marker . . ." She lifted her fingers from the button. "Shit, where are we?" Then, to Quinn: "Can you read that sign? Is that first number an eight or a three?"

The man knocked on the window.

"I called Triple A already. They know we're here. . . ."

"Sir, please, step away from my car."

Marta Lee rolled her window down farther, to better yell at the man. The window was now halfway down.

"But we need your help. Our buddy is hurt, and—"

"Wait," Sheriff Lee said, her posture and tone of voice changing. "Someone's hurt?"

Quinn could smell it now.

Alcohol.

Maybe that was why the man's makeup was smudged and how he was sweating so much on a cool October evening.

Sheriff Lee turned to Quinn: "Stay here, this will just take a minute."

Something about the smell of booze breath and sweat turned Quinn's stomach.

"How much have you had to drink tonight, sir?" Marta Lee said, and put her arm against the door handle, ready to open it onto the guy and push him back into the road, if necessary.

But the man seemed to sense this movement. He leaned against the door, closing it with his weight. Then he hiccupped and slid his forearm down over the window.

Brrrr. There was a sound, a small motor grinding.

Quinn could see, in the light of the dash, that Sheriff Lee was trying to roll the power window back up, but it wasn't moving, with the man's arm against the top of the glass.

"Hey," the drunken skeleton man said, slurring a bit. He pointed one finger into the car, more of him inside with them now. "Is that Quinn Maybrook?"

"Wait. I know you . . . ," Sheriff Lee said, surprise in her voice. And then disappointment: "What are you doing, M—"

The man leaned forward and, with his free hand, stabbed Sheriff Marta Lee in the throat.

The goofy, buzzed expression on the man's face firmed up into calm, controlled malice as he spoke: "Frendo has a posse."

Sheriff Lee's whole body tensed, and her right hand flew to her sidearm while her left pressed on the steering wheel to steady herself.

The sound of Quinn's first scream was eclipsed by the blast of the cruiser's horn.

The man at the window stabbed Sheriff Lee again. He fixed his lips into a line, and that made his skeleton makeup truly scary. He kept stabbing, motions so quick Quinn couldn't even make out the blade, until Sheriff Lee's arms went limp and blood covered the front of her uniform.

Quinn screamed one more time before he was finished.

"Hey, Quinn," the man said, skeleton teeth smiling. "Catch."

Still leaning at the window, he tossed the blade into the car.

The large hunting knife made two slow loops and landed in her lap. She pushed the weapon away, Sheriff Lee's blood smeared across her jeans, the blade's point getting caught in her outer thigh and drawing a thin gouge down denim and flesh. She winced, then kept bobbling the blade and handle until she finally had the knife that had killed Marta Lee away from her, wedged between the passenger's door and the seat.

There was no maybe.

It was happening again.

Your dad is my best friend.

Quinn flattened herself down, diving toward the driver's side of the vehicle. The engine was still running, but Quinn wasn't trying to drive. She wanted Sheriff Lee's gun. She stretched for it, body still belted to her seat, no time to struggle with it, the shotgun locked to the center console bruising her ribs.

It took her only a second to move Marta Lee's lifeless hand off the butt of the service weapon, unlatch the holster, and have the barrel of the handgun pointed out the window.

"Shit!" the guy in the skeleton pajamas yelled, turning away from her.

Not quick enough, fucker.

Quinn disengaged the safety and fired.

But she was at too odd of an angle: the partially up driver's side window exploded, but the guy was already scrambling across the blacktop. At best she'd winged him, if she'd hit him at all.

Quinn unclicked her belt and pushed open the passenger's

side door to start after him. The knife fell into the dirt beside the cruiser. She started to stand, but got tangled up in the dangling safety belt.

"Go! Go, she's got a gun," the guy yelled to his friend.

Quinn's thigh burned from where she'd cut herself, and it only took half a second to bend and retrieve the hunting knife. If they were stupid enough to give her another weapon, she wouldn't refuse it.

She rounded the cruiser's trunk, gun out, knife drawn, ready to shoot out the men's windshield as they climbed into their car to make a getaway. . . .

But neither man was getting in the rusted-out car.

Instead, the guy who'd stabbed Marta Lee was running zigzags toward the ditch, hunched over to offer Quinn as small a target as possible. She watched, unable to get a clear shot, as he disappeared into the corn.

She looked back at the car, its hood still up. The other skeleton was still watching her. He took a few steps back from the car, toward the ditch and the corn, then stopped.

Quinn pointed the gun at him.

She expected a "Don't shoot" or some resistance, maybe a weapon of his own. But instead, he . . .

He had his phone out? He was filming her, directing the camera her way, the flash turning on, making her squint in the darkness, his body losing definition behind the outstretched camera, becoming just wisps of leg and arm bones.

"Come on!" his friend, now invisible, yelled from the corn.

Quinn watched the light on the phone, thinking about how the man holding it hadn't stabbed anyone, and then she pulled the trigger anyway.

He turned the light away with the shot, ducking down under the lip of the ditch as he fled, the darkness making it impossible to tell if she'd hit him or not.

Quinn breathed for a moment. Made sure she was alone, then leaned against the trunk of Marta Lee's police cruiser.

"Goddamn it!" she yelled. Then screamed the words again. Then again until she felt something in her voice pop and tasted the copper of blood.

She looked into the car at Sheriff Lee. She thought about checking for a pulse, but knew it would do no good. Then she thought about searching Sheriff Lee's belt for the keys that would let her unlock the shotgun, or calling for help, but she only allowed these considerations to last a few seconds.

No. There was no time. They were getting away.

So, as the world grew darker and the moon and stars began to shine, Quinn Maybrook followed the two men dressed as skeletons.

She followed them into the corn.

NINETEEN

It was dark, Cole was halfway to drunk, and things were getting fully weird.

He fell forward, catching himself.

Well. Maybe more than halfway drunk.

Cole leaned against the kitchen island and peered through the doorway. He could see the dining room, the coatroom, a sliver of the front door.

Each of these rooms was bathed in shadows. Lifeless.

Cole should go around the house and turn on some lights. He should check that he'd dialed in the security code to arm the system. Which he was pretty sure he had. He always did. He didn't want fear running his life . . . but he wasn't stupid.

Aside from the solid buzz, tonight wasn't all that

different from how Cole spent most nights. But most nights Rust would come over, turning on a light in every room they entered. Turning on lights, checking behind doors, making a sourpuss face if Cole grabbed for a third drink.

But Rust wasn't here, and the house was dark and still.

"Here," Cole said to the empty kitchen, cracking open one of the large stainless-steel refrigerator doors.

Let there be light.

And there was light. And it was harsh.

Cole blinked into the fridge. What had he come up here for? The choices were limited. The fridge was . . . lean. Mostly condiments and Styrofoam takeout containers.

Oh yeah. Beer.

He looped the plastic of a nearly spent six-pack around his finger and lifted two cans up, letting them dangle there in the glow of the fridge light.

He looked at his arm. The blue-white light of the fridge wasn't doing him any favors, but his skin was so sallow and sick-looking. He needed to do something about that.

Wait. His eyes followed his arm down, over to his shoulder. He dipped his chin into his neck.

Bare. Cole wasn't wearing a shirt.

Oh yes. Things *had* gotten fully weird.

He was holding two beers. How much had he drunk before this? He was holding *two* beers. Then he puzzled it out, remembering.

Two. To offer one to his guest.

Because Hunter Duvall was here. Here somewhere in the house.

Hunter was here and Cole wasn't wearing a shirt.

Had he?

Oh fuck.

An image of Rust's face pushed forward in Cole's mind. Not Ruston Vance as he was now, with his scars and stubble, but as Cole had known him as a kid: Rusty. The boy with scabs and an air rifle. The kid that grew up to be the man Cole loved.

Had Cole done something he couldn't take back?

Had something happened with Hunter Duvall because Cole was drunk and exhausted and feeling hopeless?

No.

Cole played back the recent past.

Hunter and Cole had gotten here, what? Two hours ago? Less? No, had to be longer than that. A few hours longer. It had been light when they arrived, and it was nearly full dark outside now.

They'd taken a tour of the house.

Okay. What next?

The tour had been paused, or ended, down in the basement.

How much did he drink and when?

In the basement Cole had been showing off the projector and home theater, and that's where the buzz had come from: the bar tucked beside the theater seats.

So hard liquor then, poured straight. How much of it?

Cole shivered in the chill of the fridge light. But didn't close the door.

Think, fucko. *Why aren't you wearing a shirt?*

Oh.

Because they'd watched a movie, and Cole had been switching between different inputs on the universal remote when Hunter asked, "What's that smell?"

And Cole . . . he remembered now. This was only a few minutes ago. He'd said: "Chlorine."

Hunter made a confused face, like it wasn't the chlorine smell he was asking about.

But by that point it was too late, because Cole was up, legs shaky with booze and nerves. He pulled back the vinyl partition and told Hunter to get a load of this. . . .

Yes. The basement was split into two sections: the theater and the spa. Arthur Hill's mansion had a pool in the basement. And a sauna and steam room. But it was the pool that had impressed Hunter.

"Holy shit," Hunter said.

The moisture rolled over them both.

"Yeah, this house isn't fucking around."

The air around them *did* smell like chlorine. But it also smelled like mildew. Cole hadn't been down here in a year, hadn't run the basement fans in half as long. But Hunter was right—there was another smell down here, too. A human kind of musk and rot. A stench that felt . . . familiar.

"Too bad I didn't bring my suit," Hunter said, looking at the water.

While Hunter knelt to reach his hand in, checking the water temperature, Cole groped for a light switch in the dimness. He dialed up the pool LEDs, then set them to alternate colors, purple to red to blue to yellow.

The water was about a foot and a half lower than it was supposed to be. When was the last time the pool guy'd been out? He used to come once a month. Was the estate still paying him?

"Yeah, it's pretty cool," Cole said. "But it's small. Not like you can have a real pool party. Just a few friends over." And then he remembered the town reservoir. Where they went to have *real* parties.

Fuck.

And that thought—Victoria's blood bubbling up from her scalp—sent Cole into a kind of panic.

He'd needed something to take his mind off it. Anything.

So he'd taken off his shirt.

"No, you don't need a suit," he said.

Hunter peeled off his shirt, too. Almost too quickly, like this was what he'd been waiting for the whole day.

In the shifting light glowing up from the pool, they watched each other. Cole looked at Hunter's chest, the softness of his shoulders and slight belly. It was different. It wouldn't be like holding Rust. It would be something closer to Cole holding himself.

That idea had a certain appeal to it, but thinking about skin-to-skin contact made Cole panic more. Because he didn't want this. Even drunk. Even angry. He didn't want to be alone, shirtless, wet, with anyone who wasn't Rust.

"I think—" Hunter started. But Cole didn't want to hear it. He needed to shut down whatever was coming next.

So, without really thinking about it, he blurted: "Basement fridge is out of beer. You want one? I'll go get us one." And sped out of the basement, taking the stairs two at a time, leaving Hunter in the LED glow.

That caught him up to now, standing in front of the fridge. Gooseflesh prickled at his arms. Because he was cold, aroused, or terrified: he didn't know.

Cole burped and felt a little better.

He closed the fridge door, the shadows around him darker as his eyes adjusted.

Okay. The next step had to be figuring out a way to politely get Hunter back into his truck and out of this house.

He could do that. Shouldn't be hard. Hunter wasn't the drunk one.

He could get this half-naked guy out of his house. Politely. He just needed to—

There was a sound.

Not where he'd left Hunter, downstairs in the basement. But a creak on the stairs leading to the second floor.

Up to Cole's bedroom.

Oh shit. Hunter had somehow gotten by him.

And they'd toured the house. So Hunter knew where Cole's bedroom was. Where his bed was. If Cole had to evict Hunter from his bed—maybe less clothed than when he'd last seen him—could he?

"Hello?" Cole asked, then strained to listen for an answer. Were those footsteps? Or was that just sounds the house made? Hard to tell. There were carpet runners lining the second-floor hallways in both directions. There were two sections of the second floor: the west wing, where Cole showered and slept; and the east wing, where he rarely ever ventured anymore. Where he didn't even look down that hallway, if he could help it.

Cole moved to the door that led to the basement stairs. He stood for a moment, listening, trying to rub some heat into his chest but only succeeding in tangling up the light patch of hair into anxious knots.

"Hunter?"

No answer.

Another creak echoed through the house, out from the foyer. It was the same spot he'd heard before. Hunter hadn't gone upstairs. Not yet. He must have been standing on the stairs, waiting for Cole.

Cole left the basement door, made his way through the dining room, and before he could see the staircase . . .

Thump thump thump.

Hunter stomped up the stairs and disappeared beyond the lip of the landing.

Cole stood in the foyer, looking up to the curved staircase that led to the second floor.

"Ha. Okay. Very cute. But I—"

But something about this little chase didn't feel right.

Cole turned in place so that he was facing the front door. He reached out and tried the knob. Locked. He threw the deadbolt. And the chain. Just to be sure. Then he woke the alarm panel, the translucent buttons and the LCD screen illuminated with green light:

ARMED.

ZONES: CLEAR.

Okay. That's good.

"Look," Cole said, now more confident that he was indeed alone with Hunter in the empty house. "It's late. And it was a big day. You're a nice guy, but I . . ."—*don't want to be with you*—"don't want to play hide-and-seek right now."

No answer.

Cole started climbing the stairs, stopped at the fifth step up. It creaked under his weight. Definitely the sound he'd heard.

"Not to be rude and throw you out, but," Cole said, continuing up the stairs, stopping on the landing, "it's Halloween. Don't you have, like, very important haunted-house management duties?"

Okay. This was getting weird. Weird*er*. There was no giggling. No dares. No whispered suggestions. This didn't feel like a seduction.

But he was up here. Cole knew because he could smell him.

The stink from the pool room had followed him. The same smell Cole had noticed around the house, in pockets, over the last few months. Not chlorine. Not pool scum. But—

Cole's phone chirped. A text alert.

He blinked down at the message, the tequila-frayed synapses behind his eyes throbbing.

It was from Hunter:

SHHHHHHHH

There were plenty of notifications below the text from Hunter, missed calls from Rust, but all he cared about right now was that he'd been shushed.

"What do you mean, 'shh'?" Cole yelled. "I'm exhausted. I don't want to play, I—"

Then that ding, the default bell sound of an incoming text.

Someone in your house. I'm hiding

Cole's vision swam.

He looked up from his phone, then down the hall to his right, toward his bedroom. Not much light to see by. But there was no one there.

Cole silenced his phone, then typed:

Where are you?

The three dots bounced.

Where he'd been chilly a few seconds ago, Cole was now sweating.

The basement. Where are you?

Cole sniffed the air. The smell was back. The smell was worse.

He turned his head to look down the east wing of the second floor. The rooms he never went into. Victoria's room, untouched but for the dust. His parents' empty bedroom. Where his father used to sleep alone. Untouched since the police had turned it upside down searching for evidence.

And there, in the darkness, outlined by the moonlight cutting through the window at the end of the hall, stood a tall, bent shadow.

Cole watched the shadow. Hoping it was a hallucination.

The shadow took a step toward him. A single step, then stopped again, standing still, like its stillness made it invisible.

"Hey," Cole said, barely even able to push that small word out.

No. It was not a *tall* shadow—that had been a trick of the light. It was an average-height shadow, maybe a few inches taller than Cole himself.

Behind him, over the railing, down on the first floor, there was a knock on the front door.

Who could that be? The shadow's friend? Did it matter? Cole didn't move his eyes, kept staring into the blackness.

The shadow took another step, the image taking shape.

Where Cole was bare chested, the figure was clothed. Rumpled. The jumpsuit creased with age and use, stained dark.

The pom-pom buttons no longer heavy and full enough to puff, they just swung with the shadow's steps, matted and limp.

The knocking on the front door continued. Grew more insistent. Became a banging.

Who was rattling the frame? Cole could try running down there. Taking his chances with whoever was banging. Maybe it was help. Maybe it was the police. Or maybe it was more clowns. But even that would be preferable to *this* clown.

The clown stepped out of the shadows and inside the starlight from the foyer's large front windows. Cole could see now that the mask's smile was cracked. Cleft in two, a second, greasier smile underneath.

Cole's mind screamed at his body, begged his legs to move. He needed to turn and run down the stairs. To throw open the door and offer himself up to whoever was banging to be let in.

Frendo the Clown.

Here in Hill Manor.

Its eyes were black and glassy, shoulders dropped into a hunter's stance.

Cole's attacker had a knife out, the oxidized blade bared like claws.

There was no choice. He had to move. Had to try and fight.

Cole's muscles flexed, he took one step back, feeling the whole house spin around him.

But even rotting and decrepit, Frendo was fast.

"Wait, don't—" were the only words Cole Hill could get out before the man in the filthy clown costume was upon him, with his free hand around Cole's neck.

"I've waited so long," the man said.

His breath was putrid. His thumb snaked into Cole's mouth as they struggled. His fingernails, flaky, the skin around them inflamed, dug into the tendons of Cole's neck and chin.

And it wasn't just his hygiene—his voice had changed so much in the last year.

Cole kicked wildly in the darkness, unable to find any part of the thin man to hit. He felt his body being lifted up. The top railing of the banister pushing against the back of his knees.

He screamed as he fell. The polished marble floor of the foyer rushing up to meet him.

The front door was still shaking in its frame as Cole's body hit the ground.

As his bones snapped.

TWENTY

"That can't be good," Ruston Vance said, setting down his glass bottle of Coke and pointing out the front window of Mesa Sabrosa.

Jerri had her mouth full of burrito, so she couldn't respond.

She turned in her seat to see what he was pointing at.

What she saw nearly caused her to choke on her rice and beans.

Out the front window of the restaurant, there were three men walking down Main Street. Each stood five feet away from the other, and their steps were more or less synchronized.

The sun had nearly set, and while Jerri watched the three men, the streetlights clicked on.

They wore combat boots and canvas pants with lots of pockets, and each had a machine gun slung over their shoulder.

They looked like soldiers. Not unlike the National Guardsmen who'd been in town for a few weeks around this time last year.

Only the National Guardsmen hadn't been wearing Frendo the Clown masks.

Jerri felt her hands start to shake, so she put down the burrito foil and grabbed onto her knees. She pressed down, trying to keep herself stable.

"There's more," Rust said. Jerri hadn't seen him get up, but he was crouched beside her now, peering out the window, neck craned to look up and down the street.

There were more people out there, and more joined this bizarre parade as she watched. Most weren't dressed like soldiers. Some were in regular street clothes; some were dressed like they were headed to a sporting event, war paint to go with their greasepaint. And a few weren't armed at all. At least weren't as *visibly* armed as the three men in the middle of the street. More came into view as Rust and Jerri watched. A few of them carried signs, some simple—saying things like "Justice!" or "End the Hoax!"—and others . . . were lengths of tiny, illegible text.

And all these people marching down Main Street— every single one was wearing a clown mask.

"We've got to get out of here," Rust said, grabbing Jerri by the wrist and pulling her off her seat and into a crouch with him. Her pulse throbbed against the press of his work-calloused skin. She liked Rust, but she didn't like being touched like this.

"Hey, stop," she said, feeling her legs and muscles lock up, her wrist sore from where he had yanked her down to the floor. "We can't go out there!"

"You see this tile?" Rust tapped the floor under them. "I helped put it in. This place has a back door, and the alley connects to Oak. From there we can cross backyards and get onto Marshall and my house. I've got—"

"What's going on out there?" the restaurant's sole employee asked. The man who'd taken their order and moved back into the small kitchen to prepare their food came around the side of the counter. He took off his hairnet, letting a mop of curly hair swing down into his face.

"Louis," Rust said. He was on all fours now, moving away from the big window. "Pull down the shutter and turn off the lights."

"Put down the shutter?" Louis motioned to a watch he wasn't wearing. "I've still got until—"

Out on the street, somebody yelled something and another voice yelled back. It was the beginning of a chant.

"Give. Us. The Three. Give. Us. The Three."

"The three?" Louis asked.

But Jerri knew what the words meant. And she guessed Rust did, too. The Baypen Three. Quinn Maybrook, Cole Hill . . . and Ruston Vance.

"Just do it!" Rust yelled to Louis, then turned back to Jerri, opening and closing his hand in what must have been military sign language for *Crawl to me.*

She didn't move. Couldn't.

"Jerri, please. I know you're scared, but you need to come with me."

Jerri looked at her hands, fingertips white against the tile. The floor where her fingers could find no purchase, but she was flexing her knuckles anyway, like she could keep the world from falling apart if she just held on to solid ground.

This was just a protest or something, she told herself. There wouldn't be any violence. It wasn't happening again. It couldn't be. . . .

Outside there was the skidding of tires and then marching footsteps. More people arriving on the scene, getting out of their cars. Parking getting tight. Which meant they were out-of-towners. Probably. Probably mostly out-of-towners.

But what about those three guys in the middle of the street? They looked different. They looked . . . dangerous.

Jerri listened for, hoped to hear, police sirens or calls for the three soldiers to put down their weapons. But none came.

Louis had his keys out, pushed his hair out of his eyes in

order to search for the key that would unlock the storefront's metal shutter.

Outside, the chant died away as a new voice was raised. It was close, only a door or two down, on the same side of the street as Mesa Sabrosa.

"Go home, shitheads! You're blocking traffic. I called the cops!"

There weren't many adults in Kettle Springs who would open a conversation with "shitheads," so Jerri didn't need to see his face to know that the voice belonged to Del Ryan, the old man who owned Ryan's Thrift, one of the few businesses on Main Street that had endured both the economic downturn of Baypen closing and the fallout after the massacre.

"Smash it," a voice said, not yelling back to Del, but issuing an order to someone else in the crowd.

The sound of breaking glass echoed through Kettle Springs.

It had to be the front windows of Ryan's Thrift. Jerri imagined sun-bleached stuffed animals and secondhand varsity jackets studded with shattered glass.

"You fucking lunatics," Del screamed.

"Okay, got it," Louis said, separating a single key from the chain.

The chant was back, louder now, spurred on by the sound of breaking glass and Del's screams.

"Give. Us. The. Three!"

Rust looked up, back to the window, his eyes wide. "Jerri, cover yourself, they—"

A second later, there was no window left for the shutter to protect.

Jerri heard herself shriek, the sound like someone else's voice in her body.

A large, sickle-shaped pane of glass crashed down beside her, missing her ankle by inches. Tiny jewels of glass bounced off the tile and into her face.

The table they'd been eating at a moment ago was upturned, foil and Coke bottles scattered. A green metal trash can stenciled with the slogan "Keep KS Clean" had been tossed through the window. The can rolled to a stop at Louis's feet.

"Get out of here, kids!" Louis said, kicking the trash can out of the way and running to the window, both hands above his head, waving, either *Stop* or *I surrender* or both.

That was all it took. Jerri finally moved now, as if Louis, an adult, telling her to leave, jogged some people-pleasing part of her loose.

She stayed low, on her hands and knees, knowing that she was being cut, but too afraid to stand and make herself a target for the growing mob out on Main Street.

"Quick, come on," Rust said, crawling until they were past the small restaurant's restroom and around the corner to the unassuming service door. There was a sign that read: "Alarmed. Emergency Exit Only."

"Are you okay?" Rust asked, his hand on the metal door's push bar. There were no windows back here. No way to tell if there was anyone outside, waiting for them.

"Yes," Jerri said.

"You're cut," he said, pointing down at her hands.

She felt the air entering her wounds. The rawness of her fingers. Felt a drip of cooling blood running down her left forearm, pooling at the elbow of her new favorite, borrowed jacket, but she didn't look down at her hands to inspect her cuts. Not this time. If she did look and saw her blood and flesh, she might never come back to reality.

"I'm fine."

Rust nodded at that, then put his ear against the metal of the door.

Behind them in the restaurant, Louis was yelling. Jerri heard the word "trespassing" as glass was crunched under bootheels. They were inside, but Louis was trying to reason with them, trying to keep himself between the intruders and one of the notorious Baypen Three.

"I have first aid at my house. And plenty of weapons."

Rust winced as he pushed open the door, the expression making the scar tissue on the side of his head and face pull back into wedged dimples Jerri had never noticed before.

They listened. There was no alarm. That was good.

Rust peeked, then put his entire head outside the service door.

"Clear, come on. We need to run."

He grabbed onto her again, not her wrist, where he'd tugged her to the ground before, but his whole arm around her shoulder, not only guiding her, but protecting her with as much of his body as he could.

She'd never known this was back here, a thin strip of dirt and gravel, not wide enough for two cars, connecting the businesses of Main Street to the alley beside the Eureka. It made sense, though—this was where the shops and restaurants put their cans and dumpsters for collection. How could she live her whole life in a place and only see the front of something, what was on the surface?

"This way," Rust said. "My house, bandages, and then . . ."

"Cole," Jerri said, finishing his list for him.

He nodded. "Am I that predictable?"

Rust had been looking at his phone's lock screen for most of their meal. And he'd lapsed into an even more sullen silence after getting Jerri to imply that Cole and Hunter might still be together, hanging out at Hill Manor.

Jerri's hands hurt. But she tried to smile anyway. "Of course you'd want to get to him. You're a couple."

"A couple of something," Rust said, crouching low and

crossing the alley, head on a swivel, his arm guiding Jerri along. "Then we find Quinn if she's not still with her dad, and we get out of town. I've texted both of them but no answer—"

"Wait, out of town?" Jerri asked, interrupting Rust as he peered down at his phone, seemingly confused by the device. They were crouched behind a white fence, the bottom foot green with moss and old grass clippings. Behind the fence was one of the houses on Oak Street. One block over from Marshall Lane, their destination. "Why not go to the police station?"

"Abundance of caution," Rust said.

She thought of the cop who'd pulled a gun on her at the Eureka.

Rust went to his tiptoes to see over the fence, into the backyard. "We can stay at a hotel in St. Louis. We should be anonymous enough there. You ever been to St. Louis?"

Jerri made a sound like a giggle, but it was just for Rust's benefit. She couldn't understand what Rust was getting at. Or if he was joking, even a little. But then maybe getting out of town wasn't such a bad plan. There was no winning, when there was an army of clowns marching down Main Street. No winning, so Ruston Vance wanted to get his friends in a car and not even attempt to play the game.

"Come on, we're crossing through here." He reached up and looped a piece of plastic wiring around one finger. The latch on the other side of the fencing clinked, and the gate popped forward into the alley.

They entered the yard, and it was another pocket of Kettle Springs that Jerri was unfamiliar with. And she thought she knew the town so well. She knew all the houses on these streets, knew who lived in them, even if some were only familiar faces, if they didn't have kids. She tried to guess whose house this was, from the backyard and the color of the siding, without seeing the number or the mailbox.

It was a game to keep her sane. A game to—

Bratatattat

The sound of machine-gun fire echoed out over from Main Street. Jerri looked back up into the sky, like she'd be able to see the sound waves. But there was only a blackish-blue sky. No clouds, but a few dim stars and the moon.

"I thought we'd have more time before these idiots started shooting," Rust said, pulling them to the end of the backyard and stopping, crouching again to check their next move.

"Who are they? Why are they doing this?"

Rust shrugged. "The internet."

"No, but *who* are they?"

"The internet," Rust said again without elaborating. He pushed open the front gate and peeked out.

"That doesn't make any sense."

"It does to them," he said, then made little beauty-queen

248

wave at her and pointed, which Jerri concluded was some kind of signal he'd learned in the Scouts. Or on hunting trips. Or any of the many places that she knew Ruston Vance might have learned a thing or two about survival.

"There's a car at the end of this street," he said. "And there's someone in it. So we're not going to run, and I'm not going to hold on to you. We're going to walk, quickly, across the street and into the next backyard. Once we're through that, we'll be on Marshall and should be able to see my house."

"Okay," Jerri said. Because what else could she say? That her hands hurt and she wanted to go home? She bet Rust already knew that.

She started to head out onto the street, but Rust stopped her.

"Wait."

He pulled up the hood of her loaner coat and then took her arms and guided her bloody hands into her pockets. It was the way a parent—her mother—would get a toddler ready to go out in the rain.

"It's not a Frendo mask. But it's better than nothing," he said, pulling up his own collar, a motion that did nothing to hide the fact that he was Ruston Vance, dressed in his signature plaid and denim outfit.

They crossed the street, Jerri's eyes locked straight forward so that she didn't even see the car and person that Rust

249

had spotted. The person in the car could have been a figment of a paranoid psyche, but as more chanting and sounds of breaking glass floated over from Main Street, Jerri was reminded that sometimes a little paranoia was a reasonable response.

They crossed another yard, reaching a fence that was not flat picket boards but instead chain link.

"Shit. I worried this might happen," Rust said.

And then Jerri saw what he meant.

Not as many as there were on Main Street, but there was a second—gathering? Protest? Mob? What did you call these people?—on Marshall Lane. Which made sense. Jerri knew where Ruston Vance and Quinn Maybrook lived. Everybody in town knew. Which meant that the internet knew.

"You did?" Jerri asked. She felt exposed with nothing but chain link for them to hide behind. If the masked men and women in front of Rust's and Quinn's houses turned and looked across the street and three houses down, they would be spotted.

"Yeah, which is why I always park there." He pointed, and she followed his finger across the street, to where the crowd had thinned to nonexistence, and there was Rust's pickup truck, parked in front of a neighbor's house a few doors down.

"Really?"

"Well. I didn't know this *specific* thing was going to

happen." There was a humor creeping into his voice that disturbed Jerri. Was it just nerves? Or was Rust enjoying this? "But I try—"

He was interrupted.

"Come out," a woman yelled, her voice amplified and distorted by a bullhorn. The woman was standing on the tailgate of an SUV that'd been driven up onto the lawn and parked in the expanse between the Vance and Maybrook properties, the corner of a raised garden bed crushed under one wheel, tire treads dug into the lawn. The SUV's head-lights were on, the glare splashing the front of Rust's house.

"This is a perfectly lawful citizen's arrest," the woman said into the bullhorn, a feedback squeal at the end of the words. "We are exercising our constitutional rights."

The woman on the SUV had the bullhorn flush against her mouth, a hole cut into her fabric mask that reminded Jerri of a Mexican luchador, and was wearing . . . fishnets and a corset? It was military-themed fetish wear, and seeing it made Jerri a whole new shade of uncomfortable.

"There's something else going on here," Rust whispered.

"What?"

"Spot the difference," Rust whispered while the woman on the back of the SUV said something to the gathered crowd, pointing her mouth away from the bullhorn as she spoke to them. "That guy"—he pointed to a man in professional-looking body armor, who wasn't carrying a bludgeon or a protest sign, but instead an assault rifle—"he's like Bradly Stoughton."

"Who?" The name was familiar, but at the moment, her mind and memory couldn't function right.

"The guy we met in Philly. And the rest of them, they're just—" But he didn't get to finish his thought. The woman was back on the bullhorn.

"If the suspects, Ruston Vance and/or Quinn Maybrook, are currently home, we urge them to come out peacefully. Everyone has five seconds to comply."

The woman in the corset pointed to Rust's house.

The lights were on. Not just one or two lights, but all of them. The Maybrook home, on the other hand, stood completely dark.

Jerri hoped Quinn was still miles and miles away, with Mayor Maybrook safe in the Hermann hospital.

"Four!" the woman yelled into her bullhorn.

"When . . . ," Rust began, then stopped to breathe. Jerri looked over to Rust. He was sweating. And not from the heat—it was night now, and a chill had rushed in once the last ray of sunshine had gone. "When she hits one," he said, "we run for the truck." Jerri could see he already had his keys out, the truck key clenched like if he needed to stab somebody to death with it, he could.

"Three," the woman barked into the bullhorn.

"Wait," Jerri said. "Are your parents home?"

Rust looked about ready to cry, the unburned skin of his face and neck red and slick with sweat and his scar tissue dry and white.

The biggest of the men on the front lawn, the one that Rust had compared to Bradly Stoughton, pressed the stock of his rifle into his shoulder and began to climb the steps to the Vances' front door.

"Two," the woman said.

The man at the front door readjusted his Frendo mask and shook out his leg. He was getting ready for something.

"You had your chance," the woman said, joy in her voice, a clownish giggle like she wasn't just wearing the mask, but was playing the part of a clown: "Prepare to be breached."

The man on the front step lifted one beefy jackbooted leg and kicked in the door.

There was the crack of wood, and a half second after the door swung open, the big man exploded.

A ball of smoke, fire, and debris pushed out over the lawn, so bright Jerri had to cover her eyes. The blast had blown some clown masks off, sent a few of the closer bystanders onto their backs, and sent the rest of them running for cover. Some dropped their weapons, clubs, and blades. Many screamed. One used a "Justice for George Dunne" sign to beat out the flames on their pant legs.

On a slight delay, parts of the man who'd kicked in the door began to rain down to the earth. The SUV's headlights were tinted red as an arm, a leg, and the singed plastic of his mask floated down onto the lawn.

"Oh my god. What the hell was that?" Jerri asked.

Rust was smiling.

A man had just been killed and the front of his home was a smoldering crater—and he was smiling.

"My dad," Rust said.

"Uh . . ." Then she realized what he meant. That his dad was the one who'd *made* the explosion, not the one who'd blown up.

Then, before anyone on the lawn could get to their feet, he said: "Come on, let's go."

They piled into Rust's pickup truck and were on the road, headed to Hill Manor.

TWENTY-ONE

Quinn Maybrook, a knife in one hand, a dead cop's gun in the other, ran through the corn and thought about sleep.

She considered the quality and quantity of sleep she'd had over the last two days. And over the year before those two days.

Quinn wondered if she'd even entered REM. Either in the cruiser or in the hospital room.

At a certain point in her sleep deprivation—and she didn't know this firsthand, just from books and movies—she'd have to worry about auditory and visual hallucinations.

That thought took her mind off the concept of sleep and honed her focus.

Was that a glimpse of a skeletal hand up ahead? Or just a few threads of corn silk, flapping in the October breeze?

She pushed a yellowed stalk aside with the knife. The blood on the blade, a mix of Marta Lee's and Quinn's own blood, all blended together, had gone tacky.

One thing that kept her awake was her anger. Her disbelief that she could have found herself in this exact situation again, the cosmic unfairness of it. How was—

No. Don't finish that thought. It isn't. It isn't happening again. This isn't the same thing.

It wasn't the same because *they* were running from *her*.

Quinn had fired twice. What was the standard magazine size on a Glock 19? Or was it a Glock 17 she was holding? The number would be etched into the barrel, but she wasn't going to stop moving to try to read it now.

Fifteen-round magazine. Had to be. It was very likely that Sheriff Lee had never once discharged this weapon in the line of duty. And nothing about what Quinn had known of the woman would imply Marta Lee carried a gun with an extended magazine.

Still. The thirteen remaining bullets would be plenty. Quinn couldn't be greedy.

A corn husk crunched somewhere ahead of her. Ahead and to the left. These dumb assholes. It was late enough in the season that the corn was dried up, dropping leaves and husks. She'd be able to hear them whenever they got close.

But they can hear you just as well as you can hear them, Quinn reminded herself. And the voice she used to remind herself was not her own but Ruston Vance's. He was her redneck Obi-Wan Kenobi.

Thirteen rounds. She could spare one.

Quinn listened again, leveling the handgun to where she'd heard the crunch, ready to draw a line in the air with the muzzle.

But the next crunch that came was behind her, not ahead.

Directly behind, and close.

Quinn didn't move. She locked her joints to stay completely still. If they had guns—or crossbows—they'd be leading her. She shouldn't move how they'd expect. Not in speed or direction.

But how? How did one of these chuckleheads get behind her without her hearing them do it?

A bug wriggled between her sock and the skin of her ankle, and the sensation sent a chill up her body that ended in her knife hand, the point of the blade trembling.

Quinn picked a direction and ran. A full sprint. If she caught sight of the one ahead of her, she'd fire. If the one behind her pursued, she could stop short and hear his footfalls before he realized she'd stopped. Then she'd have him.

You're going to fire blind? Rust asked. Their training sessions were rarely about tactics, more the Zen repetition of *pop pop pop*, check the action, group your shots, careful—trigger discipline, remember?

But still Quinn knew, even without him here, even with

him only as an extension of herself, that Rust wouldn't be a fan of this plan.

She could reach out and call Rust. Her phone had buzzed with messages a few minutes ago, but on the second buzz she'd silenced the device without taking it out of her pocket. Never mind the sound—the light of the screen would make her a target. Quinn Maybrook wasn't a target tonight. She was a hunter.

Quinn slowed to a jog, then stopped. There was pulverized corn husk all down the front of her, fibers dusting the small hairs on her arms, clinging to the jellied blood on the blade that she held out, a backward grip so she could still use that hand to steady her shooting arm, if she needed to.

She listened.

Nobody was following.

Which was . . . a relief? A disappointment? It was somehow both. More than survival at this point, Quinn wanted—

Wait, what the fuck was that?

Without lowering her weapons, Quinn bent her neck to touch her ear to her shoulder, then rubbed, trying to clear her ear canal, in case there was debris rattling around. Because that had to be it, small crumbs of dirt and dried plant matter causing her to hear things that weren't there.

There was the sound of . . . voices? Was this it? Were these the auditory hallucinations she'd just jinxed herself into experiencing? It reminded her of that night over a year ago, walking through Tillerson's B-field and arriving at an oasis of teen excess.

No. It wasn't her imagination or a sense memory. There were voices out there. It was hard to tell what they were saying and how close. It was the light burble of a phantom gathering, whispers and nervous giggles carried on the wind.

Where was she? Was she close to town? She hadn't been keeping track of how long they'd been driving and what route Sheriff Lee had been taking back.

Before she had an answer to any of this, she stepped through a row and out into a corridor of corn that was unlike all the others she'd run through over the last . . . five minutes? A half hour?

What she was standing in wasn't a clearing, per se, but it was double the width of every row she'd passed. Besides the size of the aisle, the dirt under her feet looked like it'd been recently cleared of fallen stalks and husks and patted down to an even trail.

Quinn wasn't a farmer, but she had to imagine this was—what? The demarcation point between one plot of land and another? Maybe an irrigation ditch? But if it was that, then where were the sprinkler heads and hoses?

"Shh," someone whispered, coming down the row ahead of her.

It was easier to see out here, not only because of the wider row letting more moonlight reveal the dirt at her feet, but because there was some kind of . . . light pollution? Coming over the horizon.

Quinn so badly wanted to ask "Who's there?" but what if it was the man who'd killed Marta Lee? She couldn't give up the element of surprise.

"Goddamn it, don't do that," the same voice hiss-whispered. A male voice. And a scared one at that. She had them on the run.

Quinn moved her finger onto the Glock's trigger and stepped back into the corn, concealing her position for an ambush.

Then, from the other side of her. Close. Maybe two paces. There was a new sound. A sudden sound.

And it was not a voice, but a roar.

The engine of a small, powerful motor kicked to life a few feet away from Quinn Maybrook's head. The heat of the machine's exhaust blew onto her neck.

She knew that sound.

A chainsaw.

Quinn stumbled forward into the row, whirling and firing in the direction of the sound.

Pop pop pop.

Her placement was shit; she'd tripped over her own feet and was falling back into the aisle. Her body's impact with cold, hard-packed dirt compressed her lungs, the air rushing out of her in a huff that she tried to spin into a battle cry but couldn't find the breath.

She could see the chainsaw, the weight of it spinning her attacker around.

Over the man's face . . . not skeleton face paint.

Her attacker was wearing a clown mask now.

The killer loomed over her, exiting the corn, revealing himself. The corner of his jumpsuit was torn and raised from where one of her shots had found his shoulder.

It was not a killing shot. Not good enough.

She leveled the Glock. Braced one elbow against the cool dirt. No more flesh wounds.

"Fuck! Stop!" the man behind the mask yelled.

The words of protest didn't strike Quinn as odd. Most people didn't want to die.

But then he did something Quinn wasn't expecting: he let go of the chainsaw, the weapon's momentum sending it skidding to the ground, leaving big divots and kicking up dirt clods. Not kicking them up from the blade end but from the weight of the motor. The blade didn't seem to be doing anything; maybe this model had a kill switch, where the blade wouldn't spin if the user's hand let off the throttle.

"Please don't shoot!" The man's hands were up. His left hand dipped down fast to tug at his mask, and Quinn almost did shoot at the sudden movement.

It wasn't a Frendo mask, but a generic, foam rubber "evil

clown" mask, the kind you'd get at a costume store around Halloween.

The man tore at the bottom of his mask, keeping his other hand high.

But before he could get the mask fully off his head, there was someone else in the row with them.

Multiple bodies, all coming from the same direction where Quinn had heard the voices.

Still lying back, her stomach crunched in an awkward, lethal sit-up, Quinn turned toward the group, leading with her gun hand.

A girl shrieked, a boy giggled, and hands were put on shoulders and waists, young people being maneuvered like human shields.

They were kids. Well. Not kids. But high schoolers, or maybe middle schoolers. Five of them, all clumped together, four of them gripping each other, not for survival or safety in numbers but to have fun. Two girls and three boys. Possibly a double date, plus the stabilizing third wheel, a boy standing behind the others with his arms crossed.

Quinn blinked at them. The girl in front had a thin glow-stick encircling her neck, the skin on her face hued green.

The glowstick girl blinked back.

"Wait. Is that a real gun?" she asked. The boy behind her, dark eyes voids in the dark, nuzzled her neck.

"Come on, babe, keep moving—the next group's going to catch up to us."

"No, wait, that's a real gun."

"Shit," the guy in the clown mask whispered. The guy Quinn had shot had finally stretched the pullover mask off his head, the rubber tearing.

The clown-mask guy wasn't a man. He was a boy. Quinn turned back to him, unsure where the gun and knife should be pointed. Where the next threat would come from.

The guy in the clown suit was maybe the same age as the group, maybe Quinn's age, if he had a baby face. Sweat dripped from his chin, droplets glistening in the moonlight. He spoke through gritted teeth: "Can I put my arm down, please? It really hurts."

And, all at once, Quinn realized where she was.

And how badly she'd messed up.

Did you mess up, or were you suckered? Mind Rust asked.

Quinn was standing in Tillerson's B-field. Or the general vicinity.

This trail wasn't an irrigation ditch. It was the corn maze of Duvall Farm's Haunted Hayride and Scream Park.

And she'd just shot an employee.

Quinn let the gun droop and lay back in the dirt, her joints and muscles feeling pulled to their breaking point, like taffy. She had no place to sheath the knife, so she stuck the end into the ground, letting the handle stick out like Excalibur. Like a tiny memorial for Marta Lee.

"I think Brooke's right. This isn't part of the show."

"If it is, it's not scary," Brooke, the glowstick girl, said, braver now than she'd been a moment ago when Quinn had pointed the gun at her.

"Oh shit," said the guy who was standing slightly apart, no girl under his hands. Nobody to squeeze. "Don't you see who that is?"

Quinn rolled over onto her side, not yet ready to get up and check on the guy she'd shot. He was still standing. He'd be fine. She'd only winged him. She hoped.

"Oh fuck. From TV," Brooke said, fishing her phone out of her sweatshirt pocket. Quinn squinted at the logo under the girl's glowstick necklace. JHS. What school was that? How far away were these kids from? How long had they driven to enjoy a night of terror?

"We have lockers," the guy in the clown jumpsuit said, sounding on the verge of sobbing.

Quinn sat up. She needed to help him. But this was all so fucked up. And she was so exhausted. So done.

"We have lockers," he repeated, then forced more words out, raising one hand again as Quinn looked at him. His injured shoulder slumped, the arm there hanging, dead. "And my boss makes us put our phones in them. Can someone please call nine-one-one? I think I need an ambulance."

Quinn stood. The dirt had been damp under her, and the seat of her jeans was soaked through to her underwear.

"Let me see it," Quinn said. Then she turned to Brooke, took a step, reached her free hand out, and plucked the glowstick from the girl's neck.

Quinn wound the glowstick around her knuckles, then held the light up to the boy's wound. The dim neon wasn't enough to see by, but it turned the blood dribbling—just a dribble—down the boy's arm into a black line.

"You." She pointed without looking. Pointed with the gun. She was pointing a gun at an innocent bystander. "Your phone's flashlight. Turn it on."

One of the kids clicked on their flashlight and lit the trail in front of them. The wounded guy was tall—a good fit for the role of "killer clown with chainsaw"—and he had to slouch for Quinn to get a good look at his arm.

"Luckily, the bullet only grazed you," Quinn said. What were these words? Where was the emotion? She should be apologizing to this kid. She could have killed him. She'd *tried* to kill him.

"Please. Can we *please* still call nine-one-one?"

"I'm calling them," Brooke said, and the beam of her phone's flashlight bobbled as she began to dial.

"Wait," Quinn said. She turned back to the group of five, their eyes all following the gun, bouncing along as Quinn motioned. "Don't do that. There are people in this field who just killed someone. I chased them out here and—" Quinn started to explain . . . what? What was her plan here? There were probably dozens of people out in this field. Patrons and employees. More than that, because it was Halloween night.

"Hey, look," the guy standing slightly apart from his friends said, "we don't want any trouble. Could you put the gun down?"

"Listen," Quinn said. "We're in danger. I'm not going to shoot you, I—"

I'm the good guy.

There's bad people out here.

They've killed my dad's best friend. Tried to kill me.

Tears came then. The frustration, the exhaustion—it was all getting to her. Twice today. And Quinn didn't even cry in therapy. Not anymore.

Quinn used the bottom of her shirt to dry her tears, and when she looked back up, the second guy and other girl had their phones out.

"I'm not calling anyone," the guy said. "Don't shoot." Then he looked at his girlfriend's screen. "She's not, either."

Quinn couldn't see what they were doing on their devices, but could hear the bloops and vibrations of messages and notifications.

"Shay, it's your mom," the guy said, reading. "There's, uh, there's something happening."

The other girl, Shay, covered her mouth, aghast at

whatever she was watching on her phone.

"What is it?" Quinn asked, edge in her voice, a demand. "What's happening?"

"There's like, an army of them," Brooke said, then turned her phone around so Quinn could see.

It was grainy footage, taken off someone's live and saved as a video, window-boxed into someone else's stories. Quinn squinted at the footage, taking a step away from the bargain-basement Frendo and closer to the group of kids so she could see their phones.

A protest. Or a riot. Chants and broken glass. All the participants dressed as Frendo the Clown, or their best cosplay approximation.

"Oh god," one guy said. "They're pissed."

"I'll say," Shay said, intently scrolling her own screen, then stopping. She pointed a finger up at Quinn. And there was hatred in that look. "They're pissed off at her. They say she killed a cop."

"What?" Quinn said, her tears cool and numb on her face. The accusation made her stand up straighter.

"Don't say 'what,'" Brooke said, copying her friends' scrolling now. "There's video."

"Hey, what's the fucking holdup?" a guy's voice yelled from behind them. "Can we move it along? You're blocking us!"

A second group appeared around the bend, four more

young people added to this bottleneck Quinn had created.

Quinn looked at them all, their faces spotlighted by the white glow of their screens.

Both Brooke and Shay had their phones turned around, and Quinn watched herself, in double, getting out of the police cruiser, Marta Lee dead behind the wheel, Quinn's posture and expression blood-streaked and murderous.

She could feel her pulse in her ears, hear the rush of her own blood, a tiny pinprick of intense pain at the base of her neck, like a sudden headache.

No. Not a headache. She'd taken her eyes off the guy in the clown suit.

He'd . . . he'd found something to hit her with.

Hard.

Quinn Maybrook caught a quick glimpse of the sky and the stars, and then her eyes rolled back in her head.

TWENTY-TWO

Rust gripped the wheel, trying to focus on the road.

Under normal circumstances, it was a five-minute drive to Cole's house, and a decent chunk of that time was pulling up Hill Manor's long private driveway. But now that Rust was coming at it from a new direction, taking the long way around, backstreets that abutted the old Baypen Drive, it was like a puzzle.

A puzzle that he was trying to solve while his thoughts were being pulled in a thousand different directions. Many of those directions involving his mom and dad.

He needed them to be okay.

Jim Vance had been preparing to defend his home for a long time. He'd thought through a lot of these scenarios all the way to their violent ends.

No, maybe what Rust was *really* worried about was how many of these people Jim Vance was willing to kill in order to protect his home. And whether Missouri's Stand Your Ground law would extend to using a Claymore to vaporize an intruder who'd kick in your front door.

They had a plan in situations like this: Jim and Sybil would wait in the panic room, and Rust had promised that he would take care of himself. But would Jim stick to that deal?

Rust hadn't been old enough to remember much of what his father had been like before his second tour of duty, a tour extended to its absolute limit by stop-loss, but he certainly knew who Jim Vance was afterward. Quiet and paranoid. A man trying his best to hold on for his wife and kid, while still coming home with packages that he secreted down into the fruit cellar. In the beginning, normal prepper items— nonperishables, water, a generator, and a few extra guns. But after the massacre, a massacre that Jim Vance had neither predicted nor, he felt, prepared his son enough for, things had gotten more intense. The fruit cellar had become a panic room. Double reinforced and packed with munitions. Family meetings began to revolve around blueprints, escape plans, and proper handling of ordnance.

There was a car up ahead parked too far from the sidewalk. Rust didn't like it.

"Get low," Rust said, reaching his arm over, pushing on

Jerri's shoulder so she'd sink lower in her seat.

Rust guided the truck past the car . . . and nothing happened. Maybe more than a little of Jim Vance's paranoia had trickled down to his son.

Jerri didn't even look up from her lap. There'd been gauze in the glove box and there was a bigger kit in the back, and she'd bandaged her own cuts while he drove. She hadn't done a great job, by the looks of it. She had a phone on each leg, alternating between using Rust's to redial Cole and Quinn and using her thumbs to scroll and type on her own.

He understood that what the girl was doing was important, or at least seemed important to her, but her attention being so taken up by the screens made him uneasy. Why didn't she have situational awareness? What could be so compelling that she wouldn't even look up, help him watch the road for more masked crazies? It was unfair to compare them, but he wished it was Quinn there in the passenger's seat.

"This is so bad," Jerri said.

"What?"

"They're saying Quinn killed Sheriff Lee," Jerri said.

The truck surged forward, Rust's feet and hands rebelling for a moment at the shock of that news.

"Bullshit," was all he said, getting the pickup back under control, turning his whole head to look both ways down Castor before choosing to turn, making sure the clowns weren't marching down this street as well, on their way to break down the door at Hill Manor.

"I don't know if it's true she killed her, but . . ." Jerri's voice rose as she spoke; she wasn't crying or sputtering, but she sounded like she needed to scream to get the words out. "But she's really dead—the sheriff, I mean. There's video of her body. And Quinn running away from her cop car. With a knife and a gun."

Rust thought about this for a few car lengths.

"All that video means is that Quinn's alive and armed. That's good. And this is on the news? The news is saying this?"

"The news?"

"Yes, if news outlets have picked up this story, then outside law enforcement, Staties, the National Guard, they'll be here and we—"

"No, not the news, I'm on Twitter."

"Oh Jesus Christ. Try nine-one-one again. At least that's not *Twitter*."

"I tried. All calls reroute to Kettle Springs. And they're not picking up. Nothing's wrong with Twitter, as a tool," Jerri said. It sounded like Rust had struck a chord. "I'm clicking on the hashtags to try and see how these people are organizing. What they're responding to. The rest of the world has already seen this. They'll . . ."

"They'll be here eventually, we just need to—"

And before Rust could finish, they'd been spotted.

"It's him. It's Vance's truck!"

Men and women ran across lawns. It was hard to tell, dark and scattered as they were along the block, but it seemed like this was the same group of clowns from in front of his house. They must have been cutting over from where they'd left them on Marshall Lane.

Feet slapped asphalt.

Rust tried to gun it, and a man with a baseball bat—a suicidal man—jumped in front of the truck. Rust swerved, preferring to murder a few lawn ornaments and a mailbox rather than a human being.

The crowd kept coming, nine or ten of them, all different shapes and sizes. This was a different kind of attack. Very few of these people had official Frendo the Clown masks— instead they were wearing homemade versions. This was not a team of killers; they had none of the order and uniformity of Sheriff Dunne and his accomplices.

They don't deserve to die, Rust thought. *They weren't an army. They're . . . fans. And in their minds, they're doing the right thing.*

Rust pointed the truck back onto the road, and the back right tire spun out in a patch of mulch before getting traction. It was only a half-second delay, but it was enough time for a woman to jump into the back of the pickup.

The truck bounced on its suspension as they went over

the sidewalk, and a guy with a baseball bat stepped forward, swung, and took out a headlight while he screamed "Citizen's arrest!" into the passenger's window at Jerri.

"You okay?" Rust asked.

Jerri didn't answer with words, just a scared "mm-hmm" that Rust didn't have time to worry about.

There was that clatter again, and then in the mirror, Rust saw a hand-painted grin smiling at him.

The woman in the truck bed kept eye contact with Rust as she lifted a crowbar up to the glass of the back window. The woman's knuckles were cut up, dirty Band-Aids and nails caked with grime. She tapped on the window with the bend in the crowbar, softly, just knocking, not trying to break the glass, not yet.

"Pull over," the woman said, her words muffled.

The woman's mask was pantyhose pulled tight over skin, Frendo's distinctive features applied with phosphorescent fabric paint. Her nose and mouth were squished under the sheer fabric of the mask, and she had a small novelty porkpie hat hot glue–gunned to the top of her head.

She looked deranged.

"Pull over," she yelled again, punctuating the demand with another knock.

Rust nodded at her. "Okay."

And then he hit the gas.

The woman skidded off her feet, and Rust braced for the

sound of her hitting the road. He hoped she'd survive the fall with nothing more than a bump. But there was no thud, just more clattering around in the truck bed.

He hadn't shaken her loose. She was still back there.

"I know your hands hurt," Rust said to Jerri. He looked over to see that she was no longer using the phones, but now had her head tucked between her knees, elbows pressed flat against her ears. "And that you're scared. But I need you to go back there and lift up the cushion of the back seat."

Nothing. No response from the girl.

"Jerri," Rust said, turning the wheel. They were a quarter mile away from the turnoff for Hill Manor. And it looked like there were no clowns here. After this turn it'd be a straight shot. The tires under them skidded, but the woman in the back of the truck still held on, pushed into the side of the bed by centrifugal force.

"I need your help here," Rust said, trying to sound patient when he wasn't. "We can do this together, okay?"

The girl peeked up, short hair disheveled into another position, a blood-spiked cowlick added to the mix.

"The cushion. Just lift it up," Rust said.

He checked his mirrors, couldn't see any sign of the woman with the painted mask and tiny hat. Jerri wrestled with her seat belt, trying to give herself enough slack so she could bend back over the center console, between the two front seats, and lift the cushion.

The compartment under the back seat was something Rust'd had installed over the summer, tired of having his business on display in the gun rack, wanting to be prepared but not look it. Maybe a lesson he'd subconsciously taken from his dad.

"It's a gun," Jerri said, half in the front of the cab and half in the back, staring down into the compartment. She sounded surprised.

"Yes. It should be multiple guns. But do you see the short shotgun? It's in one piece. And it's smaller than the rest."

Small because he'd taken the end off an old yard sale acquisition with a hacksaw.

"Yes."

"Can you hand it to me?" Rust said, trying not to catch a knee or foot to the side of his head as Jerri wriggled.

"I think so, I—" Jerri rummaged for a second, then screamed as the back window of the cab was broken out above her.

The curved end of the crowbar rattled inside the car, one cleft end digging into Jerri's shoulder.

Jerri yowled as Rust braked, trying to slow the truck so he could help get her free of the weapon, the crowbar acting like a fishhook set into Jerri's jacket.

He grabbed onto her hood. There was the sound of fabric tearing as he pulled her up to the front seat, the seat belt engaging and pressing her back into the passenger's side.

"Look at me," the woman screamed at them.

Then she put two fingers in her mouth and ripped a hole in the pantyhose. To make it easier to scream at them, Rust guessed. "I know what you did, you fucker. You deviant. You're sick. You killed those men and women and you're going to burn. Justice for—"

Rust hit the accelerator again, stopping the woman's rant as she tumbled backward but still not shaking her loose.

Rust saw the woman dig the crowbar into the lip of the cab's window, holding herself in place, the sharp metal scratching up Rust's truck.

He looked at Jerri beside him; the girl was panting.

They needed to keep driving. They couldn't let more of these nuts catch up with the truck. And there was no time. If this was a coordinated attack, they could have already broken down the door and might be in Cole's living room by now. Who was there to protect him? Hunter Duvall? Yeah right.

"Do you know where Cole's house is?"

Jerri gulped air, nodded, then said: "Yes."

"Can you drive us there?"

"I . . ."

"Can you drive!?"

"I've taken some of the online practice tests?"

"Good enough."

They disengaged their seat belts and switched.

"Keep us moving," Rust said, and climbed into the back, taking up the shotgun. It was not the Winchester 1300, the gun from that night out in the corn. He'd never been able to touch that weapon again.

No, this short-barreled shotgun looked nasty, but *looking* was what it was good for. He wasn't planning on using it, didn't even break the action and load it, just put some shells into his jacket pocket as the woman in the truck bed screamed for help.

"I've got them! I've got them!" the woman yelled. "Help me! George Dunne did nothing wrong!"

"Hey," Rust said to the woman, gems of auto glass crunching where he knelt as he centered himself in the rectangle of the cab's back window. "Listen to me."

The woman pulled herself up the end of the crowbar, hand over hand, feet trying to find purchase on the textured hard plastic lining of the bed.

Rust noticed that she was wearing house slippers. All the other Frendo rioters they'd seen had been wearing boots, or at least sneakers. Who joined an armed takeover of a town without the proper footwear?

Someone crazy, yes. But also someone local.

Rust tipped the gun away from her for a moment, then grabbed onto the hook of the crowbar and lifted it over the edge, setting her free. Without the handhold, the woman slipped, the acceleration of the truck dragging her down the length of the bed until her feet were resting against the tail-gate.

She roared, finding her feet again and hefting the weapon, her small muscles tensing as she swung at the window, nowhere near hitting Rust.

"Hey. Stop trying to attack me or I will shoot you."

He didn't need to raise his voice to be heard. There were dark houses on one side of the road and an empty field on the other.

She stopped, tilting her head to one side, then used one finger to rip another hole in the sheer fabric of her mask. A big hole over one eye. She couldn't see in that thing.

"Just take the mask off," he said, motioning with the sawed-off shotgun.

"Fuck you."

"At least drop the weapon," he said. "I don't want to kill you, but at this range I will kill you if I pull this trigger. Best-case scenario, I'll aim low and take out your feet and ankles."

"You and your friends won't hide from us," the woman said. "We have numbers in the hundreds. Thousands."

"No, you don't. Dozens, maybe. From what I've seen," Rust said.

The street was getting sparser. Fewer houses. They would soon be on the long private road leading up to Hill Manor.

Something that Rust said must have reached this woman's capacity for reason, because she dropped the crowbar.

Losing the weight of it allowed her to straighten up.

The woman was thin, unhealthily thin, with dark blue veins on her arms and splotchy skin.

"Careful now, don't fall," Rust said. And he meant it. He was concerned. This woman hadn't tried to kill them. She really did believe that she and her friends were going to enact some kind of citizen's arrest. It was hard to tell with the mask, but this was a middle-aged woman in house slippers. She was somebody's relative. The aunt you didn't want to talk to at Thanksgiving.

The woman sat down in the truck bed and pulled off her mask.

Delicate features and worry lines.

"I hate this town," she said. She trembled. It was probably very cold out there, with the wind coming over the cab. Jerri was doing a good job, keeping the truck steady and maintaining speed.

Rust didn't recognize the woman.

"Sometimes I have my issues with this town as well," Rust said to the woman, keeping the barrel of the empty shotgun trained on her, just for show. She wasn't a threat now.

There were no sounds in the night. No bullhorn orders being barked by pinup-girl clowns, which made Rust feel better, but also no police sirens, which made him feel . . . less than better.

"My husband and son brought me here. I love them, but I hate this town."

Husband and son. Who was this woman?

"Did you kill him?" the woman asked Rust, her voice small. "Did you kill my husband?"

This was getting weird.

"Not that I know of?" Rust said.

"I thought you might have," the woman said. "Since I tried to kill the mayor."

Rust thought of Glenn Maybrook, an inch-deep gash in half his neck, and wished he had a shell in the gun. Just one.

But he couldn't let her know that.

"Did I do it?" she asked Rust. "Did I kill him? They said I didn't on the news, but the media lies. So maybe I did kill the mayor. Some of the channels I watch say I killed him."

Rust thought for a second, then answered: "No. You didn't kill him. But he's really hurt."

"That's good," the woman said. Rust couldn't tell which part she thought was good. That he was still alive or that she'd really hurt him.

"Your husband and son, who are they?"

"Oh, don't you know me?" The woman pushed her hair back off her face. No. He still didn't know her. "I'm Jane Duvall. Of Duvall Attractions?"

Okay, that . . . that kind of made sense. And it got another rise out of Rust, made him unsatisfied with the dinky, chopped-up antique gun he had in his hands. There were better weapons under him, a mag-fed Mossberg he'd been practicing with that'd take some assembly once they got to their destination.

"So you're Hunter's mom?"

"Yes."

I fucking knew it, Rust thought, anger flaring through him. The fucking Duvalls.

"And your husband's Eli Duvall? And you're saying he's dead?"

Jane curled up, getting smaller in the truck bed.

"I found him in his car, as I was heading outside, to the rally. The rally where we were going to bring you to justice."

A whole family of murderers and psychos, Rust thought, images of the ghoulish Duvall Farms Haunted Hayride advertising running through his mind.

And her son was with Cole.

The tires slowed. The grit of the turnaround driveway crunching.

"Um, Rust?" Jerri said, behind him in the cab.

"Yes."

"We're here."

Rust hoped he wasn't too late. But feared that he was.

TWENTY-THREE

Hunter Duvall wasn't sure what he was seeing.

Refracted light from the pool? The diodes and indicators in an electrical closet or control room?

He stood at the edge of the water. He was shirtless and alone. And sober. He hadn't been drinking. No, he'd let Cole drink for two. But even with a clear head, he'd gotten swept up in the house's opulence and Cole's enthusiasm and now, moments after peeling his own shirt off, he felt foolish.

Hunter had screwed it up. He'd let Cole trick him into overplaying his hand. Hunter had been eager to hook up, had needed so little convincing that he'd scared Cole away. He'd been stressed, first seeing that weird guy in the haunt and then sneaking out of the house once his dad was asleep, hunting for his mom all night, fearing the worst. . . . He'd just gotten ahead of himself, overeager.

How long should he wait down here, alone in the basement? The ridiculous basement that was both a movie theater and a health spa.

But there it was again. That light. It wasn't machinery. It was a computer or iPad. Some kind of backlit screen, visible only when the color-shifting pool lights changed between purple and green and went dark for a moment.

The light was across the water, directly in front of where Hunter was standing, the tile under his bare feet moist with condensation. He shifted his weight, and his skin squeaked across the surface. He'd taken his shoes off upstairs, because it'd seemed like the kind of house where he should take his shoes off, but why had he taken off his socks?

He stared at the source of the flicker. It was coming from behind the glass door of—what was that? The sauna? The steam room? Cole'd said the house had both.

As Hunter watched, trying to figure out what he was looking at, a shape passed in front of the light.

A human shape.

He wasn't alone down here.

Every inch of Hunter's skin dappled and buzzed in the wet chlorine air.

His first instinct was to cover his chest with his arms. But that was dumb. Whoever was in the dark didn't care about the work he put in on his Bowflex.

Hide, Hunter's brain screamed at him. But the impulse was too weak; his legs were stuck in place.

The rapid journey that Hunter's emotions had taken—from horny to embarrassed to terrified—had short-circuited his brain.

Hide now. You're out in the open. Forget your shirt. Fuck your socks. Hide.

He took a step backward. Then another, his arms out for stability.

"No Running," he read on a sign posted in his peripheral vision, his eyes locked on the glass door to the spa.

There was a silhouette in that doorway now.

Was the figure's back turned to look at the computer screen, or was the shape watching Hunter?

Then the shadow made a sound, like clearing its throat or muttering a curse, and the noise echoed through the chamber.

Hunter's left heel touched metal and he almost tripped. He looked down into the dimness. It was the metal tread runner that divided the floor of the theater room from the spa. Facsimile hardwood on one side, tile on the other.

Almost there.

His damp feet squeaked again as he did an about-face.

Behind him, there was the long whine of a door swinging open, its hinges noisy from negligence and humidity.

Hunter had to make a choice: he could run for the stairs

to the first floor, end up spotlighted by the stairway lights, and hope he was faster than the shadow, or he could try to hide down here, in the home theater.

He ducked behind one of the large leather recliners, decision made. His damp skin squeaked, and the built-in mini-fridge was cool against his body.

There were only footsteps now. Heavy, shoed footsteps walking beside the shallow pool.

Hunter listened, head down and lips clenched. After a few more steps, he tried to ignore the approach of the figure and focus on what he could hear. There was the sound of aluminum and glass shifting, someone looking for something in the upstairs refrigerator. Cole was up there. Hunter strained to remember the layout of the house's first floor. Whether or not the stairwell to the basement could be seen from the kitchen. He thought it could be, depending where you were standing—

There was the stamp of a foot, then rubber skidding across tile. The shadow had tripped on the metal bar that divided the theater from the pool. But he'd caught himself before falling, and Hunter heard him moan, like simply walking required terrible effort.

The room began to stink. A wet dog. No, worse than a wet dog. A wet dog on a hot day during a garbage strike.

Should he look? Did he even want to know what could

smell like that? What had been hiding in Cole's basement, in a room that, as Cole had admitted, nobody used?

Or did he already know what he was going to see, because he'd caught the open-air version of that same smell out in the field?

Yes. He should look. Because as terrified as Hunter Duvall was right now, there was something compelling about this nightmare.

He peeked just in time to see the shadow step into the light from the stairwell, making the transition from a frightening abstract shape into a very specific figure.

Frendo the Clown.

Hunter stretched his neck out a little more. He wanted to see more clearly, but he also didn't want to be seen.

A perverse curiosity. It was like being present at an eclipse but not having the fogged glass. It was like seeing a Bengal tiger in the wild and wanting to whisper "Here kitty kitty."

This wasn't the entertainment-only version that the Duvall family used at the haunt.

This was the *real* Frendo the Clown. As weird as that seemed, since everyone knew Frendo was a collection of people, not a single person.

Frendo turned to face the stairwell, mask angled up and seeming to scent the air like a predator. His clown suit was worn to tatters, a lifetime of dirt and grime (and blood?)

built up on the fabric. His mask had been shattered and fixed, shattered and fixed, Frendo's wide smile fractured and chipped.

Frendo's breathing was a whistled hiss. The rhythm of it at once terrifying and, if you thought about it, not much of a threat at all. Who worried about a killer with emphysema?

The knife. The knife was why you worried.

Hunter searched his memory of what had happened during the Baypen Massacre. Both the version of events that *he* believed and the insane truther ramblings that his mother subscribed to, that she filled her days with. Had Frendo, in either reality, ever used a knife like the one this Frendo was holding? A long butcher's knife? Well. It felt right. Blood-weathered and blighted. Like one tiny nick would be enough to kill you from tetanus.

The point of the knife glinted as Frendo turned the blade over between his hands.

And that was it. He was gone.

Frendo was up and away, stepping lightly, silent on the carpeted stairs heading up to the first floor.

Hunter watched him go, an exhausted kind of awe washing over him.

And then he listened, only realizing after a few seconds what he was listening for.

He was waiting for a scream. He was waiting for the cinematic *thwip-thwip-thwip* of a knife entering flesh.

And then his reason and compassion returned, roaring forward in a way that made him nauseous: *Oh shit. Cole.*

He lifted himself off the floor, his wrists and ankles numb and bloodless from the awkward crouched position he'd been holding.

He listened. No screams yet.

Something, a door or a cabinet or the fridge, clattered closed.

Shhh. Stop making noise, Cole. He'll find you.

Should Hunter yell? No. That'd give up his position, too. He wanted to help Cole, but he also had to think of himself. He was boxed in; there was only one way out. If Cole saw Frendo before Frendo saw Cole, then at least Cole had the option of fleeing out any of the ground floor's many doors or windows.

Should he call Cole's phone? He knew Cole had his ringer on, because throughout the night he kept letting a half second of the ringtone go off, then glancing down to check who it was before silencing the call. It'd always been Rust, Hunter assumed.

But the ding of a text in an empty house would make Cole an easier target, wouldn't it?

Hunter tiptoed across the movie room, looking up the stairs just as a body passed the doorway. He ducked out of sight, unable to tell if the shadow above was Cole or Frendo.

He'd text. One text. Get all the info in that he could. Be

as clear as possible that Cole was in danger.

Hunter opened his phone.

"Okay . . ." Cole's voice. Hunter was too far away from the stairwell to hear. But he was talking to someone. Hunter tried to make out the words.

". . . hide-and-seek . . . ," Cole said.

SHHHHHHHH

Hunter typed out the message but didn't send it.

Cole said something else. But Hunter couldn't tell what. He was getting farther away.

There was no time for this. Hunter had to do something.

He hit send on the message. Then heard the chime of his text being delivered, somewhere above him in the house. Farther above than Cole's voice had been, like he was climbing to the second floor.

Fuck. Hunter should have typed more.

And then, as if they were in direct conversation, Cole raised his voice. He sounded indignant: "I don't want to play" was the snippet that Hunter heard as he typed out a new message as fast as he could, sacrificing a word or two for speed:

Someone in your house. I'm hiding

Silence. An absence of sound that at least wasn't a scream and arterial spray splashing the walls.

Where are you? Cole asked back.

The basement. Where are you?

There was no answer. Hunter started counting to himself. Got to a six count before he couldn't stand it anymore.

Come on, Hunter thought, wanting to scream it. *Answer me, Cole. Where are you?*

Wherever Cole was, it wasn't the kitchen. Hunter would have heard him better if it was the room adjacent to the basement stairs. He could climb up. If not to go help, at least to be closer to an exit so he could get help.

He forced one foot in front of the other, then started climbing the stairs on all fours.

Hunter was halfway up the stairs when the knocking began.

There were short, insistent knocks echoing through the house.

What was going on? Frendo the Clown *inside* the house, and now someone trying to get in from the outside. Hunter tried to orient himself in the dark, strange mansion. The knocking was coming from the front door. Whoever was out there, they'd be able to see his truck in the turnaround. There'd be no getting past them, even if he found a way around the back of the house.

Hunter stood at the top of the stairs. The air was warmer and drier on the first floor, but still he trembled. He looked both ways and then crossed the narrow passageway into the kitchen.

The knocking paused for a moment, and Hunter could

hear the beginning of a struggle.

He was too late! Cole had gone upstairs.

Hunter felt panic rising, the swell of it pressing against his heart.

He looked around the kitchen. There were large, uncurtained windows and an island, a suspended pot rack dangling above it, and beyond that, on the far counter, every kitchen gadget Hunter could think of and a few he couldn't name.

But where are the fucking knives!?

In the foyer, Cole yelped, then gurgled. The knocking at the front door was back.

Knocking and shouting.

"Fuck," Hunter said, looking up to the rack and grabbing the first handle he could reach without climbing onto the island. The skillet was heavier than it appeared. It was made of thick cast iron.

Cole screamed and the noise ended with a thud.

The sickening smack of a side of beef tossed from a loft, onto the abattoir floor.

Oh god, Cole. I'm sorry. Hold on.

Hunter hefted the skillet, fists clenched around the wooden handle.

He peered through the nearest doorway, over the dining room table and its thin layer of dust, and beyond he could see the front door to the house, rocking in its frame. The banging had become kicks.

One. Two. Kick.

Someone was trying to break down the door.

One. Two. Kick.

"Cole!" a voice yelled from outside.

Hunter rested the skillet against his shoulder and crossed the dining room. He approached the foyer, dreading what he'd find there.

The scent of pork fat infusing the skillet would have been delicious under normal circumstances, but as Hunter crept closer to the house's entryway, the food smell mixed with the animal stink of Frendo turned his stomach.

Hunter peeked around the corner of the archway that separated the dining room from the foyer.

Cole was lying motionless on the floor. His arms and legs were splayed, elbows at odd angles like he'd fallen asleep in an extremely uncomfortable position.

And that wasn't even the most concerning part of this tableau.

Frendo the Clown was standing over Cole's body, his back turned to Hunter.

"No, don't die," Frendo said. "Not facedown."

His words sounded like an animal trying to imitate human speech. The accent, the inflection—everything about the man wearing the rotting clown suit was wrong.

Frendo reached down, grabbing a handful of Cole's hair, lifting him up off the floor by his scalp.

Cole yelped at the pain of his broken arms being left to dangle.

At least he was alive?

Slam! Whoever was at the door tried again. Wood cracked, but the door stood strong on its locks, chain, and hinges.

"You have to look at me while you die," Frendo said, turning the knife so its rusty surface could glint in the foyer light.

This was it.

"No!" Hunter yelled, his feet already moving.

He led with the corner of the skillet, not wanting to use the pan like a bludgeon but instead like a heavy, blunted ax. He took two long strides and began his swing.

Frendo turned toward Hunter, head tilted.

Hunter's swing came up a fraction too short. Instead of biting into the man's neck, as intended, crushing his spine, he caught Frendo on the chin.

A hit was still a hit, though, and Hunter was strong. He *did* use his Bowflex occasionally.

A fountain of blood and shards of rotted teeth sprinkled the foyer floor.

Hunter felt great satisfaction, then great horror, at not only what he'd done, but the stinging pain in his side as he inhaled.

And then he looked down and saw the knife, the handle

two inches from his belly button. The blade wasn't *all* the way in. But it wasn't—

Hunter's vision bubbled and shimmered. He was about to faint, at both the surrealness of the injury and at the overlapping thought that, if the stab wound was as bad as it looked, he may soon be dead.

I don't want to die.

Frendo, now disarmed, was slumped to one knee, keening through his shattered jaw. He still didn't lift his mask, even if he needed the air.

"Help," Cole said.

Hunter looked down. He tried to ignore the knife in his belly and focus on Cole.

"What do you need?" Hunter asked. "What can I do?"

"Open the door," Cole said, whimpering. He must have been thrown over the balcony. He'd been lucky—unlucky?— enough to brace his fall with both arms.

Cole's forearms had buckled and snapped like balsa wood.

"It's Rust at the door," Cole hissed. "Let him in."

"Okay," Hunter said, hunching. As he tried to stand up, he felt the knife tip grind inside him. He imagined the further damage being done to his internal organs, the infection spreading from the dirty blade.

Gotta . . . gotta pull it out. It'll be better if you do.

Hunter dropped the skillet, let it clatter, and before he

could talk himself out of it, grabbed the handle of the butcher's knife and pulled. The pain in his belly was cold, but the knife handle felt superheated with Hunter's own blood.

He let the blade clatter to the floor.

Hunter put a hand over the wound to stanch the bleeding, but he didn't feel strong enough to press and make a good seal, after all that had happened.

He looked at the door. The knocking was back.

Okay. He could do this. Open the door and Ruston Vance could pile them into his truck and speed to a hospital.

"Why's it so quiet? His truck's here," Rust asked someone.

Hunter just needed to open the door, let them in, and they'd be saved.

"Duvall, I know you're in there—open this door right fucking now."

What? Hunter limped, nearly lost his footing but held on, held himself upright and kept his guts in.

How did Ruston Vance know it was him on the other side of this door?

He thought about this, his mind dizzy. But couldn't make sense of it. Maybe there was an unfrosted window that he wasn't seeing.

"Stay there. Do not move or I will shoot."

What? Was Rust talking to Hunter?

"You better hope Cole's all right or I'll shoot your crazy

fucking son right in front of you."

Son? What?

"I'm coming," Hunter said, barely able to hear his own voice, so no hope that Rust and whoever else was rattling the door in its frame could hear him.

"I need help," Hunter rasped out, more liquid leaving his throat than sound.

"Anyone in there stand back," Rust yelled. "I'm about to open fire."

Open fire? Like with a gun?

"Don't," Hunter said.

I'm so close. Don't.

And then, before Hunter Duvall could touch a bloody, steadying hand to the metal of the lock, the wood beside the doorknob exploded.

TWENTY-FOUR

Something with a lot of legs crawled over Quinn Maybrook's eyelid and across her forehead.

She stirred closer to awake.

There was dirt in her mouth. Topsoil crunched as she ran her tongue over her teeth.

Quinn didn't have the energy to open her eyes. Not yet.

She tried to lift her head, maybe flick away the centipede, if that was what it was, but didn't have the strength.

Her hands were bound behind her.

Oh yeah. She'd been holding a gun on a group of kids and had been knocked unconscious by a blow to the base of her skull.

Her bad.

But still . . . did this count as sleep? Quinn had that

same urge that came after snoozing an alarm. Like if she could keep her eyes closed, she could continue to rest. She'd reached a dreamy, mostly unconscious state and she'd like to stay there, please.

And besides. The danger was over. Probably over. She could hear the squawk of walkie-talkies, the hubbub of young people consoling each other.

Quinn Maybrook knew these sounds.

This was the aftermath.

Whatever had happened, whoever the casualties and whether those responsible had been brought to justice or not: she'd missed it.

And it wasn't her problem anymore. Here and now, mouth full of dirt and blood and her hands tied, Quinn was simply happy to be alive.

She could mourn later. Or not. Whatever. She'd need to be caught up on what had happened. Who had survived. But for now . . . just let her—

"You did good. You did the right thing."

It was an adult male voice. Or maybe barely an adult; there was still a slight teenage squawk in the voice.

"Damn," he continued, "you have no idea how lucky you are, Taylor."

"Tyler," whoever he was talking to grunted.

"What did I say? Anyway, we're going to try and keep it out of the news for a while, but between us, you should know that she's killed more than one person tonight. And she could have killed you, too, if her aim was better."

Okay. Who was negging her aim?

Quinn opened her eyes to see . . . not much.

However long she'd been unconscious, she hadn't been moved. She was lying on her side and could feel the leaves and bent-back stalks of the corn maze behind her.

Quinn lifted her head and was able to see the boy she'd shot. He looked a little better now. Without his face scrunched in pain, pleading for someone to call 911, he was even handsome. Tall too—he needed to tilt his head down to talk with the cop.

Quinn couldn't tell if the cop was someone she knew or not, only seeing him in profile. But she could tell, from his badges and the tan of his uniform, that he was a Kettle Springs deputy, not a state cop.

She bent her legs a bit. They were unbound. Just the hands, then. She flexed her fingers and tried to assess the situation. No. She wouldn't be able to pull free of whatever was tying her. Either the kids had found something tight and unyielding to cuff her with or the cop had restrained her with a zip tie.

The back of Quinn's head throbbed where she'd been hit, but she felt alert enough that she could probably maneuver herself into a sitting position if she needed to.

But let's not do that yet. Let's see what's going on first.

She remembered the fucked-up pictures of herself that the girls had shown her on their phones and the footage of armed Frendos marching down Main Street. Apparently, none of this had been cleared up while she was out. It had gotten worse, if anything, because this cop just said that she'd killed *multiple* people.

Which she hadn't. She didn't think. Not recently, at least.

"The bandage is great, but I still think I need an ambulance," Tyler said, then seemed to remember something. "And the guests. Oh god, the guests. My boss isn't here. Nobody can reach him, and the guests—"

"The guests will be just fine. My partner is watching them," the cop said, talking with his hands. "There's still unrest in town. The safest place for them is staying put right here. We send them back to their cars and someone could get hurt."

Quinn thought about this. This implied that there were two cops.

Only two cops. That was . . . disappointing.

Quinn lifted her ear from the ground, not sitting up, just checking what she could see from her current position. At the next row of corn, there was a light casting shadows over the trail. More light than before, actually. A Duvall Farms employee must have turned the house lights on or put the attraction into some kind of emergency mode. But no ambulances yet and no sirens or flashing lights. That meant what?

That she hadn't been unconscious that long?

She guided her wrist over to her pocket and felt for her phone. Nothing.

Hands tied, no phone. If she was under arrest, she certainly couldn't remember being read her rights.

"Whoa there, big guy, you all right?" The cop put a hand on Tyler's shoulder, steadying him. This made the cop turn slightly and gave Quinn a clear look at his face. The cop had a black eye. "You know, why don't you walk that way?" The cop pointed down the trail. "Go sit with your friends and Officer Cody."

As the cop talked to the swaying teenager, he turned and Quinn could see more of his face.

He had not one but *two* black eyes.

"You've had a big night," the cop said to Tyler. "And you did something very brave, helping us apprehend this . . ."

The cop looked over to Quinn and stopped talking.

Shit. He'd caught her looking and knew she was awake.

The cop had a slightly upturned nose and boyish cheeks. And his black eyes weren't bruises. They were the stains left by someone who didn't have the time or know-how to properly remove makeup.

The kind of stains you'd have if you'd just been wearing black-and-white skeleton face paint.

This wasn't over. She hadn't missed the danger.

The danger was just getting started.

She began to pull at her hand restraints, the material at her wrists cutting first circulation, then skin.

"Oh shit," Tyler said. "She's awake."

"Like I said, buddy," the cop said, keeping his eyes on Quinn but grabbing onto Tyler's uninjured shoulder and pushing him down the path. "Go be with your friends. She isn't getting away, don't worry."

Fuck.

Quinn stopped pulling. She was only going to hurt herself.

Where did Quinn go from here? What was a way out? Did she try to be patient and wait for an opportunity to present itself?

Or was she dead the second Tyler turned his back and there were no witnesses?

"Okay," Tyler said, sounding reluctant. "But you should be careful, Officer Miller, she—"

"Tyler," Quinn said, starting to sit up but finding it more difficult than she imagined. Her body cramped, and her elbow slid out from under her in a puff of dust as soon as she was upright. "Tyler, don't go anywhere. Look at his eyes, Tyler. Ask him why he was wearing black makeup tonight."

Officer Miller smiled wide at Tyler, then turned to Quinn and scowled. The look was all she needed to see to know she was right. She remembered how Marta Lee had recognized the one skeleton and had started to say something. This was why. The uniform hadn't been stolen off a real cop. And it wasn't another Halloween costume. One of her own deputies had killed Marta Lee.

Frendo has a posse.

"You know what, Tyler? You're right. She is dangerous," Officer Miller said.

"Fuck you!" Quinn turned her eyes to him. "You killed her. She was trying to fix this fucking place and you killed her!"

"Hey," Tyler said, "maybe don't go near her if she's having some kind of . . . episode? PTSD? I've heard of stuff like that."

"Looks like you're right," Officer Miller said, leaving the boy and walking over to stand above Quinn. She wanted to scream at him some more, but what would that gain? It'd only reinforce the narrative he'd built, that she'd snapped and gone on a murder spree. "But I think it's best if instead of waiting for backup, I just walk her back to my squad car."

Miller reached down and grabbed Quinn by the wrist restraints, hoisting her up, plastic clicking tight and widening the cuts she'd started on her own.

"Come on, Squeaky," Miller said. "Let's get you in the car. Walk."

She fought him, whirling to face Tyler, trying to plead with her eyes. If she kept screaming, he would continue thinking she was in the middle of a breakdown. Which maybe she was. But she could do this. She could *reason* with Tyler, convince him not to leave her alone with this guy.

"Wait."

Yes, Tyler. Yes.

"Your squad car?" the boy asked, forehead creased in concentration.

Tyler stood where Officer Miller had left him but had begun swaying again. The dressings over his wound were shabby; whoever'd wrapped it, maybe Miller himself, had gone the wrong direction over his shoulder, and wet gauze was falling out.

"Yeah. I think I remember where I parked," Miller explained. Then, lower, more to Quinn than to Tyler, he said: "Just a short stroll through the corn, isn't it?"

She thought of that rusted-out car. He was going to kill her.

"Like," Tyler said, puzzled, "through the corn?"

"God. Yes, Taylor. Now go find Officer Cody before you pass out. I'll take care of this."

Officer Miller pushed Quinn forward and she took two stumbling steps into the corn, the world around her getting so much darker.

"Tyler," Quinn started. Just because she could no longer see the boy didn't mean he wasn't there. "I know I sound crazy and you were probably right to be scared of me before. I'm sorry I shot you. But think about this. You *know* what happened last year. You *know* that Sheriff Lee and my dad worked together." She raised her voice to be heard over their crunching footfalls, but also tried not to sound too frantic. "You *know* there's something happening in town and this guy's pa—"

Quinn's last word was silenced by a tug at her elbow, Miller swinging her around so that he could punch her in the gut. With his free hand flat on her back, the officer pushed his other fist as far as it could go into her stomach.

She couldn't breathe.

Had Tyler heard the punch? Or was he too far away, too loopy from blood loss?

"Don't gimme that shit, Maybrook," Miller said. "We both know you're tougher than that."

Quinn gagged, dry at first and then wet. Speckles of puke hit Miller's shoes, and she was able to breathe again.

"I'll kill you."

"Sure you will." He pushed her forward. "Walk."

She could've stepped over her hands in order to get her arms in front of her. Why hadn't she thought to do that earlier, when she'd been on the ground?

"You ever heard the term 'useful idiot'?" Miller asked, trying to sound calm, but with a nervousness in his voice that he couldn't hide from Quinn.

"No, is that what they call your mother?" Quinn said, tensing for another blow that didn't come. Miller didn't care about a "your mother" joke; he was on a roll now. Talking. These people always talked. Why?

To rationalize. Not for their audience but for themselves.

"I like politics. As a hobby," Miller said. "And a 'useful idiot' is someone—they don't even have to be on your side, or understand a particular issue at all—who is used to further a cause . . . in this case, to be used for *the* cause."

They were getting farther away from the light of Duvall Farms Haunted Hayride and Scream Park, the night getting stiller and darker, but it was impossible to tell if they were headed back to the road. They probably weren't. And it didn't matter anyway—when he got to the end of his civics lesson, he'd almost certainly be shooting her in the back of the head.

"Those people in town? Most of them are useful idiots. Most of them. And most are harmless. Weekend warriors. But there's some of us out here doing the real work."

"The real work of murdering kids just because you watched *The Baypen Hoax*?"

"Oh please. Not that there's not *some* interesting ideas in that video. But I grew up in Kettle Springs. I don't need a documentary to tell me right and wrong."

Quinn let that one lie. The layers of bullshit and conspiracy, she couldn't keep them straight. She'd rather not dig any further, make him angry by saying the wrong thing about his "cause."

They walked . . . until Miller felt like talking again.

"You know," he said, "when he was alive, I used to think George Dunne was a pretty hokey guy. The hat. The sunglasses and the mustache. The cowboy attitude. I thought it was dumb. But then he died, and the stories came out. And, if you think about it, all that swagger? It was the real deal. Real as fuck. Guy really did live by a code. And died by one. And killed by one."

Yeah, he certainly died by one. I blew his brains out, Quinn thought but didn't say.

"Reminds me of Buford Pusser," Miller said. "You know that story?"

"No, tell me more."

"Sarcasm. I'm surprised you still have it in you," Miller said. Then he stopped her short before she could respond to that with more sarcasm.

Maybe she was going about this the wrong way. If getting him angry could get him to make a mistake . . .

"That's far enough. I've decided you don't get to hear about Buford Pusser."

Her hands began to tremble and she balled them into fists. No. She wouldn't beg.

"Turn around."

"Why not just shoot me in the back?"

"Why? Because you rushed me, remember?"

She didn't turn.

"Remember how you rushed me, and I had no choice but to shoot?"

"How old are you?" Quinn asked.

"Turn." He poked her with a gun barrel. "Around."

"Over twenty, for sure. Maybe twenty-five? A teen girl younger and lighter than you rushed you and you felt threatened? That's not going to fly."

Miller grabbed her by the shoulder, spun her around.

He was sweating, not just droplets on his face, but pit stains completely through his uniform.

He hadn't done this before. And as she looked at his expression, it didn't seem like he'd be able to do it now. Quinn studied his face. Had he been the one who'd stabbed Marta Lee? Or had he been the one filming? Without the skull makeup, it was hard to tell.

Officer Miller may have talked a big game with his buddies, or in message boards if those buddies were online, but now that the moment was here, he was a scared little boy.

Quinn could get him to stop.

"You don't have to do this," she said. "Think about it. Forensics, ballistics. They *will* catch you. It's never as perfect as you think it is. You're a cop. You know that."

He had a pistol pointed at Quinn, and another still in his holster. For whatever reason, like that'd add to his story of how this had played out, he was going to shoot her with Marta Lee's gun.

"No. They won't catch me. There's too many of us. And there's a plan. We all—"

"All of the people that followed George Dunne—your hero?—they're dead or in jail. You *think* you have a plan. And you've been tricked into thinking you're playing an important part. But you're a—"

"Don't say it!" He raised the gun, took his finger off the trigger guard.

And she had to say it.

Even if the next thing that came from Officer Miller was a bang.

"Useful idiot."

"I told you not to say it." As he spoke, he put the gun even closer to her face. The barrel touched her forehead, made tiny crosses on her skin. "I know what I'm doing." A kind of Halloween Ash Wednesday. If she were Catholic.

Maybe she'd misjudged him. All that stood between life and death was a flexed finger. A tiny application of pressure.

I'm sorry, Dad, Quinn thought.

Then there was a sound like a roar, and a large, polka-dotted body flew at them from the neighboring row.

Tyler.

He was holding something heavy . . . the chainsaw!

A chainsaw with no chain, but still.

He allowed the weight of the chassis to swing down, the

body of the chainsaw colliding into Miller's gun hand with a satisfying crack.

But still Miller held on to the gun, and the barrel swept over Quinn's body.

Don't go off. Don't go off.

It went off.

The muzzle flare was warm against the cut in Quinn's thigh, but the bullet had missed her.

She needed to do something.

Tyler was no fighter.

But she couldn't help with her hands behind her back.

Quinn crouched down, then tried to hop over her hands in one smooth motion . . . but she couldn't get her elbows past her waist in a single hop. She fell back onto her butt, the cuts in her wrists growing deeper and more painful.

Tyler and Miller continued to struggle. Tyler was wailing on the cop with the blade of the saw now, the blows doing about as much good as a pool noodle. But at least he'd gotten Miller to drop Marta Lee's pistol.

Quinn's arms came loose with a last swipe of fabric burn against her elbows. Her wrists were still bound, but at least her arms were in front of her now.

She stood and searched for the gun, but it was impossible to see in the dark. It could have bounced in any direction, been swallowed in a pile of browning corn husks.

Tyler screamed.

Officer Miller was throttling the boy now, had a thumb in Tyler's gunshot wound, new blood welling up through the shoddy bandaging.

When it was clear that Miller had Tyler beaten, the boy down on one knee under him, the cop's hand went to his belt and he reached for the second gun there.

There was no time.

Quinn threw her arms, still bound, over Miller's neck and pulled back.

The fight became a three-person piggyback ride, Quinn and Miller leaning against Tyler for a moment, the tall boy putting his hands up, crumpled into a wedge, the strength in his arms keeping them all upright.

But then Miller shot both hands up to his neck and tried to stop Quinn from choking him.

He shouldn't have done that.

By lifting her up and straightening his own posture, Miller let Quinn's feet touch the ground and gave her all the leverage.

She pulled. Hard. Trying to get his windpipe as flat as possible, digging the plastic nubbin of the zip-tie fastener into the thin skin of his neck.

Quinn felt a pop and didn't know if it had come from her body or his. Either way, the pain was immense.

Miller fell backward, on top of her, but the collapse

happened in slow enough motion that she was able to get her feet under her and cushion the fall—so she didn't get the air knocked out of her for the third or fourth time tonight.

Miller's legs began to kick and shake.

This was it.

She had him.

He wouldn't be getting up.

Quinn pulled, ignoring the tearing of her own skin. Her biceps burned. She knew from training that she'd reached the very limits of her endurance, how much she could lift and how many reps she could complete, even with Ruston Vance cheering her on.

Her shoulders felt ready to dislocate.

And still Officer Miller bucked against her, arms flailing, trying to grab onto her. He got a finger up her nose, then another past her lips. The skin of his hands tasted salty.

Moments ago, when it'd come time to shoot her, Miller had hesitated. It was possible he hadn't wanted to kill her. And now he seemed even less enthusiastic to die.

And he *was* going to die if she kept this up. If she kept regulating her breathing, kept repositioning a millimeter at a time so she could get the plastic tie under his Adam's apple, feeling the bump of it crunch as he sucked in tiny pockets of air through clenched teeth.

Had he learned his lesson?

Should she let him go? Attempt to handcuff him, keep

him prisoner until the real cops showed up?

Then Miller stopped trying to grab her and put his hand on his belt, reaching for his gun.

No. She shouldn't let him go.

Quinn undid one leg from where she had them wrapped around his waist in an MMA submission, and kicked down. Her range was limited with his weight on her, but she stamped her heel against his gun hand, not letting him get the grip clear of his holster.

Tyler didn't help during any of this, just held his shoulder and cried, slumped in the shadows.

Officer Miller stopped moving. But Quinn waited to remove the pressure from his neck until a full count to fifteen.

And even then, she'd picked his head up and shook him like she was a terrier with a rat, just to make sure he wasn't faking.

Quinn had widened the cuts in her wrists to nearly an inch in some spots. But she hadn't hit a vein or artery, merely rubbed the ligaments there raw. She'd need some medical care, but it was okay. She could go on.

Miller's neck looked worse than her wrists.

"Hey," Quinn said after a minute of waiting for Tyler's cries to subside. "Thank you, Tyler. You saved my life, but I still need your help."

She pulled herself up to her knees, then started going

through Miller's pockets, finding it difficult with her hands tied.

First, she found his key ring, which had a small utility tool they could use to cut the zip tie.

Then she found her phone. The screen had cracked in the scuffle but not badly enough that she wouldn't be able to use it.

"Tyler," she said, waving at him, trying to center his focus again. "I need you to cut me loose. Then I've got to call my friends. But I need you to bring me to where the other cop is keeping everyone."

"You think he's . . . going to shoot the guests?" Then another quick sob. "And my friends?"

"No, don't worry, Tyler. This isn't like last time. They're not after all the teens in Kettle Springs. They don't want to hurt your friends."

"They don't?"

She undid the clasp on Miller's holster and pulled the gun free.

"No. They just want to hurt mine."

TWENTY-FIVE

The outside of Hill Manor was dark and cold—all arches and columns. This was a house built by someone who wanted you to know they had more money than you. Even if it was a house sliding into disrepair. White paint in need of power washing; loose flashing; and dead, overgrown ivy.

Jerri shivered, then followed Rust and Mrs. Duvall through the door that Rust had just blasted open with a shotgun.

The inside of Hill Manor was dark and hot. The air was humid and smelled like sewage. The sensation of entering the house was like walking inside the body of an animal that had recently died.

"Light. Light!" Rust yelled.

Oh yeah. She had the light. Using both hands, her palms

padded by bandages, Jerri swung the beam of the large flashlight across the floor in front of them.

It could have been a trick of the glare, but she thought she caught a glimpse of motion, a figure headed deeper into the house, though there was no time to squint at shadows.

Both Rust and Mrs. Duvall were screaming.

"Cole!"

"Hunter!"

The names they yelled were different, but the worry in their voices was the same.

Someone they loved was hurt.

Jerri moved the light between the boys and felt her stomach drop. Both were shirtless, their bodies splayed across the floor.

Cole's thin muscles were no longer lithe and sexy under the harsh beam of the Maglite; instead he looked broken and emaciated.

Hunter . . . looked even worse. His skin was waxy white in the areas where it wasn't streaked with brown blood.

"Jerri, I need you to check to see if we're alone, okay?"

Carefully, Jerri aimed the flashlight around the foyer, up at the curved staircase and down into the connecting rooms, but Rust didn't wait for her to reply that the coast was clear. He stood and crossed to the wall. He felt at the molding until finding what he was feeling for: the chandelier above them began to glow. But it was rich-people lighting, mood lighting, and didn't do much to brighten the house.

"What's that noise?" Jerri asked. It was an electronic chime, like a more insistent doorbell.

"The alarm." Rust took a hand from the shotgun, then pointed two fingers to where Cole lay on his stomach, forearms bent unnaturally. "We'll leave it. It'll call the cops or the security company or something. Maybe the alarm company will have better luck reaching someone than we've had. Come help me."

"What about her?" Jerri asked, aiming the flashlight at the woman who not five minutes ago had been menacing them with a crowbar.

"Hunter's not armed," Rust said, not whispering, pointing to the boy, then his mom. "Neither is she. Let her try and save him. If either of them starts to get violent, I'll shoot 'em."

Rust put both hands back on the shotgun, squatting above his boyfriend. It wasn't the stubby, antique-looking weapon he'd asked Jerri to hand him in the truck. This shotgun, which he'd needed to assemble once they'd parked, machined tubes and handles clicked and fastened with practiced haste, was new and sleek. Varnished black metal and rubberized plastic grips, and a side-loading magazine that jutted out from the body. It looked less like a real weapon and more like an exaggerated power-up in a video game.

"Good of you to join us," Cole said, his chin squeaking

against the polished tile floor. Then he began to cough, his body shuddering.

"You shot him," Jane Duvall yelled at Rust, sitting cross-legged next to her son. "You shot my boy."

"Peppered him," Rust said, then to Jerri: "The case. Give it here."

Rust set down his gun, and Jerri unslung the first aid kit from over her shoulder and handed it to him. She didn't know how to fire a gun and really didn't want to try for the first time tonight. So her role in the group had become that of the pack mule. The kit was bigger than a lunchbox but smaller than a duffel bag. She wondered how many bags Ruston Vance had like this in his life. Surely at least two, one in his truck and one at his home.

"Here," Rust yelled over to Mrs. Duvall. He tossed her two shrink-wrapped packages from inside the bag, then rolled a bottle of liquid antiseptic over the tile. "I'd worry about the other side of his abdomen, if I were you. The buckshot's not going to be what kills him."

Rust looked up to Jerri and pointed down at the floor. He didn't speak, just urged her to follow the tip of his finger as it glided around the fan of blood splatter nearest them; then the large butcher's knife, the puddle on its blade still dark and liquid; and then the frying pan, one edge gooier than the other.

She could see what he saw. Kinda. He was putting

together what had happened before he'd shot open the door.

"That knife went into Hunter, I'm betting," Rust said, and then began running his hands over Cole's chest and stomach, the way a veterinarian or a farmer might grab an animal and massage its flanks, checking for injury or inflammation.

"Ow," Cole said, not struggling against inspection, nose still flat against the floor. "Look, Rust, we're in danger. He's—"

"Shh. Don't talk," Rust said. There was care in his voice. "You got him. Your arms are broken, you're probably coming in and out of shock, but you got him, Cole."

Then Rust did something Jerri wasn't expecting: he lowered himself in a kind of one-armed push-up and kissed Cole on the back of the head. "You stabbed him. You did what you had to and I'm proud of you."

"Wait," Cole said, the word muffled. "Stabbed?"

Rust shushed and cooed, but Cole only grew more agitated.

"Come on. Flip me over! I've licked the fucking tile clean."

Jerri looked at Rust.

"Shock?" she asked.

"Maybe not," Rust said, his expression lightening. They were in a room full of blood, but Rust seemed relieved, like all he'd wanted was for Cole to be alive and he was, and now it was all good. "Help me lift him," Rust said. "Grab from the shoulder. Try not to bend his arms."

Cole screamed, Jerri groaned, and Rust stayed silent except for his breathing.

They propped Cole onto his side, Rust's knees like a pillow under his boyfriend's shoulder blades.

Cole blinked against the light, then moved his eyes over to the Duvalls, first mother and then son.

Hunter was still. The boy looked dead until his mother peeled open a packet of sterile gauze, tipped the bottle onto the wound, and then pressed the handful of fabric down into his side. Hunter screamed, but it was a subdued sound, like the boy didn't have enough strength to open his mouth all the way.

Then Cole seemed to remember something, and his eyes searched around as much of the room as he could see. He tried to twist in his half seat to look behind Rust.

"Where is he?" Cole asked.

"He's there," Rust said, pointing over to Hunter. "You got him. You stabbed him."

"Not *Hunter*," Cole said, confused, his eyes seeming ready to go cross, frantic. "I didn't stab Hunter. Hunter tried to save me. Hunter hit *him* with . . ."

Cole pointed to the skillet, trying to snap his fingers, the word not coming.

Jerri could remember being like this, a year ago, how it'd

taken her hours to be able to speak with the cops and tell them who she was, why they'd found her out in the middle of a field, and what had happened to Dorothy.

Rust took a steadying hand off Cole, letting him sink farther back into his chest. Rust rested the free hand down next to the shotgun.

"Wait. Him who? Hunter hit *who* with that pan?"

"*Him*," Cole said. Like the emphasis he was putting on the word made it obvious.

"Look, shock or not, I'm tired of this." Rust spoke the words slowly, but it may not have been for Cole's benefit. It might have been because he was on the edge of panic himself. "I need you to say the name."

Jerri didn't know what was about to come out of Cole's mouth, but suddenly the inside of Hill Manor matched the outside and she felt cold all over, under her jacket.

"My dad," Cole said, "and he's still here."

God.

His face.

What had the Duvall boy done to his face?

Don't worry about how you can't swallow. How you're drooling blood down the front of your buttons.

Arthur Hill pushed that voice away, the sick part of himself that reveled in his failures, that delighted at the torments and misadventures of the last year. Especially those of the last twenty-four hours, what was meant to be his final victory but hadn't worked out that way.

Hadn't worked out that way *yet*.

Arthur Hill removed his shoes and stepped as lightly as he could, panicked voices coming from the front room.

Then the chandelier light illuminated, throwing long shadows into the dining room, urging him to move as fast and quietly as his old, ruined body could manage.

If you want something done right, you have to do it yourself.

He tried to mouth his mantra, but could only wiggle his tongue against broken teeth and the numbed pain of a compound fracture, his jawbone jagged in his open mouth.

Yes, but you've strayed from that motto a bit. Haven't you, Arthur?

So few things you've done right, even the things you've done yourself. That dime-store Rambo you hired in Philly? Bradly Stoughton? Pathetic.

That was true. It stung to admit it, but it was true. He'd had weeks in this house. Plentiful opportunities. And he'd decided to outsource as soon as Cole had left to go on his trip. . . .

Damn.

Why was it so hard for him to act?

It wasn't the killing. He'd killed before. Plenty of times

in the last year. Just today he'd killed Eli Duvall, that pretender, that profiteer, that carpetbagging new-money Branson scum.

It was harder for him to end it with Cole, though. Never seemed like the right time. Never seemed like all the pieces were ready. Why was that? It wasn't the act of killing itself. No. He looked forward to that.

But when the light went out from his son's eyes . . . what would be left for Arthur Hill to do?

Follow him into that good night? Or emerge from his hiding as a new man. It was possible. It was a new world, a new America, from the one he'd left last year.

It seemed preposterous, after all he'd done. But he *did* see a pathway there for his rehabilitation. After his jaw was wired. After he'd had a shave and several showers. And after he hired the right PR firm. Maybe pled out to lesser crimes. It was possible.

The Baypen Hoax, in its myriad versions and uploads, had been watched millions of times. And Arthur Hill had nothing to do with the video's creation. No, the conspiracy theories and revisionist histories had sprouted on their own, organically. The seeds of it all, skepticism that the news media wasn't telling the whole truth of what happened in Kettle Springs, those rumors had started spreading almost as soon as Arthur Hill had landed in Cuba.

Not that he'd known that. Arthur Hill didn't know much about the internet. But he knew about advertising and how to spend money. And he knew that you could pay to put an idea into people's heads. And that throwing money to recommend *The Baypen Hoax* to users, in those early days, before all the takedown orders, was surprisingly easy.

Arthur was sixty-three. He'd become a father late in life. He wasn't supposed to outlive his wife. Or either of his kids. Both of his kids.

Wait, what year was it?

No, he was older. He'd turned sixty-four at some point during his exile. That must have been when he was somewhere in the Eastern Bloc. When he'd gone in search of an army that hadn't existed.

Sixty-three or sixty-four, it didn't matter. What mattered was that he was feeling his age. At least he wasn't feeling his jaw, or not as acutely as he could be. He was already taking painkillers and antibiotics, whatever he could scrounge from Hill Manor's medicine cabinets, to take care of the weeping scabs and infected dermatitis under his jumpsuit. So maybe those drugs were helping with his jaw.

He knew he smelled bad. That meant something in him was going rotten. And the drugs were probably too little too late.

How had he let it get this bad? No. That wasn't fair.

It hadn't been easy to take care of himself, body or mind, lately. Getting back into the country had been months of work and . . .

Arthur stepped forward into the doorway to the basement, letting his foot hang over the top stair.

Then he stopped.

Was this the direction he should be going? If Hill Manor's uninvited guests pursued him, would he find himself trapped and wishing he had more points of egress?

There were other places in the house where he could go, places where nobody went.

The sauna was home base, though. That was where his iPad was, what he could use to call for backup. It was also where his canned foods and jerkies were. He felt himself wanting to retreat to the warm cedar smell of the sauna, of home.

But no. The basement wasn't the right choice. Not right now.

He had to be logical about this. Yet it was hard to be logical when his face was split in two.

He should take the high ground. The first floor was too open, vaulted ceilings and large rooms with clear lines of sight. The second floor was all adjoining rooms and dust-covered furniture and close quarters.

And he didn't need the staircase to get up there. He knew a secret way. The secret way was how he sometimes went upstairs, to watch Cole sleep. Sometimes with Ruston Vance beside him.

How many times had he stood over the boy's bed just like that? The musk of Arthur Hill making their noses twitch. His blade against their necks, the tip tracing the outline of Vance's scars.

But first . . . what was first?

Think. You've trained for this. You've thought about it, fantasized about what you'd do when the time came.

First he had to go to the laundry room.

Which was on the way to his secret spot. Perfect.

He stepped forward. There were holes in his socks, and the exposed flesh gave him extra traction on the hardwood.

"Do you understand me?" a voice called from the front of the house.

Arthur Hill pulled open the door to the laundry room. Nearly tripping over a pile of dirty clothes, not in a hamper, but *next* to an upturned hamper. Cole hadn't done laundry in weeks, the boy opting to order packs of fresh undershirts from Amazon rather than running a load.

Someone was coming. Leaving the group. They were in the kitchen. Two rooms away.

And the only one of that group—a boy, a middle-aged woman, and a child of indeterminate gender—the only one who *could* be pursuing was . . .

Oh Ruston, Arthur Hill thought.

He took the second blade, his contingency blade, from one of the folds in the jumpsuit. Then he reached a hand up to pull open the fuse box, a spit trail of blood leaking out from his ruined jaw.

If you want to play, we can play.

"Try to help her patch him up," Rust said to Jerri. At some point in the last minute or so, Hunter Duvall had stopped screaming and the puddle around him had widened. "And once you're able to move him, get them both out into the truck."

"Wish we had my car," Cole muttered. "Shouldn't have trusted wasshername."

"Yes. I'm sure you'd be able to drive just fine with two broken arms," Rust said.

Cole started to respond, but Rust put a *Quiet, the adults are talking* hand up. Rust didn't have time for what would came next, Cole making some joke about his pickup truck's speed and/or gas mileage.

Rust turned to Jerri, not touching her jacket, but putting a hand near her shoulder. She seemed to get the idea, that what came next was important, and locked eyes with him.

"If I'm not out front thirty seconds after you hear the first gunshot, you drive them out of here and get to a hospital."

This was a flawed plan, and a voice in Rust's brain was screaming that. But the rest of his body was yelling back:

He's alive. He's here. You have *to get him.*

Jerri didn't respond to the instructions, getting a faraway look in her eyes that made him think she'd heard him, processed the plan, and was mentally moving on to next steps.

"Do you understand me?"

"Yes. Okay. Thirty seconds. First gunshot. I can do that."

"Great."

And Rust swept the mag-fed Mossberg around in front of him, turned, and moved on to the living room.

As he went, Ruston Vance turned on lights and checked his corners. The sweep wasn't just best practice, tactically—it helped him to stay focused.

You shot Hunter.

Sure, Hunter and Cole had both been alone and shirtless before calamity had struck, something that Cole and Rust would have to discuss. But Hunter hadn't deserved to be shot for that.

From the sound of it, Hunter was one of the good guys.

And yet Rust had experienced a feeling of serves-you-right pride sweep over him as he'd shot open the door and seen that he'd clipped the boy.

Maybe more than clipped. Maybe gutshot.

These were thoughts he couldn't afford to be thinking right now. He crossed the dining room and pulled the Mossberg up, ready to fire as he approached the kitchen.

The boogeyman who'd hung in the shadows of their lives

for the last year was real. And he was in this house.

Rust needed to find Arthur Hill and kill him.

As Rust entered the kitchen, he swept his arm over the row of switches on his left. The overhead lights, the ceiling fan, and the surface lights under the cabinetry all came up to full brightness. He wasn't worried about being seen or giving away his position. Cole's dad had attacked Hunter and Cole with nothing more than a knife. If Arthur Hill wanted to reveal himself while Rust stood in the center of a well-lighted room, Rust was fine with playing a quick game of "Knife, Paper, Shotgun" with him.

He listened, tried to hear footsteps, anything that might hint as to where Arthur Hill was hiding.

Nothing.

That was fine. What was in here he could use?

He opened one of the under-sink cabinets with his foot, then another. The first had liquor bottles, some half-full, and the second had a mix of plumbing tools and cleaning products . . . and also a few liquor bottles.

Could he do anything with the Mr. Clean? What would Jim Vance do? Create an oil slick or something?

He was thinking this, began to think what a stupid, *Home Alone*–minded thought it was, when the lights went out.

All of them.

Two rooms over, Rust heard Jane Duvall start to panic

and Jerri say something to calm her.

Good girl. He trusted Jerri. She may not have had Quinn's killer instinct, but she had something else: empathy. He'd left her liquid sutures and butterfly bandages. If Hunter could be saved, she would save him, and then she'd grab Cole and get out like she promised she'd do.

Cole and the rest were safe—at least for the moment.

Because Rust now knew where Arthur Hill was.

To plunge the house into darkness, turn off all the lights at once, Cole's dad could only be in one place. Where Rust had to go any time he was over when Cole used too many appliances at once and flipped a breaker.

The laundry room.

Rust hurried through to the doorway, putting himself in the center of the three-way junction that led to the front of the house, the back of the house, or down the basement stairs.

He forced himself to picture the layout of Hill Manor, to double-check, think if he could be wrong. But he didn't think he was. If Arthur Hill was in the laundry room, there was now nowhere for him to go except deeper into the back corner of the house or out the sunroom that led to the backyard.

You're older, Rust thought, *but you're not smarter.*

He would push forward, make sure Arthur Hill couldn't run away again.

And with that, he pointed the Mossberg ahead of him, ready to blast anything that moved.

"We know you're in there. We saw the lights," the woman outside said into her megaphone.

Jerri looked over at Cole. He was closer now that she'd dragged him over to sit beside Hunter. Then she looked to Jane Duvall.

Jerri didn't look down at Hunter. It was hard for her to look at him. The boy was still alive. He occasionally choked and sputtered as he fought to breathe, but it was still too painful to see him, the deep pockmarks of the buckshot slowly leaking, the abundance of glue and bandages they'd used on his knife wound still not seeming like enough.

Cole shrugged.

"Do you know these people?" Jerri whispered to Mrs. Duvall.

"Just from online."

"Vance," the woman outside said. "We know this is your truck."

"That's Red Nose Trixie. With the microphone," Jane Duvall explained. "Don't think that's her real name. Just her clown name."

"Clown name," Cole said, shaking his head.

Outside, a hushed male voice, still perfectly audible in

the dark foyer, said: "The door's already open. Why don't we just—"

"Don't you—" the woman, Red Nose Trixie, said, then put the bullhorn away from her mouth. "Don't you remember what just happened? Nobody attempts to breach that door. Not until we're sure it's safe."

Jerri remembered what Rust's father had done. Even if the clowns were being more careful this time, Jerri still couldn't shake the idea that the people outside were idiots.

"Hey," Jerri said, putting a bandaged hand on Mrs. Duvall's arm. "You're one of them. Can you go out and talk to them?"

"Yeah. That's a great idea," Cole said. "Get them to leave. Tell them we're not here."

"Or," Jerri said, "talk some sense into them, tell them we need to get Hunter to a hospital."

"Yeah," Cole said, pointing his chin at his two crooked arms, looking embarrassed. "I guess that's good, too."

Jane Duvall looked down at her son, patting his hair, the part staying where she put it, the blood on her hands like hair gel. He was still. Too still.

Mrs. Duvall's face twitched, small lip spasms and eyelid tics visible in the SUV headlights pointed at the front of Hill Manor.

"I could try," she said.

"Thank you," Jerri said, then reached out to touch the woman, but Hunter's mom recoiled against her.

Jerri crawled to the nearest window, but couldn't bring herself to peek over the sill. There weren't just the head-lights. There was the orange flicker of flames out there as well. If this was an old-fashioned mob, she couldn't see if they had pitchforks, but they certainly had torches.

Mrs. Duvall bent, kissed her son on the head, and then stood.

"I see something," one of the men outside said. "There's movement in the window." He said it "win-da."

"Don't shoot," Mrs. Duvall said. Even raised, her voice wasn't strong.

Jane Duvall stepped into the full light, shadowing her eyes with her hands. "I said don't shoot, I'm one of you! Big-TopKnits2020!"

Jerri looked over to Cole, who shrugged and mouthed: *Clown names.*

"Come out with your hands up," Trixie said into her megaphone.

Jane Duvall obliged, needing to use the toe of one of her house shoes to pull open the remainder of the shotgunned front door.

"Mom," Hunter said. Jerri looked over to where he lay, but it was unclear if he was conscious, aware of what was happening, or if he was having a bad dream, calling for his mother.

"I'm one of you," Mrs. Duvall said again as she stepped out the door.

"Where's your mask, then?" one of the men asked, the "win-da" guy.

"They took it from me," Jane Duvall said. "Like they took my son. They're in there. Two of the Three. Hill and Vance. And they killed him," she sobbed. "They killed my boy!"

"Fuck," Cole said. "Hunter's mom's fucking crazy."

Jerri didn't bother to agree. There was no time; she had to listen.

There was a hushed discussion going on outside. Then it ended, a decision reached, and Jerri heard Red Nose Trixie say:

"You heard her. Burn them out."

Then the windows broke and the torches were thrown inside.

Rust couldn't worry about the new voices outside. Or the screaming and the breaking glass.

Because something had just moved, right in front of him.

There it was again and—

The smell.

The stench was like the unnerving sensation of walking into a spiderweb. It almost tickled but was also deeply gross. Even more troubling was the realization that this smell had been all over the house, in pockets, for months. Rust had noticed, but he figured the smell was just Cole being a slob, attracting pests that'd died in the walls.

It was too dark. There were no windows in this part of the house.

Rust could risk moving for his penlight, but if he wasn't quick enough, he'd need to fire the Mossberg one-handed and that could go bad.

Here, trapped in the back corner of the house, there were only two directions Arthur Hill could be going: forward to meet Rust—or deeper in, the laundry room was followed by a few storage rooms, a linen closet, and then, at the far-east corner of the first floor, the old servants' quarters. What Cole called "the Butler's Bedroom" even though they didn't have a butler.

Something crossed in front of Rust then, a heel squeak on hardwood, and he fired at the sound.

The muzzle flash lit the hallway in front of him, not revealing a pale and broken Arthur Hill, as he imagined it would, but an empty expanse. He got enough of a glimpse to see that the door catty-corner from the laundry room was ajar. Rust breathed, ears ringing, working the pump to feed another shell of low-recoil double-aught buck into the chamber.

The extended magazine was bulky, but it gave him ten shots without having to worry about reloading.

He was down to eight.

When are you ever going to need that? he could hear Quinn asking, the memory from one of their last sessions before she'd headed off to college.

I'm hoping never, was how he'd replied then.

There was a small sound ahead of him in the hallway.

Got you, asshole, Rust thought. A sensation of great relief cooled his blood, easing the burn in his scar tissue.

Yes, he was counting the chickens before they hatched.

Rust approached the closet door, groping in the darkness for the knob before finding it, resisting the urge to throw the door open.

Instead, first he listened. There was a commotion out front, screams and more breaking glass and one word "Fire!" then "Put it out!"

No. No more fire. Rust couldn't take it.

Something moved behind the closet door. There was a muffled thud and a grunt of exertion.

If Rust opened the door, he'd be giving Arthur Hill one last opportunity. If the old man was somehow quick enough, or had better low-light vision than Rust had, he'd get a chance at Rust before Rust could fire.

Should he say something? Something that would serve to put a tidy ending on this last year of hell, this waking nightmare?

No.

He didn't feel like giving Arthur Hill that opportunity.

Rust moved the barrel of the shotgun to the middle of the door. He tried to estimate where center mass would be, aiming so he wouldn't miss if the man was crouched.

He squeezed the trigger.

With the barrel inches from the door, the wood vaporized in a puff of air. The muzzle flash gave the glimpse of a circle, a foot in circumference, punched into the center of the door.

Inside the closet there was movement, possibly Arthur Hill's body slumping to the floor.

And there was the smell. The pent-up animal stink in the small closet released like Rust had just lanced a boil, liquid putrefaction filling the hallway.

For safety, he expelled the spent shell and advanced another. That done, he took his hand from the forestock and dug into the pocket of his flannel for the penlight.

The hole was ragged and smoking at the edges. But inside the closet there were singed bedsheets and feathers from exploded pillows, though . . . no blood.

How?

Rust bit the end of the penlight, holding it in his mouth, and put the Mossberg back up on his shoulder. Then he swung the ruined door toward himself and . . .

There was nothing in the closet. No body. No Arthur Hill.

Then why the smell?

Something hung loose in front of his light, like a pull chain to an exposed bulb but . . . thicker.

Rust reached out and grabbed the rope, pulling it forward.

Two wooden slats hung from the rope.

A ladder. He'd shot a rope ladder, destroying one side so the footholds hung loose.

Rust looked up just in time for a ruby gem of saliva to drop into his face, the glob of spit hitting him on the cheek.

Frendo the Clown's face leered down at him, the human jaw underneath the broken mask unnaturally distended.

That was Hunter's doing. He'd smashed Arthur Hill's jaw open with the skillet.

Arthur Hill didn't say anything, just smiled the best he could with his mouth hanging open like that, a rippling twitch of his neck muscles and a snort into his mask.

Rust pointed the Mossberg up and fired.

His target was expecting that, though, and had ducked out of the way, back into the second-floor hallway, before Rust even had his finger on the trigger.

Above him, harder to hear over the din at the front of the house, Cole's dad made a delighted squeal, a taunt yelled at Rust that the old man could no longer put proper words around.

Let's see how fast you can run, Rust thought, stepping back out of the linen closet, pointing the shotgun a few feet down the hallway, at the ceiling, and firing.

Plaster exploded, falling debris making Rust's eyes water. He racked. His muscles were beginning to strain, and he was sweating under his clothes. This was harder work than he remembered.

He ran two more steps down the hallway, toward the direction he'd heard Arthur Hill hobbling, and fired again, more plaster and this time . . . a scream, an anguished yowling sound, a hunted animal that would need to be tracked and put out of its misery.

Got you.

Rust felt himself smile now, the sweat against his scalp itching his scars as the droplets rolled against the smooth, poreless skin. He stopped clenching his teeth, and the penlight slipped from his lips and onto the floor.

It was fine—he didn't need it.

You're the reason I have these scars.

You're the reason I scream at night.

The reason your son screams.

Let's hear *you* scream a little more.

Rust glided the tip of the Mossberg, trying to follow the keening sound in the second-floor hallway above him, leading it by about half a foot.

He fired again, then took three more steps, bringing him to the intersection of the first floor. . . .

Wait.

Someone had gotten the lights back on.

No, that wasn't it. Rust took his hand from the forestock, shook the muscles of his arm out. Low recoil, my ass. He wiped his brow, trying to clear his vision so he could get a better idea of what was going on.

The lights weren't on.

The house was on fire.

Hill Manor was going to burn to the ground. He took a few more steps, felt the heat, understood now why he was sweating so heavily.

And the flames weren't the worst part.

There were men with guns here. Men in clown masks. One of them approached Rust from the foyer, and the other one flanked him, coming around through the kitchen.

"I repeat. Stop firing!"

There was a flashlight in Rust's eyes.

"Drop it. Drop it now," the man in the kitchen said, coming up alongside him.

Rust considered his options. If these men wanted to honor the legacy of the masks they wore, they were going to kill him anyway.

Should he try to get a shot or two off before they took him down?

What about Arthur Hill? Was he lying in a pool of his own blood somewhere on the second floor, ready to let the flames take him? It seemed anticlimactic, if that was how it was going to end, and if Rust wouldn't get to see it.

"Let go of me!" Cole yelled from the foyer.

Cole was still alive. That was good.

No. Rust shouldn't try to fight these men. He'd die. He wanted to see Cole one more time before then.

"Okay," he said.

Ruston Vance showed his hands and put his gun on the floor. There were five more shells in the weapon, and he only wished he'd gotten a chance to use them all.

TWENTY-SIX

The cop had his back to Quinn. He was keeping an eye on the clearing, not the trail behind him, and talking into the radio clipped to his shoulder.

Dummy.

"Dispatch, I know you've got other concerns, but any word from Miller?"

Officer Cody then switched, taking a small walkie-talkie from his belt. The device was camo-patterned plastic, the type of thing a kid would get for their tenth birthday.

"Hey man," Officer Cody said into the toy, probably his direct line to Miller. "What's the issue? Over."

Quinn crept forward, timing each step with his words and sighs. They were playing a high-stakes game of "Red Light, Green Light."

"A lot of people are heading back to their cars, and there's not much I can do to stop them," Cody said, a whine in his voice. He was a follower, not a leader, and he needed Miller to tell him what to do.

Miller couldn't come to the phone right now.

"Don't move," Quinn said, flicking the front sight of the handgun against the cop's earlobe, then pressing the barrel into his neck.

"Wh—what is this?"

"I killed your buddy," Quinn said, low. She didn't want everyone looking over here. Not yet. There were other people in the clearing, some sitting on their haunches, faces illuminated by their phones, others milling around the reconstructed barn and other set pieces that the Duvalls had installed out here. "This is the only chance I'm going to give you so you don't end up like him."

She reached down and pulled his gun from his belt.

Her small armory was growing.

Throw them all into the ocean, she thought. Then remembered she'd just killed a man with a zip tie.

"Tyler," Quinn hissed, wiggling the gun behind her back without looking, hoping he'd take it from her.

Nothing.

"Tyler, a little help."

She was ready to pull the trigger and kill Officer Cody

if he moved. It would make things easier, actually. No need to babysit.

But it might make it a little harder to execute the next part of her plan, to convince the kids in the clearing that she wasn't a crazed murderer.

She chanced a look back at Tyler.

The boy was sitting in the dirt on the trail behind her, knees up, uninjured arm covering his face like the slacker kid in math class that "just wanted to sleep, Miss."

This was bad. He needed a doctor.

And you *did that*, she told herself. You *put a round in him.*

Keeping the barrel of Miller's gun under Officer Cody's high-and-tight buzz cut, she looked down at the gun she'd just taken from his belt. She checked that the safety was on, used her thumb to drop the clip, then tossed the extra gun somewhere into the dirt behind her, freeing up a hand.

She then began to unclip the cop's handcuffs, fumbling with the metal snaps for a second. One or two Duvall Farms employees had noticed her. Shoulders were tapped, *Look without making it obvious* whispers exchanged, and by the time she had the handcuffs free, most of the clearing was watching her.

"Hands," Quinn said.

"What?"

Quinn pressed a cuff to his wrist, but the loop didn't

budge. She tried a second time, really needing to karate-chop the ring down to get the mechanism to work.

Click-click-click. She tightened the cuff, relishing in that ratchet zip, a sound that meant halfway there.

"The other one. Behind your back. Now."

"Hey," a girl in the clearing said. She wore a wedding dress with a large ragged hole where the heart should have been. Most of the kids in the clearing were in costume, girls in need of an exorcism huddled next to DayGlo killer clowns and mid-transformation werewolves. Which meant that they were the staff of the haunted house, all drifting over from their different-themed zones to this clearing to figure out what was going on.

"We're fine," Quinn yelled over to the girl and her coworkers. "Everything's fine here. Stay over there."

"She's got my gun!" the cop said, his voice sounding scared. It was a nasal voice. Quinn tried to recall how *Frendo has a posse* had sounded. It had to have been Miller who'd said that, she was certain. Which meant it was Miller who'd stabbed Sheriff Lee. Which made Quinn feel better about crushing his windpipe.

"Does anything you know about me make you think I'm bluffing?" Quinn asked. If she was going to live in these people's heads as some kind of murderous mastermind, she'd lean into it. "Your hand. Now."

"Okay—" he said, and slowly moved his arm down,

offering her his wrist. She tightened the cuffs, shook the chain a bit to make sure it was secure, then kicked him behind the knees.

"Sit," she said, not helping him to the ground but instead letting him fall. "Stay."

"You can't do that, he's a cop," another girl said. She had the neon fletching of crossbow bolts sticking out of her body and one fake arrow through her neck, an effect probably achieved with two ends of a shaft and a headband. It was too much. Too grotesque. It reminded Quinn of Ginger Wagner, the first to die.

Quinn tried to ignore her, turning her back to the clearing now that Cody was neutralized. She collected the stray magazine and then opened the slide catch to check that the gun didn't have one in the chamber.

Then she started walking back to Tyler, the boy nearly in a fetal position now. She hoped he was still conscious.

"Okay, big guy. Stay with me—I need your help talking with your coworkers."

The boy didn't speak, but did remove his arm from around his head and let her help him stand.

They walked to the center of the clearing, Tyler leaning against her.

Quinn looked at the faces around them.

Then at the features of the clearing itself.

God. Why would someone do this? Even if they weren't

using the actual Frendo the Clown costumes, they'd reconstructed the barn and the silo. Each structure was resized and repositioned so that they aided the flow of traffic through the attraction, but even so, *why* do that? What's the fun of fake scares on a real mass grave?

Being back here, surrounded by all of this, it made Quinn's heart beat a little faster, made her feel more awake, and not in a good way. She shook the rising panic away. There was no time for it. Neither Cole nor Rust had picked up their phones, and 911 was unstaffed. She wondered if the dispatcher was in on whatever was going on or if the Municipal Building had been completely overtaken by the mob.

"Okay, listen up," Quinn said. "Most of you know Tyler, right?"

There were a few nods.

"Right?" she asked, louder.

The nods grew more emphatic. And she realized she was still holding the gun in one hand. She wasn't pointing it at anyone, but it couldn't have been comforting.

"Well, that means Tyler can vouch for what I'm about to say."

She pointed back to Officer Cody, who was watching this, dirt and dead grass stuck to his forehead. "That cop's partner killed Sheriff Lee—while *he* filmed it."

The man looked like he could have been crying, but this far away, with only the floodlights at the top of the barn to see by, it was hard to tell.

"And his partner was willing to kill me to trick people into believing their story."

Quinn looked up to Tyler.

He nodded.

She kept looking at him, pleading. He needed to sell it. If she was going to get help, he needed to sell it.

"Yeah," he said. It took obvious effort for him to project his voice. "It's true. That other cop was going to shoot her and leave her in the field."

"And I'm only alive because Tyler saw what was about to happen and saved me," Quinn said.

The teenagers in the field were listening—there was still the glow of screens, but most phones were down at their waists, or shining through the inside of their jacket pockets.

"Show of hands," Quinn said. "Who here has a car?"

A smattering of hands, fewer than she would have liked, went up.

"Tyler needs an emergency room. Someone's going to have to volunteer to get him to a hospital. Fast."

"I'll do it." Another tallish boy in a clown costume, his with zigzag stripes instead of Tyler's polka dots, stepped forward. "He's my friend."

"That's good," Quinn said. "Thank you. And then I'm going to need—"

Quinn tried to think. What was next? She'd had the

thread of a plan, and then all the steps so far—taking care of Cody, getting the kids to listen, etc.—had gone so well that now she didn't know what to do with herself.

Then she remembered.

"Before I was knocked out . . ."

Tyler started to apologize, but she ignored him, addressing the small crowd.

". . . I saw some videos. Of people around the town. People marching on Main Street. Does anyone know if that's still happening?"

She looked around, gaze lingering on the kids with phones visible. Most seemed reluctant to speak.

"Not rhetorical."

"They're still there. . . ." It was the zombie bride speaking up. The kid next to her held up his phone. "Nobody's stopping them."

Quinn looked back at Officer Cody.

The Kettle Springs Sheriff's Department was not a big office. And if two of their deputies were ready to lead a mutiny, then Quinn didn't have much hope for whoever was left.

"You, with the car," she said, then lifted up her shoulder to try to get Tyler on his own two feet. "Take him, get going."

"The rest of you. I know it sounds insane. A lot of things today have been insane. And I'm fucking sick of it," Quinn said. She thought of her father, in a hospital bed, so far from home. And then she thought of their home, how it wasn't Philly anymore, and how there were people out there that wanted them dead, that didn't believe even the basic facts of what had nearly killed her a year ago. "But I need help. They're in town. Right now. *Our* town. Fucking it up. Terrorizing *our* neighbors. And sure, some of them, like these dipshits"—she motioned back to Officer Cody—"are locals. But I bet most of them aren't."

"They're not!" someone from closer to the silo yelled, holding up a phone screen that Quinn couldn't see at this distance.

"And they're here because my friends and I stopped them last year. The people that killed your classmates. The kids you knew. Your brothers and sisters . . ." Quinn felt her voice starting to break. "I'm worried for my friends, and I need help. So, please," she said, ready for this to be over: "Can you help me? Can we ride into town and maybe put an end to all the bullshit, all the lies, all the times where no one listened to us? Because we lived it. We nearly died. Can we say for once, you know, enough? That it's fucking enough already."

There were a few cheers and some guy yelled, "Hell yeah!" but most of the gathered costumed employees said nothing. Some looked down at their shoes or phones.

"Good enough," Quinn said, ready to take any help she could get.

"Wait," one of the girls on her phone said. "I'm sorry, but . . ."

Quinn crossed to the girl. The air in the middle of the clearing felt crisp, a chill fall breeze.

The girl tipped the phone to Quinn.

It was a video.

No. Not just a video but a live video—there were reacts and comments streaming by that Quinn didn't even attempt to read.

"Look what we've got, y'all." The man in the video had a canvas Frendo mask pulled up over his mouth, squeezing the sides of his balding head like a sweatband. He was riding in a pickup truck bed, stars and corn streaming by behind him as the truck trundled down a dirt road. Then he turned the camera, Quinn catching a glimpse of the lights of downtown Kettle Springs in the distance before he pivoted enough to show the other side of the truck bed.

Leaning against each other, their heads banging against the glass of the truck cab as they rode on bumpy terrain, were Cole and Rust. The boys each looked various levels of broken and defeated. Rust scowled up at the cameraman; Cole didn't, just staring straight forward. His arms were crossed in front of him, and it was hard to tell on the small screen, but they somehow seemed wrong.

Out the open windows of the truck's cab, a song was playing, the cameraman pointing at the boys, getting ready to sing along with the lyrics: "Oh here comes, here's the chorus."

The song was "Two Out of Three Ain't Bad."

Quinn looked up from the phone, then around her at the employees of Duvall Farms. These were young faces, frightened faces. And more than half of them were already wearing clown costumes.

"Everyone put your phones down. Nobody film this," Quinn said, fearing that if even one electric eye was on her—if she were somehow, unbeknownst to her, being broadcasted live right now—then the new plan she'd just come up with would be ruined.

She turned in a circle and couldn't see a single phone angled her way.

"Okay," she said, then pointed at a kid dressed as a clown. "How many masks like that do you have?"

TWENTY-SEVEN

Glenn Maybrook floated in a haze of painkillers and love.

The hospital's fluorescent lights hurt his eyes, so he kept them closed.

But he felt himself getting better. Cells rejoining, cartilage and tissues knitting back together. All because he knew the important women in his life were just there, just beyond that curtain of semiconsciousness. He knew they were there, and he knew that they loved him. That he was safe. That the worst was over.

He wanted to see them.

Rest was important, but in his dream Quinn and Izzy had been standing over him, watching him. Marta Lee too. Even though he was sure that, by now, she'd left to go do some police work.

Sam too—since it had been a dream, that was possible. She could still be alive. They could still be married. Beams of amber light emanating from all of them, a healing golden halo around his sliced neck.

He had to open his eyes.

He was so thirsty. He wondered how long it'd be until he could eat. The doctor might have said, but he couldn't remember.

He peeled his eyelids open, a gentle gluey pull joining his lashes as he did.

The room around his bed was empty.

There were no golden beams of love. No daughter, no girlfriend, no partner, and—not that he was really expecting her—no dead wife. There was flickering white light from the hall window, and the rest of the room had a murky blue tint from the TV, an episode of *Property Brothers*, the volume way down.

"Shit," he said. Whether it was due to the pain that came with alertness or the pain that came with disappointment, the wounds under his dressings began to throb.

Without turning his body, he turned his head and eyes and looked around him for his phone.

It was on the tray attached to his bed, currently swung into the away position so he could sleep without shifting and bumping into it.

Too far. And too much of a hassle to reach his good arm

over to pull the tray in. He could check his phone later.

For all he knew, Izzy was in the hallway or at the vending machines and would be back in a minute.

He would rest now. He'd hear her come in and wake again.

Yeah.

He reached his good hand down in order to readjust the thin, scratchy hospital blanket and . . .

His fingers hit something?

He grabbed onto the item, something heavy and wrapped in paper. He lifted it, not to his face where he'd be able to see it, but just a few inches off the mattress, to test its weight.

It was small but heavy.

While he slept, had someone left Glenn Maybrook a gift?

The idea put him in better spirits than waking up to a cramped, empty hospital room had.

He used the pinkie of his bandaged hand to work the remote and get his bed adjusted to a sitting position. Then he lifted the small, heavy paper-wrapped cylinder to where he could see it.

Oh.

It wasn't wrapping paper. Just a single sheet of plain white printer paper, curled into a scroll around something black and heavy, a rubber band to fix the paper in place.

He swallowed, the sensation like dull razors against his throat, then began to unwrap the note.

Getting the rubber band free with one hand was harder than it should have been. He snapped himself a blood blister, then, trying to uncurl the note, got a paper cut, lengthwise along the knuckle of his middle finger.

With the paper free, he could see what he'd been left, what it'd been wrapped around.

It was Quinn's combat baton.

"Thanks . . . ," he said to no one.

He held the note up but couldn't read it. After an annoying, painful few moments of effort, he had his glasses on.

The note wasn't from Quinn.

He knew his daughter's handwriting. And this wasn't it.

He skipped ahead, read to the bottom of the page.

Your Izzy

Funny how he could know someone so intimately, in all senses, or at least feel like he knew them, and still not recognize their handwriting.

Too much texting. He'd have to change that, when he was out of here. Get to know all of her.

He started at the top, angling the page toward the TV for a little more light.

Glenn,

We haven't said the L word, the love word yet, but I'm sure we've both felt it.

What I'm not sure of is how that love makes you feel.

Since I'm not Sam. But it saddens me that I'll probably never find out.

I think it could have been great.

I know how that love made me feel. It made me feel undeserving, but that was only when you weren't in the room with me to sweep that feeling away.

I'm leaving you this note wrapped around this baton. Your daughter gave it to me, but it's because she doesn't know me. Like you, she doesn't know about the weapon I keep in the projection booth closet. I can no longer keep it at home because I'm afraid that one day you'd find it and ask me questions I never want to answer.

The world is sick. Sicker every day. There's not an hour that passes that I'm not tired and ashamed for the part I played in that sickness.

I hope that you do not have to use this baton, but if you do: aim true.

If I don't see you again, or if you see me differently when you do, know that today I'm making a choice to try and undo some of the harm I've done.

Love,

Your Izzy

By the end of the letter Glenn Maybrook was crying, even if he didn't fully understand why. More than a breakup letter, it felt like a confession, and there were a few things that jumped to mind, what a lifelong resident of Kettle Springs could be confessing to—

A shadow fell over the room.

Someone blocking the light from the hallway, obscuring the small safety-glass window.

Glenn dropped the letter and picked up the baton.

Aim true.

But before he could figure out how to extend the tip of the weapon to its full, dangerous length, the person at the window was turning the doorknob, pushing their head inside the room.

"Oh, you're awake," a female voice said, turning on the overhead lights in Glenn's room.

Glenn's eyes stung, but only for a moment. It was a relief to see the nurse. Kindness in her eyes and pastel cartoon cats and dogs on her scrub top and matching scrub bottoms.

He put down the weapon, embarrassed that she might understand how he'd been scared, how he'd been ready to clobber an intruder.

"Mayor Maybrook?" the nurse said. "The commissary is closing for the night. Would you like some Jell-O?"

"My . . ." Glenn swallowed. It was so hard to speak. "Can you hand me my phone?" He needed to talk to Quinn. Needed to let her know about this and know she was safe.

If he could keep his eyes open, maybe he'd call Marta, too. He needed to hear if anything else was going on in his little insane town.

The nurse guided the phone into his uninjured hand. Like the baton, the device felt heavy.

"And the Jell-O?" she asked.

Yeah, Glenn Maybrook was tired, stressed, and heart-broken, but he'd take some Jell-O.

TWENTY-EIGHT

There were shards of wood in the bottoms of Arthur Hill's feet, his scabby legs studded with shotgun pellets, but the pressing, life-threatening issue had been the fire.

So he'd jumped.

From his bedroom window he'd jumped, hoping to spin into a roll at the last moment, not only to break his fall, but to extinguish some of the small flames that had caught on the cuffs of his costume, begun to melt the material.

The jump hadn't ended well. The world literally reached up to slap him in the face. The cool lawn hard and unforgiving.

Everything went black.

"We got a brother down back here," was the first thing he heard when he woke from his daze, body smoldering.

Someone else came over, heavy footsteps on brittle dead grass.

Don't take my mask off.

"Get him in the truck and . . ."

Please. I need it. Don't take it off.

"Yeah. Maybe I'll put down a towel first."

I'm not ready to take it off yet.

"Exactly what I was thinking. Phew. Maybe crack a window, too."

Hands were lifting him up. But nobody tried to remove his mask.

Thank you.

He chanced a glimpse out of the side of one swollen eye. These men. They wore masks, too.

"You're going to be okay, pal. We don't leave a man behind. . . ."

Arthur Hill would not die.

Could not die.

But he did need to rest as they drove into town.

He'd rest and then he'd tell these men who he was, remove his mask and reveal himself.

Arthur Hill was not their brother. Or their pal.

They were his retinue. He was their leader. And they would learn some respect. And foist upon him the admiration that, after a trip around the world and months in hiding, he was due.

Jerri sat, listened, and wondered whether or not she was going to be killed when the truck got where it was going.

It was hard to tell if they considered her one of their prisoners. Neither man riding back here had pointed a gun at her; they'd simply set her in the corner of the truck bed and paid all their attention to Rust and Cole.

But she wasn't completely off the hook like Hunter seemed to be. Hunter, she assumed, had been granted VIP status because of his mom. The two of them had been ushered into an SUV that now followed directly behind the truck. From where Jerri sat in the truck bed, she could see the clown driving and Red Nose Trixie in the passenger's seat. Jerri thought there was at least one more truck behind that, their convoy three vehicles deep.

"We're so fucked," Cole said. He kept weaving in and out of consciousness, his head lolled against Rust's shoulder. Jerri couldn't imagine the pain Cole must be feeling. The bones in his arms weren't set, and with every bump and jostle, the jagged ends of his fractures would be grinding against each other.

Rust wasn't saying anything, just glaring at the clown standing over them in the truck bed, the man's legs bent to stabilize himself. The clown didn't care that Rust was glowering at him. The guy was too busy snapping selfies and singing along with the radio. The men in the truck's cab were having a good time, too. The radio on, they joined in on the karaoke.

The other clown in the truck bed with them was more serious. He was one of the soldier clowns Jerri and Rust had seen marching through Main Street at the start of all this. And Rust's dad had blown up one of those guys. So this guy probably wasn't happy about that, if they all knew each other.

"Get ready," the clown with the long gun said, then pointed at the other clown's phone. "Put that away."

Ready for what? Jerri wondered. If the plan was to kill Cole and Rust, she would have assumed they'd be driving out to the fields that ringed the Hill property, where it'd be quieter and easy to bury them.

But instead they were driving *toward* civilization. And while the one clown had just been told to get serious and look alive, the truck's radio switched to that "Celebration" song. . . . Jerri didn't have it on any of her playlists and didn't know the artist, but it was played at every wedding, barbeque, and older relative's birthday party she'd ever been to.

The driver turned up the volume as they approached Main Street.

Not only had the clowns who'd been chanting and breaking out shop windows an hour or so ago not dispersed, but there were more of them now. Way more.

"Patches is watching the scanner, too. He thinks they're around thirty minutes out. For party over," the clown with the phone said, no longer filming himself but reading his messages. "Said the decoys and the blowouts seemed to work, for speed-trap Staties and stuff."

Speed traps? Scanner? Like a police scanner? And what did "party over" mean? Was it a good thing or a bad thing?

"Half hour's cutting it close. We should get this over with quick," the man with the gun said, talking to his friend, but also waving at the approaching crowds. First a ticker-tape parade wave, enjoying his "celebration," and then yelling for people to make way, let the truck through so that they could drive up the street.

"Shouldn't take too long. The trial and all," the man with the phone said, then pointed at Rust and Cole. "They look plenty guilty to me."

There were two loud booms, somewhere in the crowd.

Jerri flinched, thinking they were under attack. But it was just a firework, a mortar lit and launched. A pink flame bloomed above the Eatery a few seconds later. The Eatery's windows were broken out, one flickering light on in the kitchen, visible through the service window.

Most of Main Street was dark, the lights and signage extinguished. The streetlights were on, though, and a handful of the windows above shops glowed behind drawn drapes and shut blinds. People were likely up there, barricaded from the madness happening out on the street.

The marquee to the Eureka was illuminated and flashing,

the effect enough to light the block party happening on either side of the theater.

That was strange. The marquee lights weren't on a timer. They needed to be turned on manually, two separate switches, one for the neon and one for the filament bulbs.

"You guys are fuckin' heroes!" someone screamed, and the crowd applauded, fist-pumping at the clowns on the back of the truck.

Two shirtless men, pom-pom buttons applied to the front of their chests with body paint, ran up behind the truck and slapped their palms against the tailgate, leering at Jerri through the eyeholes of their masks.

"Back up, you jackasses. This isn't Mardi Gras. Let them through," the more serious clown said, pointing to the SUV behind them with one hand, waving his gun with the other. The guys in the body paint shrank back into the crowd with a muttered "Sorry . . ."

But it *did* seem like Mardi Gras or, at least, Founder's Day.

The soundtrack coming from the truck speakers changed to the first few chords of "Free Bird."

Jerri remembered her days of DJ-ing, what felt like a lifetime ago, and realized that this wasn't the radio.

Somebody was *selecting* these songs in real time. . . . They were building a mix for what was shaping up to look like a public execution.

Cole groaned and lifted his head. "I fucking hate this song," he said.

"I like it," Rust said. "But I don't want to die to it."

"Quiet," the phone clown said. "It's a long song, so you're probably gonna."

The clowns in the back with them held on to the sides of the bed, and the truck pitched to the side, the driver pulling the left tires up onto the sidewalk in front of the Municipal Building and putting the vehicle in park. They were all leaning now, Cole needing to shift, Rust trying to slide his weight up so he wasn't crushing his boyfriend or his fragile arms.

Above them, on the Municipal Building, someone had climbed the steps and spray-painted "No More Lies!" across the doors. Then, under that in a different style and paint color: "Frendo Lives!"

Which seemed like two contradictory messages, as Jerri thought about it.

These people couldn't keep their stories straight. Were last year's events an elaborate conspiracy by the kids of Kettle Springs to kill the town's authority figures? Or was the issue with Frendo that he just hadn't killed *enough* teens? She had a feeling that none of the people partying on Main Street would be able to articulate why they'd chosen to wear a clown mask tonight, if asked. They'd offer some bullshit about personal liberties and freedom, but they'd lose the thread of their logic along the way.

"Okay, let's go," the soldier clown said to Rust, then tapped him with the side of his boot. "Climb out. Onto the steps."

Rust continued glaring, stayed seated.

"Something in your ears, tough guy? Get out. Get the twink up, too, or I'll tell Bobo here to just toss him over the side."

"Pogo, man," the clown who'd spent the ride on his phone said.

"What?"

"I'm not Bobo, I don't know a Bobo," the other man said, offended. "I'm Pogo Sixty-Nine."

"I'm not going to remember your internet name, fanboy," the man with the gun said. "Just do your job, monitor the chatter, and tell me when we need to pull stakes."

While they argued, Jerri looked across the street and a half block down, toward the Eureka.

Had the clowns broken into the building? Had they turned on the marquee lights on purpose? To be able to see better, out on the streets? Jerri worried about whatever mess they were making. It was a silly thought, but she hoped she'd get a chance to clean up their mess, because that'd mean she survived tonight.

By the time she looked back, Rust had hopped over the side of the truck and was holding out his arms to help Cole down.

Was it a good thing that the boys weren't tied up? If they were *really* prisoners awaiting a "trial," they would be shackled, right?

Jerri didn't know why she was looking to make sense of it all. But then again: a year ago a woman in a Frendo the Clown mask had killed Jerri's sister and then . . . let Jerri live.

For a moment, that had seemed like the end. Until it wasn't.

There was still a chance. There was still hope.

Rust had his arms around Cole, scooping him off the curb as his feet touched down.

The front two doors of the SUV, parked at an angle across the steps from them, headlights pointed up at the stairs, opened.

Cole was shirtless and small. Rust cradled him in his arms as he walked up the steps, the two of them casting one long shadow.

"That's far enough," the clown with the gun said, hopping down onto the sidewalk himself.

"Watch him, Lawrence," Red Nose Trixie said, coming around the front of the SUV, pulling at the laces on the back of her mask.

Hmm. No snazzy clown name for Lawrence, Jerri figured.

Trixie lifted her megaphone.

"Ladies and gentlemen," she said, the crowd already

cheering and clapping, so she tried again. "Lady clowns and gentle clowns." Laughter this time. And more cheers. She was good at this. Was this woman—this pinup-slash-psychopath—was she their leader or merely the best of them on a microphone? Was this truly the voice of their movement?

"We are gathered here today to witness the trial of Ruston Vance and Cole Hill."

And the crowd went wild.

This wasn't a good plan.

This was barely a plan at all.

Quinn sweat into the latex mask. The powdery texture of the rubber was irritating the corners of her mouth. Was she allergic and had never known until now? She wished that she'd given the spare gun to one of the Duvall Farms employees. Or that she'd tried a little harder out in the field to recover the third gun after Miller had dropped it. But it was too late now.

The show had started.

"First of all," the woman with the bullhorn said, "a quick apology. There was supposed to be a gallows. But thanks to a miscommunication and logistical problems, we do not have a gallows."

"Look. I said I'm sorry," someone toward the front of the crowd said, but he was ignored.

Was this . . . comedy? Were they doing a rehearsed bit?

370

It didn't matter.

Quinn looked at the crowd around her, trying to spot her new friends. It was harder than she thought it'd be. One clown mask looked a lot like the others. There were even a few repeats among the gathering, Heath Ledger Jokers mixed in with the generic clowns, the ones with the kids' show masks and Frendo face paint under a porkpie hat, and then the occasional *real* Frendo mask, a collector's item worn like a status symbol.

It was easier to look for the jumpsuits, mud and dirt on the knees from being out in the fields.

The employees of Duvall Farms Haunted Hayride and Scream Park were standing here beside her, though. Many of them brandishing baseball bats or other improvised weapons they'd found in their cars or at the lockers at work. Others had found weapons here on Main Street, picking up broken bottles of half-finished Miller High Life, since so many in the crowd were treating this like a tailgate party.

Quinn was the only one of the good guys who had a gun.

"Pardon me," Quinn said, trying to push her way to the front of the crowd. The fewer people between her and the executioner, the better chance they had of this working.

Her gun was the signal. The signal to rush the steps, grab her friends, and get ready for the chaos that'd come as soon as she started firing.

But how could she possibly hope to save Cole and Rust?

There were a hundred people out here on the street. Maybe even more—she was terrible at estimating things like that.

No, she told herself, these people were weak. Hiding behind screen names and masks. All she had to do was worry about the ones with the guns.

"Quinn Maybrook will answer for her sins. Maybe not today. But she'll answer," the woman in the skirt and military corset with the megaphone said, pushing back on a chant that had risen up, insisting, "We want the Three!" and "Where's Quinn!?"

"Justice!" a man yelled right in Quinn's ear. He smelled like a brewery, his eyes so lidded behind his mask, he may not stay awake long enough to see the conclusion of this show. Maybe after she shot the guy with the AR-15, she'd shoot this guy next.

The Glock felt sweaty in her pocket. The slickness made the weapon feel eager, hungry . . . alive. Its friend, the spare service pistol, was tucked into her waistband. Which meant it was under the clown jumpsuit, harder to get to.

"Justice requires a trial," the woman on the stairs said, then waved to Cole and Rust. Rust had taken a seat on the second-to-top step, Cole draped across his lap.

"Defense makes its statements first," the woman said. "What do you two have to say for yourself, regarding the charges against you?"

The stockinged woman did a little two-step dance up the

stairs toward Rust and Cole—she was a real entertainer—then put the megaphone under their chins.

She clicked the button to engage the microphone, and after a quick screech of feedback, the only sound on Main Street was the sound of Ruston Vance's breathing.

This was their idea of a "trial": they would stop cheering and hooting long enough to hear Rust and Cole's last words. Hopeful they'd get to listen to them beg for their lives.

They didn't know the two boys like Quinn did.

There were eight to ten feet and a row of spectators separating her from her target. Quinn watched the citizen-soldier clown check the ejection port on his AR, then release and reattach the magazine. He was making final preparations, making sure everything was in good firing order.

"Just do what you're going to do," Rust said into the bullhorn. "Every single one of you people are going to pay for this. Just like your idols. They're dead. And I can't wait for you"—he looked up to the woman with the wrestling mask and fishnets—"to rot with them."

The woman kept the microphone engaged for an extra beat, moving the receiver to over Cole's mouth, but all he did was cough on the plastic.

"Damn," the woman said, deadpan. "Okay then, defense rests, I guess," she said, the bustle of the crowd resuming with a few laughs and jeers.

"Then what say you, the people of the prosecution?" She

swept a manicured hand out to the crowd.

"Murderers!"

"Fucking psyop!"

"That one's not even a teenager—he's thirty and stays young by drinking blood!"

The woman on the stairs let this outpouring of venom go on for another few seconds, nodding at everything the crowd had to say, her megaphone stowed under crossed arms.

Quinn looked around her. It had become easier to tell who in the crowd was a teenage haunted-house employee and who was here for the show. Her backup wasn't cheering. It'd be conspicuous, if anyone in the crowd was astute or sober enough to notice.

Spittle flew from masked mouths, plumes of hatred rising in the cold Halloween air.

Quinn could feel that the show was almost over.

She took one more step forward while everyone was jostling and cheering, elbowing herself a front-row space, needing to drop her voice and yell "Yeah, kill them!" so as not to draw suspicion on herself.

She was perfectly positioned. The second the clown in front of her raised his rifle, she'd have her own weapon clear and would start firing into the back of his head.

And then . . .

Quinn noticed a smell. A stink like burning trash.

A new body pushed its way through the crowd and onto the stairs.

Not a man. And not a Halloween costume. But some kind of monster.

Yes.

Oh yes.

His whole body hurt. But this was everything he'd worked for.

Everything he'd sacrificed had led to this.

Those weren't *murders*, a year ago. They weren't even a conduit for Arthur Hill's revenge, which is what he'd thought they'd been at the time.

They were a movement.

A cultural awakening.

And he had to do it now.

He had to take off his mask and reveal himself to this crowd.

The mask had kept him safe, had been his second skin for a year while in hiding. But it was time for Arthur Hill to reemerge, now that so many more volunteers had offered to take the weight of Frendo from his shoulders.

"Scushe me," he said, his own voice sounding foreign to him, his broken jaw not letting him make the words right, not supporting his tongue like it should.

He stumbled out onto the stairs, the crowd parting in front of him as he approached. As if they knew who he was, just from his aura. Knew to make way for their leader.

"Waiii," he said, trying to tell them to wait on the ceremony.

Oh yes. His son would die. His son's lover, too. But not until Arthur Hill had a chance to reveal himself. A chance to deliver a speech on the microphone. To inspire these gathered masses.

"Looks like somebody's a little eager, folks," the woman said. Arthur knew her. Red Nose Trixie. She would occasionally reshare the videos he paid to boost. She was part of the cause. Though Arthur Hill didn't see the need for her . . . boudoir pictures to constantly be posted in the comments. But she had her fans, knew how to spread the good word.

"Sit down, asshole!" someone in the crowd yelled at him. Arthur wished he knew who. They'd be punished for that.

"But please, everyone." The woman, Trixie—though he doubted that was her real name— approached him, holding a hand out.

She was trying to redirect him offstage. She didn't understand. This wasn't *her* show. It was his.

"Please stand back and give us space to continue the trial. . . ." Red Nose Trixie pulled her hand back, where she'd come so close to touching Arthur Hill.

She was disgusted by him.

Trixie didn't speak into the megaphone, instead pointed behind Arthur and said: "Pogo. Or someone. Come get this guy, maybe hose him off."

While her attention was elsewhere, he grabbed the microphone out of her hand. The floor was now his.

They'd listen.

He depressed the button on the megaphone's handle, then peeled back his mask.

There was a slight tug of pain, scabs and skin pulling free from where his face had started to heal into the eyeholes of the mask.

"Peale. I am Abpur Helll," he said, trying to enunciate and finding it harder than he imagined, even yelling.

He pulled the microphone back, didn't want to let it block his face.

They needed to see it was him.

He straightened up his posture the best he could, though his shredded feet hurt. He presented himself to his audience. Ready for these people to appreciate the return of their king.

But instead, a half-full beer can was tossed from the crowd and collided with his shoulder. Pain from his burns and bruises reverberated out through his body.

No.

This was all wrong.

No.

Why didn't they recognize him?

Yes, many of the posts online were about George Dunne. Many of the signs these people carried had Dunne's name on them. But that was because George had died. He'd been a martyr. Arthur Hill *couldn't* be reduced to a footnote in his own story. The *real* patriots among the crowd would know who he was.

They would recognize him. They just needed a second.

"Peese," he said, forgetting to depress the button, his words not amplified.

The machine squawked, started working. He needed to make them understand in as few words as possible. He wasn't just some face in the crowd. "I . . ." He forced the word out, loud, confident, amplified now. His jaw was bleeding again, wounds reopening. "I am Fer-en-doe."

I am Frendo.

Now they'd get it.

"Oh my god," a familiar voice said behind him.

Yes. That was realization. That was validation.

"My god, Rust."

Yes.

"It's my dad," Cole said. "And none of these people care."

Arthur Hill turned to face his son. Awake now, curled in the arms of the boy who wouldn't be able to protect him.

Not this time.

Cole smiled up at him. A heinous, evil smile. Smug.

Why hadn't Arthur killed him weeks ago? Cut those

lips, scalped that beautiful hair?

Then, with a sudden jolt of pain he couldn't remember having before, Arthur Hill felt weak in the knees.

And there was a line of blood running down Cole's face.

Had it begun? Had the crowd waited long enough? Had Cole been shot?

No. There'd been no bang. No pop of gunfire.

"Peese," Arthur Hill said, the word even smaller and more slurred.

Please.

Because there was something blocking his windpipe.

Something cutting through his vocal cords.

The arrowhead bobbed in front of him, so that he had to cross his eyes to see the glimmer of his own blood.

Arthur Hill fell forward on the steps.

His life was leaving him.

As he bled out, the last thing Arthur Hill heard was screams and gunfire.

I can't die.

But he did.

Izzy Reyes took a deep breath. Under her feet the tin and steel of the marquee groaned, but nobody on the street below seemed to notice.

All attention was on the spotlighted stairs leading up to the Municipal Building.

And all of Izzy's attention was on the guys with the flak jackets and long guns.

There were three of them out there that she'd been able to spot.

But the one next to the pickup, at the bottom of the stairs, would need to go first.

He was the one-man firing squad. It was becoming clearer that when this floor show was over, the woman on the bullhorn would drop her arm and the boys would be shot.

Izzy may not be able to save their lives. But she could delay their deaths.

And do some damage in the process.

But it wouldn't save her from the hell she believed in, where she *knew* she was going.

Jerri was in the back of the truck. Once the executioner was taken care of, Izzy would try to pick off anyone who went for the girl. Hopefully Jerri would have the sense to run away from the action, hug the sidewalks, and move around the swirl of chaos that'd be kicked off, the second the gathering of clowns realized they were under attack, that there was someone up here shooting down at them.

It was thirty, maybe thirty-five, yards to the bottom step. And the angle was right, her being on an elevated platform like this.

She'd shot much farther and kept her accuracy. But she hadn't been training, and her best shots had been in flat fields, target practice into bales of hay. Bales of hay didn't move. And the wind down Main Street could do funny things, blow signage around, with gusts strong enough to take letters off the marquee she was currently standing atop.

Stop it.

You won't miss because you can't miss.

She lifted the bow. No maintenance. No restringing, no bolt tightening; she hadn't even applied a dollop of bow wax. There hadn't been time.

Izzy hadn't touched the weapon in over a year. Didn't even want to now. But she had to.

But as she tried to draw back the arrow, Izzy realized there was a new body on the steps. She looked up from her target and saw the new clown slip off his mask and try to say something into the stolen megaphone.

Arbor Heel?

No.

She knew that man.

Across the street and nearly a block away, his facial features had changed, but she knew him.

Arthur Hill.

The man who'd started all this.

The man who'd ruined her life.

"I'm sorry," Izzy said. And she wasn't sure who she was apologizing to: Cole, Rust, Jerri, Glenn, his daughter, the whole town, her past self.

All of them and none of them.

This was a mistake. She was about to make a mistake. She knew that. She should be nocking, pulling to full draw, and taking aim on one of the men with the semiautomatic guns.

Arthur Hill was a broken man. He couldn't even speak. He was a low-impact target. Killing him wouldn't help anyone. Wouldn't save any lives or bring anyone back.

I am Frendo.

And that was it. His confession. His boast.

Izzy Reyes had to kill him now.

So she did.

She'd been aiming down the peep sight at his chest, but he'd turned at the last moment and she caught him in the back of the throat.

Izzy took another arrow from her bow-mounted quiver—she had four more—but couldn't even nock before she'd been spotted.

"Up there! On the sign!"

She drew, tried to sight onto the man with the machine gun, now turned to look up at her.

He was too close to the back of the truck. She could hit Jerri.

"People. Please stay calm!" the voice came over the megaphone. "But . . . whoever's firing isn't one of us."

Izzy stepped back. She stumbled on one of the anchors that held the marquee to the building, but stayed upright.

Pop . . . then a moment later two more: *pop pop.*

There were three distinct gunshots as Izzy let the tension off the bowstring and tried to move back so she wouldn't be visible from the street. The woman on the Municipal Building stairs screamed a long "No!" into her megaphone, the word cutting off halfway, the end of the pained yowl still audible, though unamplified.

And then the semiautomatic weapons fire began in earnest. Shots pinging all around Izzy, neon tubes flickering and exploding. Sparks and redbrick dust, stinging her hands as she tried to dive back into the maintenance hatch that led out to the top of the marquee.

"Don't let her get away!"

Oh god. They were going to get into the theater.

There was an even mix of screams and cheers as Arthur Hill fell forward with an arrow through his neck.

Some attendees were horrified to see a kind of violence they hadn't been planning to see, and others sounded happy that at least *some* violence was finally happening.

Arthur Hill, his hair patchy and thin, scabs and sores on his scalp, dropped out of the way, allowing Quinn to see that there was a gout of blood on Cole's bewildered face.

Cole's evolving mix of emotions seemed to mirror what the crowd was feeling as their bloodlust turned to panic.

"Up there," someone yelled, "on the sign."

Quinn blinked for a moment.

Okay. This didn't change anything.

She still had a target.

The clown with the AR had turned, his eyes searching Main Street for the mad bowman.

She pulled the pistol free from her pocket. It didn't matter now if anyone saw she was armed.

Panic was overtaking the crowd. The man with the rifle must have found what he was looking for, because he raised the barrel.

That was all Quinn needed.

Here she was again. Shooting clowns.

She pointed her gun so that the bullet would enter his chin below the mask, blow his brains out the top of his skull.

She squeezed the trigger.

And the guy beside her with the beer breath ran right into her, knocking her aim off, sending her shot into one of the few unbroken windows at the front of the Municipal Building.

"Huh?" the man with the rifle said, voice muffled and confused, as he changed targets, sighting down the barrel at Quinn. He seemed to track the gun in her hand. He *knew* that it'd just been pressed flush with his skin, but still he hesitated, probably because she was dressed like one of them, had been standing beside him and the parked truck this whole time.

Lying back, elbow down on concrete to steady her shot, Quinn fired twice more.

The man's eyeball exploded, and the white glare of the SUV headlights turned the gore into a strawberry-jelly burst of color. He was already weapons-free, though, so as he fell back into his death spasms, the muscles in his hands and arms tensed.

Two three-shot bursts of semiautomatic weapons fire strafed not only the crowd of bystanders, but also the side of the truck. Sheet metal punched through with several muffled *thunk*s.

God. *Please don't have just shot a bunch of the people I brought here to help.*

Quinn stood, gathering herself, trying to triangulate where the rest of the gunfire was coming from.

Deeper in the crowd, there were two more sources of muzzle flashes. But the clowns weren't shooting at her. They were concentrating their fire at the Eureka's marquee. Sparks, plastic, and glass rained down onto the sidewalk. Some of the braver clowns with bats and blades had already begun trying to kick in the heavy double doors of the theater. But there were plenty more people in clown costumes who were making a run for it, were trying to get the hell off Main Street. There was a series of overlapping stampedes as bodies were pushed into alleys and groups tried to stay together while running north or south.

Whoever had just put an arrow in Arthur Hill, they'd taken all the heat off Quinn. Probably saved her life. At least temporarily.

"Hey, what the hell did you do!?" The beer guy was on Quinn, shaking her, grabbing at her mask.

She couldn't see, the brow of the mask slipping down over her eyes. But she felt rubber tearing as she pressed the gun into the meat of the man's arm and fired.

He screamed so hard a cloud of stomach acid hit her in the face, the air hot and wet, the latex around her eyes snapping back as he let go.

She could see a little.

The man grabbed at the gunshot on his arm, yelling an unbroken string of "Owowowowow" like he could have been a runner-up on *America's Funniest Home Videos*.

Quinn looked down, finding some portions of her vision expanded by the mask's eyeholes having torn wider, but, overall, her sight more obscured.

She found what she was searching for—the AR, its barrel still smoking.

"I saw what you did!" a woman wearing a "Search Baypen Cover-up" shirt said, clawing at Quinn's mask. The woman stomped a sneaker down, crushing Quinn's outstretched hand.

Quinn tried to raise her gun, but the woman slapped the pistol away, raking press-on nails across the fabric covering Quinn's forearm, then across her face.

Quinn's mask was in tatters now, a few latex strips lying across her face and shoulders, and the woman's eyes went wide under her own mask.

The woman recognized Quinn.

"Hey. Everyone! Hey," the woman started to yell, but the people around her weren't paying attention. The crowd had either dispersed, some fighting with the teenage clowns among them, or was streaming into the Eureka.

"It's her!" the woman yelled. "Help—"

The woman stopped yelling as a bottle was broken over the back of her skull. Her eyes rolled white, and she collapsed into the heap of bodies that was now forming beside the truck.

Quinn looked up. A neon-spotted clown with black-light paint on their jumpsuit gave Quinn a nod and a thumbs-up.

"Sorry, good luck," they said as they ran up the stairs, trying to cross in front of the SUV to get as far from the gunfire and chaos as they could.

Whoever they were, Quinn didn't blame them for running. She appreciated the help and she wanted to get out of here, too.

Quinn pulled at the strap of the rifle, trying to get it free from the tangle of bodies, then lifted it up.

Unmasked, Quinn started to climb up the stairs to the Municipal Building toward her two best friends.

Jerri only caught a glimpse of Izzy Reyes before she disappeared back over the lip of the marquee.

What the hell is she doing? Jerri asked herself, the answer coming the second before the first gunshot: *Protecting me.*

The bang was close, so close.

Jerri turned back in time to see the clown—Lawrence—shot in the face. He turned toward her, one of his eyes a ragged, jellied hole, but his one good eye seeming to see her. . . .

Oh no.

His weapon began to fire, the recoil of the unbraced rifle pushing the man's arm up into the air as he squeezed off his death rattle.

Jerri was up and over the side of the truck bed so fast, she didn't have a chance to protect her face as she flipped over and onto the asphalt of Main Street.

"This one's getting away!" a man yelled. It was one of the guys in body paint. He pointed down at Jerri. Standing over her, he looked even bigger than he had when he'd been banging on the tailgate. He wasn't all that tall, but still had to have been twice, maybe three times, Jerri's weight.

She hadn't done anything! This wasn't her trial! What was she "getting away" from?

When the shirtless man realized that nobody cared, that most people around him were scrambling for cover, he splayed his fingers and grabbed a handful of Jerri's short hair.

She locked onto his forearm, taking some of the pressure off her scalp, the cuts in her hands howling under the gauze.

No. She couldn't have survived all this to let this guy hurt her. The very idea of *this guy* killing her made her furious.

"How does that make you feel?" Jerri imagined Ms. Slade's voice. All those missed gym periods. All that reliving the past.

The shirtless man lifted Jerri aloft, her feet leaving the ground.

How did it make her feel? It made her feel like she wanted to live.

She kicked. And kept kicking until one foot found the fleshy patch under the man's third painted-on button, the area below the curve of his belly button.

"Shit," the man hissed, letting her drop a little. "You'll get it now, little man."

"Little woman," a voice said out loud as Jerri thought the same thing.

And there was the satisfying wood crack of a grand slam, the man's nose and mouth disappearing in a crunch of blood and cartilage as he was smacked in the face with a baseball bat.

The man was unconscious instantly, one ankle buckling one direction, the knee of the other leg going the opposite way as his hand unclenched and he dropped Jerri back onto the asphalt.

The clown with the baseball bat was somehow even scarier than her attacker had been.

How did this keep getting worse?

The clown stood over the man's body, choked up on the bat, looking ready to hit the man again if he moved.

When it was clear he wouldn't move again, the clown turned to Jerri.

"Don't hurt me." Jerri put her hands up, hating how quickly the fight had left her. She tried to inch backward from where she lay, but her shoulder hit the pickup's rear tire and there was nowhere else for her to crawl.

"It's okay," the clown said. "It's okay." The voice was familiar. Kind. Friendly. A voice that Jerri thought about a lot. Sandra Wright took one hand off the bat, used a thumb to lift her mask enough to wink at Jerri.

The girl's corpse-bride face paint was smudged but still beautiful.

Sandra replaced the mask and offered Jerri a hand up.

Jerri took it.

"Fuck. Get back!" someone in front of the Eureka yelled.

The clowns had the doors broken open now, but as soon as they began streaming in, they were tripping over themselves to get back out.

One person who fell away from the door had an arrow through their stomach, fletching bobbing under the half-extinguished lights of the marquee.

"Let me through, let me through," one of the soldier clowns yelled, pulling people out of the scrum with one hand.

"Ms. Reyes," Jerri said, looking over to Sandra, "we've got to help her."

It was impossible to read the older girl's expression through her mask, but Jerri could read the hesitancy in her body language.

"Please. She's"—*like a mom to me*—"a good boss."

Sandra nodded, wiped the blood off her bat and onto one leg of her jumpsuit.

"Okay. We can clear a path."

And they did, Jerri staying low and agile in Sandra's shadow, the bigger girl wielding the baseball bat like some kind of Amazonian warrior.

Did Sandra even play sports? Or was she just naturally this fierce? Jerri, who thought she knew everything about everyone, couldn't remember right now.

There were minor scuffles around them, groups of teens disarming and beating the hell out of out-of-towners who'd come to Kettle Springs to make trouble, but mostly: the battle was over. And the clowns—the bad clowns, that is—had lost.

The crush of bodies trying to get out of the Eureka had slowed to a drip as Jerri and Sandra approached.

But then came the sound that Jerri had been dreading as they'd run across the street.

Three quick blats from an assault weapon. The darkened lobby of the theater flashing bright for a quick moment, then going still.

Jerri surged forward, but Sandra caught her by the arm.

"Don't," Sandra said. This close, Jerri could smell the rubber stink of Sandra's clown mask, but also . . . the sweet-mint-and-smoke smell she'd noticed on the junior girl what felt like a lifetime ago, the last time they were both standing in front of the theater.

"I have to," Jerri said.

And before she could push forward, or had even tracked that Sandra's mask had come up, there was a quick kiss on Jerri's lips.

It lasted one, maybe two, heartbeats.

"That was for luck. Not romance," Sandra said.

"That's cool," Jerri said. And even though there were men and women bleeding and screaming all around them, she was blushing, ready to pass out from the sudden glow of her skin.

Jerri nodded and nodded and used that momentum, the heat of the kiss, to send her into a jog. She reached the front doors of the Eureka, one door completely off its hinges and laid across the front of the lobby.

She waited there for a moment and listened.

There were no more gunshots.

There were no voices. No movement of any kind, really. For all the activity that had been happening in here minutes ago, it was dead quiet now.

"Ms. Reyes?" Jerri said into the dim, smoky lobby.

No answer. She stepped over the doorway and inside.

The lights were off, except for the bulbs above the candy counter, which ran on a separate switch along with the glass window of the popcorn popper.

Someone in front of her moaned, and she stepped over broken glass to find the gunman she'd seen run inside.

He was alive, but wouldn't be for long, the way he was breathing, sucking in air in big gulping "gak" sounds, but exhaling only blood.

The arrow was on the right side of his chest, probably straight through his lung, the arrowhead poking out where she couldn't see it.

Jerri frowned at him. Still a person. Even if he was a killer. And then she kicked his weapon away from his hand, just to be sure. But even as she did that, she noticed that the sucking sound of his lungs had ceased.

When she found Ms. Reyes behind the candy counter, the woman didn't look much better than her attacker.

Isabelle Reyes's head slumped against her chest. She was leaning against a box of nacho-cheese cups and had Sno-Caps scattered around her like rose petals.

The gunshots had hit her in the belly. There were at least two, maybe more—it was hard to see the holes against her dark sweater.

Jerri sobbed to see her, and the sound brought the woman back awake.

Ms. Reyes didn't try to raise the compound bow, just looked up at Jerri, then, recognizing her, smiled.

"You're okay," Ms. Reyes said, and then the smile wilted into a frown, a burdened, deep-thinking look.

"We need to get you help," Jerri said, but they were just the words she'd practiced saying on the walk over to the concessions counter.

Then Jerri looked at the scene a little closer, thought about things, scrutinized the details, like Rust had shown her how to do, in the foyer of Hill Manor.

Ms. Reyes was pretty good with that bow.

A bow that looked so *familiar* to Jerri.

A realization that felt like it may have been the final straw, the final ounce of her sanity, latched on and rolled over in Jerri's mind like a death spiral.

"No. It's okay," Ms. Reyes said, a quick cough that she

seemed more annoyed with than pained by. "I deserve this."

"What are you saying? You don't deserve this." Jerri bent, held the woman as much as she could without hurting her any worse.

"No. I do," Izzy Reyes said. "I'm so sorry for what I did to you. For what I did to Dorothy."

And there it was. A deathbed confession.

"I tried, though . . . I tried to protect you. Tried to . . ."

And Izzy's whispers petered out.

Jerri thought for a second.

Then made up her mind to say it, just in case Ms. Reyes could still hear.

"You do deserve this."

But as angry as she was, Jerri still stayed with the woman as she died, this woman who'd betrayed her, ruined her life, lied to her, and then tried to make things better with a thankless job and free day-old popcorn.

Jerri held on to the body until it began to cool, then exited the Eureka once Main Street was filled with the flash of police lights.

As far as last stands went, Rust was fine with this being his.

Here at the top step, with his friend and the boy he loved. And armed.

"Should we get to cover?" Quinn asked, looking back at where they'd laid Cole behind them. She'd made a small pillow for him with the spongy remnants of her clown mask. He was wearing Rust's flannel draped over him like a blanket because his arms were too injured to use the sleeves, but it didn't do much to stop his shivering.

"If they're going to come, they're going to come," Rust said, lifting up the dead man's rifle. The thing was a joke, so much extra plastic hanging off it in the form of useless tactical scopes and grips that it felt like Rust was holding some kind of toy, a Super Soaker.

If the clowns regrouped from their panic, remembered that "the Three" were up here for the taking, then Rust and Quinn could fire on them. And if the clowns found their courage, the three of them would need to fire until all their rounds were spent.

There was a chance they'd make it out alive, but if one of the clowns got in a lucky shot, they'd be finished.

But then after a tense few moments of waiting, the unexpected happened: nobody bothered them.

Nobody bothered them for a long time.

They sat there, perched on their exposed high ground, slightly in the shadow of a mailbox so the SUV's headlight glare wasn't in their eyes, and watched. They watched the clowns dust themselves off, gather their injured, and get chased out of town on foot by the teenagers of Kettle Springs High.

Rust was tired.

And Quinn had to be, too, because she was leaned against him, breath warm and gun hand dipping. Leaning there, she might have even been asleep with her eyes open.

That sounded nice.

Sleep sounded good.

"Don't move," a man said, stepping out from where he'd been crouched behind the bumper of the pickup truck.

And, fuck, if he hadn't gotten the drop on Rust.

Rust sighed. Exhausted. He was exhausted by this.

The man was skinny, couldn't have been that much older than the kids patrolling the alleys of Main Street, their masks now off, their weapons heavy with blood.

The man had black circles around his eyes and wore a Kettle Springs Sheriff's Office uniform, the bracelet of a handcuff tight around each wrist.

He pointed a pistol between Rust and Quinn.

Quinn stirred and the cop flinched, looking ready to shoot. "Drop it, both of you."

"Officer Cody," Quinn said, an incredulous tone in her voice. "How'd you get the cuffs—"

"Do I sound like I'm kidding?" the man said, voice twitchy.

"Fair," Quinn said, lowering her already dipped weapon to the step beside her.

"You know him?" Rust asked.

"Yeah, I killed his buddy."

The cop took a step up toward them, then another, his raccoon eyes wild and pink with bloodshot.

"Is he serious or . . . ," Rust started to ask.

"Don't," Quinn said. "Don't do it."

Yes, she'd read his mind. If he could get the man's pistol aimed back at him, he was ready to take a shot. It'd be a small sacrifice, a big risk with high reward. If he could get the barrel over in time and save Quinn and Cole, Rust was fine with being shot.

But in the end, Rust didn't have to do that.

The car was quiet, the roar of the engine inaudible until the last half block, as the driver revved.

The cop, Officer Cody, turned just in time to see what was about to hit him.

If he'd gone over the hood, the hit could have been funny, but the way he was standing on the stairs, his legs were the first point of impact, ankles smashed as he was rolled over by the car.

There was nothing funny about it.

The wheels chewed up his body as the fiberglass of the fender crunched against the stone steps, pulling up four or five steps toward them before stopping on an angle.

Officer Cody was crushed under the car's fender, arms and legs broken so badly that they were almost in knots.

Quinn and Rust sat in stunned silence.

"Yikes," Cole said. "But that's a cool car."

And of course he'd say that.

Because it was *his* car.

The 2021 Dodge Challenger SRT Hellcat had made its way back from Philadelphia just in time.

But as the driver's side door opened, it wasn't Quinn's roommate, Dev, who stepped out . . . but Jim Vance.

"Dad!" Rust yelled.

"Jim!" Cole echoed Rust's tone, but his voice was significantly weaker.

Rust's dad looked around the car, gun raised. There was nobody else on the street that presented a threat. Some of the clowns were peeling off their masks to reveal young people, younger than the three of them were, at least. Some of them were crying, huddled over friends and loved ones with broken bones or bullet wounds. Homemade "Get 'er Dunne" flags were being wrapped around injuries like tourniquets.

"A girl dropped this off at our place," Jim Vance said, climbing the couple of stairs up to them and pointing back at the car. "You mind that I drove it, Cole?"

"Our place?" Rust asked, confused by pretty much everything that had just happened.

"I wasn't," Cole said, struggling to sit up, "going to give a stranger from the city *my* address."

Jim Vance sat down next to Rust, checking Cole's wounds.

"You want a hospital, or you want me to set them back home?" he asked Cole.

"Look," Quinn said.

And she stood, pointing.

South, where the road out of Kettle Springs began to turn, there was a line of cop, ambulance, and fire truck lights.

"Took them long enough," Quinn said, and sat back down. She was so tired and sounded so done with this shit.

Rust couldn't agree more.

THE FINAL CHAPTER

"Everything looks good, but . . . let's go with the crab cakes."

"You won't regret it. They're house-made. Lump meat. Delicious. Best in the state, really."

Quinn doubted that, but she'd play along.

"When in Rome," she said, and handed the menu back.

The server left her, heels clacking.

Maryland. It had been a long trip. A lot of miles on the new car. Quinn's lower back was aching. There was a bruise down there that, three months later, still hadn't healed right. She should see if she could do some physical therapy when this was all over.

But it may never be over . . .

Quinn took a sip of her coffee. Weak.

She didn't hold out much hope for the crab cakes.

She'd glanced at the page to get directions, but while she waited for her food, she checked this place's Yelp score again.

3.3 stars.

Best in the state. Sure.

But it was fine—Quinn wasn't here to eat.

Her phone buzzed with a notification.

Wish you could have been here! Hope you're having fun! <3

Her dad wasn't wasting his last days in office. He'd gotten the votes to rename the Municipal Building to the Sheriff Marta Lee Civic Center.

A second later, there was another message, a picture of the new sign. The photo was slightly out of focus and too small in the frame. Glenn Maybrook still didn't know how to take a picture with his phone.

If these truly *were* his last days in office. He said they were, but Quinn wondered. Glenn Maybrook's recovery had been tough, but he seemed better, even if the doctors said he'd have swallowing problems and nerve damage the rest of his life.

But Quinn guessed the physical recovery had been the easy part, in comparison to the loss of Izzy. The loss of the Izzy he'd built in his mind, not the one that had come out in the investigation later.

How had they missed that the first time? Not just the cops, but Quinn and Glenn themselves had missed it.

Because Izzy had seemed so nice? Because she'd been trying to make amends?

Quinn didn't FaceTime with her dad as much as she should, but she wasn't too worried about Glenn Maybrook. Jerri Shaw was checking in on him often. The girl was acting as kind of a second assistant, when Kendra was overwhelmed. And this was when Jerri wasn't busy at the Eureka, the theater under new, background-checked management. Again.

There'd been no manhunt for Jane Duvall. She'd sat in the back of the SUV for the duration of the gunfight, her son's head in her lap. When the cops reached her, the first thing she'd said was how she'd like to confess. How sorry she was.

Quinn didn't know everything that happened with that whole situation, the Duvalls, but it seemed like one day she'd look into it, talk it out with Cole and Rust, if they were ready. It sounded depressing, a whole family destroyed. Rust had never said it to Quinn directly, but she knew that Rust blamed himself for what had happened to Hunter. And that was after the coroner had deemed the buckshot wounds "superficial" and listed the cause of death as a stabbing. Arthur Hill's final victim.

But enough of that. If she thought about the dead too long, she'd spiral and her hands would shake. She couldn't have that now. It would blow her cover. So she tried to think about some of the nicer things that'd happened in the last few months.

Cole and Rust were moving.

Technically, the Vance family was moving, and Cole was moving with them. But he'd also put up half the money for the ranch, so that made things confusing.

Minnesota? Montana? It was one of those *M* states that wasn't Missouri. Quinn would have to visit one day. The place looked nice, big skies and mountain ranges. If someone was going to try messing with you there, you'd see them coming.

Quinn scratched at the base of her neck, the feel of it still new, kind of weird, the buzzed scrape.

She had cut her hair. Cut *all* of her hair. She'd done it herself, in a Holiday Inn Express with a size-zero clipper. Then after a couple days of growth, she'd spread hair dye over the buzz cut with the back of a comb, just in case someone should recognize her natural color.

The haircut felt like giving something up, a last connection to Samantha Maybrook through her curls, but it also felt like a fresh start.

The server was on her way back, heels on tile, the sound rhythmic.

"Here we go," she said, laying down a sad-looking plate of formerly frozen crab cakes on a bed of wilted spring mix.

Best in the state. Liar. This woman was a born liar.

"Anything else I can get you?"

Quinn looked up. She'd gotten good at this. At doing her research, but still there was always the chance—the slim chance—that she'd gotten something wrong.

"Mm-hmm. Looks great. Thank you, Trixie. I think that'll be it for right now."

"What was that?"

Quinn held the woman's eye contact. Yes. That was it. That was the look. Guilt. Panic.

"I said that'll be it for right now?"

"No, I think you called me the wrong name."

"Did I?" Quinn asked, turning their eye contact into a glare. *Daring* the server to recognize her. "Sorry about that."

"It's okay," the woman said, flicking her plastic name tag.

Allison.

Sure.

Allison Rainier. 33. Columbia, Maryland. Two cats and a fiancé.

It wasn't like Quinn was going to dox the woman. She wasn't looking to release this personal information to the public. But it hadn't been too hard to find.

Red Nose Trixie turned on her heels, away from Quinn's booth, and started walking back toward the kitchen.

Quinn tucked a twenty-dollar bill under her plate and then grabbed for the baton she'd been keeping under her leg.

She'd go somewhere else for lunch.

Quinn Maybrook flicked her wrist, the baton extending, and was on "Allison" as the woman whirled, trying to splash Quinn with a lukewarm pot of stale coffee.

"Weak," Quinn said. Then set to work. Four or five whacks and probably as many fractures, if she'd done it right.

She was out of the restaurant before the fry cook could run out of the kitchen, before any of the handful of patrons moved to stop her.

The woman known online as Red Nose Trixie was still screaming as Quinn let the door swing closed.

There were a lot of names on her list, and Quinn wanted to be out of Maryland before dusk.

ACKNOWLEDGMENTS

"They made a *Clown in a Cornfield 2*?!"

Is something I'm sure a lot of people in bookstores will say. And I feel like I would have been just as incredulous, if you told me there'd be a sequel back when I was handing in the manuscript for the first book. But the slasher sequel is a long and storied tradition and I'm so grateful that I've been allowed the opportunity to return to Kettle Springs.

I'm so unbelievably proud of what I was able to do with this book, so I'd like to take a moment to thank everyone who made it possible.

On the publishing side of things, everyone at HarperTeen, Temple Hill, and Writers House. Specifically, David Linker and Petersen Harris for their encouragement and insight. Alec Shane for his patience during long phone calls. Jen

Strada and Jessica Berg for their invaluable edits and notes.

It was a real honor to be able to work with illustrator Matt Ryan Tobin again for the cover. If you took a chance on either book, odds are it was because his beautiful paintings caught your eye (and maybe tore it out). And a cool illustration needs equally cool design, so thank you to Sarah Nichole Kaufman and the rest of the Harper team for that.

Would like to re-thank my writing heroes, those who generously took the time to blurb the first book . . . because we're *definitely* reusing those quotes for this one.

On the home front: my wife, parents, in-laws, and the friends in text threads who *feel* like family.

I'd like to thank the Horror Writers Association and its voting members for the tremendous honor of giving the first book the Bram Stoker Award for "Superior Achievement in a YA Novel."

But most of all thank *you*. Without your support I wouldn't be writing these words, may not be writing at all. Every single reader who read the first book, told a friend about it, left a review online, or posted about it on their socials: I am indebted to you.

Books live or die on their word of mouth, so if you enjoyed what you've just read, please consider taking a minute to help spread the word. A quick, honest review on Amazon or Goodreads is worth its weight in gold.

And who knows? Maybe if enough people read this one,

somewhere in the future there'll be a befuddled shopper exclaiming:

"Wait. They made a *Clown in a Cornfield 3*!? Come on!"

Thank you,
Adam

.